WHY THE MONSTER

Sean and Rachel
Qitsualik-Tinsley

Illustrations by
Toma Feizo Gas

INHABIT
MEDIA

Published by Inhabit Media Inc.
www.inhabitmedia.com

Inhabit Media Inc. (Iqaluit), P.O. Box 11125, Iqaluit, Nunavut, X0A 1H0
(Toronto), 191 Eglinton Avenue East, Suite 301, Toronto, Ontario, M4P 1K1

Design and layout copyright © 2017 Inhabit Media Inc.
Text copyright © 2017 by Sean Qitsualik-Tinsley and Rachel Qitsualik-Tinsley
Illustrations by Toma Feizo Gas copyright © 2017 Inhabit Media Inc.

Editors: Neil Christopher and Kelly Ward
Art Director: Danny Christopher
Designer: Astrid Arijanto

We acknowledge the support of the Canada Council for the Arts for our
publishing program.

This project was made possible in part by the Government of Canada.

Library and Archives Canada Cataloguing in Publication

Qitsualik-Tinsley, Rachel, 1953-, author
        Why the monster / Rachel and Sean Qitsualik-Tinsley ; illustrations by
Toma Feizo Gas.

ISBN 978-1-77227-141-6 (softcover)

        I. Qitsualik-Tinsley, Sean, 1969-, author II. Gas, Toma Feizo, illustrator
III. Title.

PS8633.I88W59 2017   jC813'.6   C2017-904760-4

Printed in Canada.

PROLOGUE:

Huuq's Sky Time

Huuq was born in the Sky Time.

This was not a sort of time that ran on, beat by beat, night chasing day, with no concern for the lives caught in its rhythm. It was living time. Deep. Strange. Never taking one route, like a river.

Its flow could cause anything to be.

Not to say that Sky Time was magical. Not exactly. The Sky Time included everything that was. And was not. Being. Non-being. It was all that could exist or fail to be. One living imagination, dreaming only itself: that was Sky Time.

Set in this Sky Time was the Land. Inhabitants of ordinary time might have simply called that the "Arctic." But whenever Huuq and his people (*Inuit*, which sort of means "Inhabitants") spoke of the Land, they never imagined borders. Or maps. Or geography.

The Land was so vast that one could stand on any hill and see something—Sea, Sky, more Land—forever into the distance. There were no trees. A few bushes, though. For only a couple of months, the Land painted itself with flowers. The rest of the time, it was so cold that the Sea became a single, rigid sheet. Ice and snow. A white horizon in every direction.

For Huuq, Summer was one long day. The Sun circled the Sky, dipping low and blazing red as it brushed the hilltops. But it never set. Winter, on the other hand, was one grand night, a time when Huuq's people switched from boats to dogsleds. On clear Winter nights, the stars seemed to shiver fiercely, and Huuq wondered if they felt cold.

He had always watched the Sky.

Huuq's favourite sight was what his people called "Many Players." They were lights, but quite unlike the stars. On special nights, the Many Players streaked like coloured ribbons across the Sky, as if flown by giants bigger than the World. Huuq stared, never smiling, at their show. They held something for him. He sensed that. They felt like a crowd, a dream-folk who called to him, their words unclear and slightly frightening. And he never whistled under them. He believed that if they heard him whistling—disturbing their play—the Players might swoop.

Who knew what they would do to him?

The lights knew that he was there. He could feel it.

They were watchers.

Alive.

Most things were alive in the Sky Time. It was before people had convinced themselves that much of the World was dead.

There was even life, of a sort, running through the Land. Plants had sap and people had blood and the Land had its Strength. Every pebble or mountain was part of this power.

And every plant that sprang from the Land.

Every creature that ate a plant.

Every creature that ate a creature.

And, of course, people. They were part of it, too.

Huuq was sure of such facts. He had heard them from only one person in camp, but that individual seemed reliable. The same reliable person had told Huuq many things about the Land.

For example, though it was alive, it would be a mistake to think that the Land had a mind. It never really thought. Or wondered why the Sky was blue. Or who its parents were. It could only *feel* the lives on its surface. Like someone holding a seashell up to their ear, the Land could listen to any living heart.

Especially when that heart was angry.

Or frightened.

Or in grief.

Those facts were not important to Huuq. Not at first. They were a bit like hearing that white bears were left-handed, or that the Sun was a woman, or that the World was actually a great, big ball.

The facts became important when he changed.

And met the Land.

Sea.

Sky.

And learned that they knew him.

Part One
HUUQ THE THIEF

The Storm

Stating that Huuq lived "long ago" means nothing. In the Sky Time, every chunk of long ago was equal to every other.

It matters, however, that Huuq was from a poor community. Most of the time, Inhabitant camps were made up of a few travelling families. It was typical of an Inhabitant camp that people got along with each other. They enjoyed company and helped each other through the difficult parts of life. If there was someone in a group who could not (or would not) get along with others, they were eventually asked to leave.

Yet there was a problem with that way of doing things.

Sometimes, the worst minds from various places found one another. It was rare. But it could happen that a lot of unlikable people came together, and then there was a new camp.

All of unlikeable folk.

Huuq wondered about his own camp.

Sometimes, just before he fell asleep, his mind worked very hard. He thought about the events of the day. Words. Deeds. And he wondered if the families of his camp were too bitter. Humourless. Every day, it seemed, he labelled someone greedy. Biting. Dark.

(He tried to avoid the violent ones.)

If someone from camp had asked for his opinion, Huuq would have shrugged and lied. He would have described the place as "normal." But normal meant that people laughed at the mistakes of others. If a family had poor luck in hunting, other families smiled. Normal meant very little laughter. Games were competitive, rarely fun. No one was allowed to be good at anything, or their neighbours would grow jealous. Normal meant that a dull, foggy fear crept in and out of every brain. And to most camp folk, it seemed, that was fine.

In his *isuma*—the secret bundle of his most private passions and opinions—Huuq suspected that his camp was abnormal. He remembered, from time to time, that his parents had not originally travelled with this group of families. Huuq had relatives elsewhere. He held only threads of what those aunts and uncles and grandparents had been like. When he had last seen them, he had been tiny. Small enough to be carried by his mother, in a special pouch inside her parka, close to her hood: an Inhabitant way of carrying babies.

There had been an argument. Mostly between his parents. Raised voices. Those were easiest to remember. Squabbling— over an object, maybe. Huuq had been too small to understand, too little to do anything but block his ears.

After that, his parents had become boring. Sour. Sullen. A bit too quiet.

(And they'd come to live in this place.)

Huuq mostly tried to recall smiles. The smiles *were* there, in his memory, from relatives who had been left behind. He seemed to remember strange men and women kissing him in their delighted, snuffling way. Dream-faces came to him when he slept. And in such dreams, he hoped that those faces were of the normal folk. Characteristic of how people were supposed to be.

Huuq's real treasure, however, was his dream of being gone. Not away from family. Just camp. He was up in the Sky, among the Many Players. There, he was not a person at all, but made of coloured lights. And every time he felt something, he lit up in different hues.

(But he hadn't had that dream in a while.)

When awake, Huuq loved to steal. Not in order to profit. He just liked the unnameable *shift* that followed a theft. The community changed. It was filled, for the briefest time, with a special energy. Life. In the chaos of a simple object gone missing, the camp folk became less stagnant, less dark. For a while, they were no longer like water stuck in a dirty puddle.

To Huuq, the shift was a beautiful thing, on the heels of such a simple action. He would take bric-a-brac from someone's tent or snow house and move it to another. One stolen object was the same as another. He enjoyed watching his victims go from home to home. Asking if anyone had seen their belongings.

He was no true thief, he told himself. Huuq never permanently kept whatever objects he pinched. He felt that the camp folk should have thanked him. He kept them from thinking that their dull, foggy fear was normal.

Huuq feared that fear more than anything on the Land. More than freezing, more than bears. Though he could not have said why.

Huuq was stealthy. He had only rarely been caught stealing. But he had never been caught returning objects. That seemed unfair to him. If he had been spotted putting more things back, people would have realized, by now, that he was no thief.

When he'd been little, perhaps eight or nine seasons ago, everyone had laughed at his antics. But now, grown-ups levelled unfriendly, even frightening, looks at him. He wondered if it had something to do with his age. Was he an adult? Only a little while ago, Huuq had discovered something strange about himself: he suddenly cared how he looked. If his hair or clothes were untidy, it bothered him. He wondered if that meant that he was growing up. But he still had no idea what older boys meant when they said that certain girls were "pretty."

Last year, his father had told him that it was time to stop stealing. Time to help out, to do some chores. And Huuq never complained aloud while fetching ice for drinking water. Or coiling rope. Or feeding the dogs.

But he had not stopped taking things, either.

Why couldn't people see the humour in it?

Lately, there were people who automatically blamed Huuq whenever anything went missing. Then, they came to Huuq's parents, asking something like,

"Why does your son act like this? Why?"

Huuq's mother and father had asked the same question. Guessing, as though the right try might finally untie something in his brain, Mother had especially pressed him on one occasion. Huuq had remained silent. She had walked off in a huff, saying that his "head was broken." Then, Father had taken a turn, asking in his quieter way. Huuq had remained stony with him, as well. The man just shook his head. Looked disappointed. Muttered that Huuq's "heart was empty."

Since then, Huuq's mind had often chewed on their words, thinking that his parents were right only somewhere between their opinions. Yes, something in him was on its way to breaking— some organ that was neither heart nor head, but connected to both. It sat in an otherwise empty hollow within him. Like a length of bone tensed almost to snapping. It never quite gave, but he could feel the pressure on it. And he knew that that was coming from the camp around him. Yet he could not have said why.

Often, he sat by himself. In those times, he whispered his own name. For that was what "Huuq," as a word, meant.

It meant "why."

One year, a terrible winter arrived.

Outside, the air was almost too dry to breathe. Bands of powdery snow snaked over the white Land. Folks had to blink rapidly whenever the wind gusted, because the cold would freeze the eyes in their heads.

At this time, the Land was too chilly for tents. So the families with whom Huuq's parents travelled built domes made of snow blocks. Their word for such a dome was "*iglu*." And it simply meant "snow house."

With a lamp burning seal oil in each snow house, it was warm enough for people to survive. But the adults, even the older kids, grew grim. Grimmer than usual, that is. All the families portioned their oil with care, as though it were the very measure of life. And in such a storm, no one disputed that that was normal.

Even Huuq knew why the camp was grim. But that did not mean that he could feel concern for the storm. He dimly understood that no one had caught seals in quite a while. The oil that families now used had been stored from previous seasons.

If the oil ran out?

Huuq did not care.

Oil was boring and had nothing to do with his greater concerns.

All he felt, as snow and wind clawed at the little camp, was the press of stagnation more unbearable than any he had previously known. It was as though the dull, foggy fear had solidified, trapping him in a World of emotional slush.

There was difficulty in moving from home to home while the storms blew. It was hard to steal. Suddenly, the World had become very bad, and it had accidentally forced Huuq to be very good, keeping him from having any fun at all. Flurries came and went, coiling around the camp like great, raking phantoms. He could barely stand it. The harder the storms pressed, the lower Huuq became. He could feel himself becoming a typical camp dweller. Damp in head and heart. Foggy. Fearful.

There was wrongness present. Where? How? He was unsure, but he could sense it.

There were plenty of chores for Huuq to do. Ice needed to be chipped, melted for water. Caribou sinew needed to be pulled and tied. Huuq's father even invited him to help bore holes in antler (how thrilling!). Sometimes, Huuq was tempted to learn how to fletch arrows. It was *almost* interesting to watch his father carve arrowheads. He wondered why some heads were barbed and others were not.

Yet Huuq knew that, once he began to help, it would lead to expectations that he help with everything else. So he pretended to be clumsy, dimwitted—until his parents grew frustrated and kept all the work items away from him.

Huuq hated games more than anything else. It seemed that, in gaming, camp folk were at their most dull, peevish, and petty. Who wanted to toss around seal knuckles with such folk? Who wanted to pretend at poking some object hanging from the snow house roof, only to be "accidentally" struck by a neighbour?

Other than stealing, there was no good game that Huuq could play by himself.

Sometimes, when Huuq felt especially dark, he sat wondering if people were capable of disliking him as much as he disliked them.

Huuq had only two friends, but neither were camp folk. Not in the usual sense. One of them lived without family, in his own little snow house at the edge of camp. The man had a long, silly-sounding name. But Huuq just called him Aki. This meant "gift." Huuq called him Aki because grown-ups, even Huuq's own parents, brought the man gifts from time to time. No one ever said why.

Huuq didn't see Aki very often. But sometimes he visited the man in his home. If Huuq was lucky, Aki would be in the mood to chat. Then they would have a time free of normal life and its twin—boredom—as they gabbed about all the strangeness that Aki had experienced across the wide Land.

As for Huuq's other friend, he played with her every day. She was his dog, Qipik. It was rare for Inhabitants to have pets. Huuq knew a girl who had been given a duckling one summer. It had followed her everywhere, nibbling at the bits of algae she carefully collected from streams. She had awakened one morning to find that her sister had rolled over on it in her sleep. Huuq also knew a boy (the tallest in camp), who had been promised a baby falcon. The boy had been promised that falcon every year, but had never actually received the pet. These days, the boy no longer spoke of the falcon his father was going to find for him. He spoke only to say things that seemed stupid or cruel.

Qipik had been given to Huuq as a gift from Aki. Up until two seasons ago, she had been his blanket, and he had refused to sleep away from the smell of her smoky fur (though it had made him itch).

One day, Huuq had suddenly realized that she stank of her meals: mostly char salmon, great, red-fleshed fish as long as Huuq's arm. In subsequent months, he had cultivated the tendency to sleep apart from her.

Yet she had kept her name, which meant "blanket."

Huuq no longer wanted to use his dog as a blanket. But that didn't mean that he wished for her to live outside of the home. Huuq's father, a man milder than most hunters in camp, had suddenly become a tyrant on the issue of dogs. Less than four seasons past, when Qipik had been small enough to carry under Huuq's arm (a warm, squiggly bag of fur), the dog had been tolerated indoors.

Now that she was a full-sized husky, grey and white with streaks like the colour of rusty rocks, she was no longer part of the family.

At least, the way Huuq saw it, if Father had wanted her in the family, she would have been allowed to stay inside whenever she wished. Qipik was outside almost all the time now, curled into a little ball against the cold. She was allowed to live outside the mouth of the family's snow house. But more and more, she was becoming a typical dog. Worker, not pet. Resource, not family.

And it filled Huuq with rage.

How could one be family in one moment, an outsider in the next?

How long before Father expected her to pull a sled?

At times when the wind howled loudest and the family snored around him, Huuq lay awake, thinking of poor, freezing Qipik. In those moments, when his eyes were wide and staring in the dark of the snow house, his rage became hate.

Here is how Huuq's mind connected it all together: once, when Huuq had been hiding in Aki's home, his odd friend had pointed out odder facts about the oddest thing of all—the Land and its ways.

Snowstorms were made of light gusts.

Glaciers were made of crystals too small to see.

If the temperature dropped just low enough, the Sea went solid.

Once the temperature changed its mind, people could no longer dogsled across the Ocean.

It was possible that the leader of a caribou herd might say to himself, "Let's try a different route this year." And an entire community starved because it could not hunt the animals.

It might happen that the leader of a wolf pack said to herself, "I want our dens to be in the hills, not the valleys, this year." And their cubs grew up stronger than ever before.

The path of a summer bee, the nod of a blossom, the shiver of snow at a mountain's summit. The slightest things of the

World, in their multitudes, caused the Land's Strength to move.

(Aki liked to talk that way.)

Huuq remembered what Aki had told him: little things mattered. So, as Huuq lay awake, thinking of poor, freezing Qipik, he decided that his father was making a terrible mistake. Maybe the man had thought that putting Qipik outside was a small matter. A trifle. But maybe Father could not know that he had also exiled a part of Huuq himself. It felt like Huuq's heart was freezing along with his Blanket.

Did Huuq not have the right to resist? To stick up for himself?

He did. He was sure of that. And so, armed with this conclusion, Huuq spent days in silent, righteous indignation. It was the Inhabitant way to insist that family was one. Yet, what if part of the family turned against another part? Huuq had an obligation to defend Qipik. He was sure of that. And it meant defying Father. But that was only fair. Father had defied the Inhabitant way of life. Father had decided to mistreat Qipik. Father . . . the man had refused to respect Huuq's feelings. In a way, he had stolen Huuq's choice. His free will. Was that not a kind of attack? A theft, at least? And his parents called him empty, broken—thieving! He was the only honourable soul in camp . . . .

One day, when the fogginess and fear of ordinary camp life seemed to press on Huuq so strongly that he thought tears might come to his eyes, he went and snuck Qipik into his family's snow house. There were plenty of blankets piled about the place. All of thick caribou hide.

My Blanket, he thought, *should sleep with the blankets.*

She was family.

No matter what Father said.

At a moment when both of Huuq's parents were outside, talking to other grown-ups about weather (as usual), Huuq hurried his dog inside.

To his frustration, Qipik did not want to come in at first, treating the snow house doorway as though it were some kind of barrier. But with Huuq's harsh hissing, and a bit of dragging, she suddenly rushed inside. Then it was a simple matter to pile blankets over Qipik, making her sit still on a low platform against the curved wall.

Huuq was quiet and tense after his parents re-entered. But he was pleased when the dog went undetected for some time. He watched, smiling to himself, as his parents cut up bits of frozen caribou meat and passed them around. He chewed his piece, wishing that it had more fat on it, while his mother, singing softly, fed a sliver to his baby sister.

Huuq's meat disappeared.

He looked and saw that his hand was now empty. He stared at his own fingers, even wiggled them, as though the gesture could make the meat reappear at any moment.

It took him a heartbeat or two to realize what had happened. But the situation made sense when he saw Qipik gulping down the last of his food. The dog's head had emerged from the blankets, snapping the meat out of his grasp.

Huuq, no longer smiling, glanced at his parents.

Their eyes were wide.

Staring at the dog.

Before Huuq could say a thing, Qipik burst out from under the covers. Huuq's mother, a spidery, nervous woman at the best of times, let out a screech. Huuq's baby sister, a blob of chewed meat and saliva tumbling from her mouth, began to cry.

The dog bounded toward the snow house doorway. Huuq's father tried to kick her as she went. He missed. Fell.

Looking a bit like a dog himself, Father spent a couple of heartbeats chasing after Qipik on his hands and knees.

Like a sudden cough, a sharp laugh emerged from Huuq. He stopped himself, putting his hands over his mouth—but not before catching Father's attention.

The man stood, panting, eyes on Huuq.

Father was not a large man. His voice tended to squeak, almost childlike, past his overgrown moustache. But now, his sinewy throat let loose a roar that Huuq had never before heard.

"Why do you do these things, Huuq? Answer! Why!"

Huuq froze, staring. He had never before realized that his

father's eyes could look so round. They looked like brown bird eyes.

"Bad enough we don't have that dog on a team!" Father hollered. "What if she'd eaten all our food? Chewed through our hides? Knocked a wall down? Don't you care about your family?"

At first, Huuq sat startled, even a bit mad that his father was taking this tone with him. But as he heard the words, saw the anger in the man's amber face, Huuq became afraid. Tears welled in his eyes. Father had never before yelled at him.

"Don't be too hard on him," Huuq's mother whispered. "The boy's funny. Strange. Something in him is broken, empty . . . . "

"I don't care!" roared Father. Then he coughed, because he was not used to his own volume.

"I'm done with this," the man added in a lower voice. "From now on, I'm breeding that dog. She can at least give us pups. I'm not going to have my son pretending a dog is his sister!"

Then Father held his hands out to Huuq.

"Why can't you just be a member of the camp, Huuq? Why can't you be normal?"

Yet a sudden, mild tone could not make up for the outburst. Huuq felt a tear dripping from his chin. He seized his mitts and ran to the snow house entrance. He was still in his winter clothes, including boots, and pants made from beautiful, white bear fur.

On hands and knees, he crawled out of the snow house.

Qipik was waiting for him, grey and rust-coloured tail wagging. Before he put on his mitts, Huuq yanked one of her ears. It was an old play gesture.

"You're my dog," he muttered. "Not Father's."

Qipik gave him a stinky lick. Her saliva immediately iced Huuq's cheek in the cold wind.

"If you had pups," Huuq told her (really speaking to himself), "you'd change. You'd be part of this camp. Normal. Dull. Foggy . . . . "

"Are you talking to a stupid dog?" came a voice.

Huuq turned to see who had called out above the wind.

Of course, he thought. *Coming like seagulls.*

The local camp bullies.

There were five of them, mostly boys a few seasons older than Huuq. The tallest was Paa. Their leader. Their mouth. To Huuq, he was well labelled, since his name meant "opening." Ever since Paa's father had brought him on his first hunting trip, the boy's mouth was at work. Talking. Talking. And always about himself. Paa seemed to think that he was a grown-up these days. As such, he assumed the right to pick on all smaller kids.

Huuq was already in a bad mood, so he stood up, dusting snow from his knees, to glare at Paa. He wasn't worried about getting beaten up. In Huuq's community, everyday life resulted in many sad happenings. But it did not include people openly attacking each other.

Cutting words. Those were the preferred weapons.

"I am talking to somebody stupid," Huuq called back in a loud voice. "Just not my dog."

"Huuq talks only to dogs," said a bully over Paa's shoulder, "because he can't get along with people."

"You're right," said Huuq. "I talk only to dogs. So, when is someone going to hitch you to a sled?"

"Don't forget," Paa said to his fellow bullies, "Huuq has another friend. Aki. Does he count as a person?"

The bullies all began to snicker, saying things like,

"Aki, the freak . . . ."

"Aki, the crazy . . . ."

"Aki, the Monster Man . . . ."

"Don't call him Monster Man," warned Huuq. He didn't like any of the names the bullies had for Aki. But, somehow, Monster Man was the worst.

So, Aki liked to live by himself!

So, he didn't like to play in community games!

Yet Aki still had the respect of other grown-ups. They brought him little gifts, didn't they? Wasn't that respect? Who were these gulls that they felt any right to mouth off about Aki?

Why did being special make one a monster?

"What can you do to silence us?" asked Paa with a grin.

Then Huuq roared.

The sound arrived on its own, as though his throat had

developed an independent opinion of the bullies. There were no words attached to the roar. It was simply barked out. In all its lovely horror. A single expression of Huuq's frustration.

Huuq's tone, a more animal version of his own angry father, stunned the bullies into silence. Glaring at them all, Huuq put up his hood against the chill wind. He turned and walked toward Aki's home.

2

The Monster Man

When Huuq crawled into Aki's snow house, Qipik was close behind him. Aki was sitting on piled hides, some old and patchy, others new and fluffed. He was chewing meat. Dark and dry. It was caribou with very little fat on it. Lately, the whole camp ate the stuff. That, or the little dried fish that was left. It had been a long time since anyone had caught a seal.

The caribou made a ripping sound as the man's teeth pulled on it.

Aki smiled at the boy and dog, as though unsurprised to see them. While Huuq stood and grabbed some dried meat for himself (groaning when he realized that there was nothing with fat on it), Qipik approached Aki. Her tail was still and her head was a bit bowed—the strangest dog greeting that Huuq had ever witnessed. But then, his friend had never been an ordinary person.

Aki gave the rest of his snack to Qipik.

"My parents," said Huuq between bites, "are the ones with broken heads. Empty hearts."

He was now sitting cross-legged on the floor, which was covered in the oldest of Aki's hides.

"Why would you say that?" asked Aki. He brushed back his silver-streaked hair. Then he adjusted a thin leather cord that he always wore tied around his head.

"They don't like me," Huuq told the man. "They don't like Blanket, either. My father wants her to have pups. Like a normal dog. He wants me to be normal, too. All he cares about is whether we're useful to him."

Aki smiled, showing huge, yellowed teeth that reminded

Huuq of old walrus ivory. As usual, they had dark bits of dried meat stuck between them. Huuq was the only person in camp who never got nervous when Aki smiled.

"Normal people," said Aki, "always think it's best to be normal. But what happens when things become abnormal? They always go running to someone like me. Maybe even yourself, someday. Don't worry, my Little Tooth. You just scare them. That's all."

Little Tooth: it was something Aki had always called him. The name made no sense, but Huuq had never questioned it. Why bother? It was a secret, which made it good enough to treasure. Nicknames were shadowed things. Like thefts. And that made them shine against the dull, foggy fear.

"I just want to be left alone, not scare anyone," said Huuq. He thought for a moment. "No, actually, scaring people would be great," he said. He smiled as he spoke. It felt as though a sudden ember were burning inside of him.

"Scaring is even better than stealing. Don't you think?"

Aki said nothing, but stared eerily while Huuq thought some more. Somehow, the man always seemed to know when Huuq needed time to sort out his thoughts.

"That's what they need," muttered Huuq. "A good fright."

The idea energized him.

Aki narrowed his eyes, smiling. "To make someone fear," he told Huuq, "is the same as stealing from them. Fear steals control. It takes away the human part of a person, leaving only the animal behind."

But Huuq barely heard Aki's words. His thoughts had become like windblown snow. As they swirled, he grew more excited.

"Aki," he said, sitting up with eyes wide, "you know about all kinds of scary things across the Land."

Aki narrowed his eyes. "Why would you say that?" he whispered.

"It's that Paa," Huuq told him.

"The tall boy," Aki said, nodding. Paa was the tallest boy in camp.

Huuq answered in the Inhabitant way, saying *yes* by widening his eyes. "He thinks he's smarter than smart," Huuq continued, "just because his father lets him hunt now. He's always trying to impress his friends. He even calls you names."

"Young folk talk about me?" asked Aki.

Yes, indicated Huuq, again using his face.

"What do they say?" asked Aki. The man looked a bit bored, however, not truly interested in gossip.

"They say," said Huuq, gulping a great breath, "that you're the Monster Man."

"Why is that?"

"Because you deal with . . ."

Aki leaned back, laughed a bit. He seemed amused at Huuq's hesitation.

"It's true, though, isn't it?" pressed Huuq.

"What's true?" asked Aki, rocking gently as he spoke. He no longer looked Huuq in the eye, but seemed to watch something through the walls of the snow house; as though he were staring at a bird in flight far out over the Land.

"You know about them," Huuq insisted. "About the Its."

Now, Huuq did not actually say that word: "Its." Because he had spent some seasons speaking with Aki, he used various words that even Inhabitants might not have recognized. The word that he used instead of "Its" was one known to his people, though not one of their favourites.

Huuq actually said,

"Tuurngait."

It was a slightly grim word. Like the crunch of ice underfoot. Or wind as it whips at one's ear. The first syllable was a sound like the first three letters of "took," but lengthened. It was followed by an "r" that was mostly made in the back of the throat, almost becoming a "w" sound. Then, there was a "nguh," followed by an "iht."

All together.

Fast.

And the dread word was out.

Aki at last locked eyes with Huuq. He, better than anyone,

knew what the word meant. Tuurngait were the Its of the World. As to what they were: it was better to characterize them by what they were *not*. They certainly were not Inhabitant. Mostly. Not exactly "him." Or "her." Not quite alive. Or dead. There were many, many Its. Some seemed exactly alike. Others varied as widely from each other as did seaweed from falcons.

Its dwelled in the Sky Time. Just like Inhabitants and animals and plants. But they existed in deeper spaces.

The shaded paths of existence.

(Or non-existence.)

As Huuq had heard from Aki: if a person, even a very old and wise person, were to envision all that they knew—everything thought true, untrue, or wished for—they might be able to focus those thoughts for a short period of time. Then, they might store those ideas and wishes and experiences. Using will, imagination, they might place those bits of heart and mind in a sort of cave.

A cave, so to speak, of the soul.

Yet, if this were to happen, the cave would not be alone. It would become one more of a series of caves, all interconnected and unseen by most. A person might deal with the thoughts stored in their own cave. He or she might pick them up. Re-imagine them. Study or change them. But, unless they were a very rare sort of individual, they could never reach the items in other caves.

The other caves were where the Its dwelled.

Their caves were countless. And the Its could reach any other cave they wished. Though Huuq's mind was disturbed at the thought of it, Aki had tried to explain that reality was not quite as reliable as folk assumed. Wide as it might be, the great World was unfinished. Unset. Existence was such that objects, even creatures, only appeared to rest. Or move. Or have shape. Or be anything that they seemed to be.

The Its could see into the "suchness" of it all. They could enjoy, in their strange way, how each cave led to countless others, with the World never settling.

In such suchness, the Its were always *between*. Between order and chaos. Real and unreal. Something and nothing.

"You know something about Its, don't you?" Huuq repeated.

Aki said nothing.

"Well, what if we could bring some Its here?" asked Huuq. His voice became featherlight, almost as though he were speaking to himself. Or talking in his sleep. "What if we could scare the whole camp by bringing in—"

Aki cut him off sharply, saying,

"No. No, my Little Tooth. I wish you had listened more carefully to the stories I told you. If you had, you'd know that Its are nothing to want."

"But I did listen!" said Huuq, growing angry. "You told me all about the Its."

"In stories," muttered Aki. His gaze returned to Huuq. Not for the first time, Huuq noticed that one of the man's irises was oddly coloured. Blood-red. When Huuq and Aki had last spoken, the red iris had been on the right. At this moment, it was on the left.

"But the stories are true, aren't they?" asked Huuq.

Aki laughed, sounding like an old, loose drum. "Stories are never true, Little Tooth," he said. "There has never been a story that was true."

"Then you told me lies," Huuq said, fuming. He was very short on patience today.

"No," said the man, "I told you the opposite of lies. The opposite of lying is not truth, you know. Something better than truth. That's what stories tell. Better than truth. Better."

Huuq fell silent, hugging himself in anger and frustration. All he could think of was his father. Hollering. His mother being spidery. Dismissive. He hated it when Aki spoke in his roundabout way, putting left and right together—making nothing in the middle. It was like being told to shut up. And Huuq was sick of that.

He was tired of older folk telling him not to *be*.

Perhaps realizing that he had offended his only friend, Aki's face softened (though the red iris had switched to the right).

"My Little Tooth," the man said, "outside of storytelling,

I will talk to you of the Its only this one time. You should have realized, from the stories I've told, that you must never wish to bring Its into camp. Wishing to see, or talk to, or be assisted by Its . . . those are dangerous things."

"Why?" asked Huuq. His voice was suddenly full of curiosity, anger set aside like an overused toy. "The Its don't all sound bad. Not in the stories you tell."

As though begging for patience, Aki held up a leathery hand. The fingers were capped with the thickest, most yellow nails that Huuq had ever seen.

"Not all of the Its are foul," said Aki. "But that is because there are many kinds of Its. For as many creatures and objects and powers that there are in the World, there are Its. And many are Strong. With the Strength of the Land. Would you have such Strength brought here, to your own family, before you know whether a given It is foe or friend?"

While Huuq struggled for an answer, Aki fingered an ivory amulet about his neck. "Too risky," the Monster Man added. It now almost seemed as though the man were talking to himself. "Like I said, Its are nothing to wish for."

Huuq threw down the rest of his dried meat. Sensing that he was upset, Qipik licked at the back of his hand.

"No one around here likes change," Huuq said.

"I wasn't speaking against your idea," said Aki. "I just want to make sure it stays an idea. I . . . my kind, we usually keep Its away from Inhabitant places, Little Tooth. We don't bring them into camp unless it is to get rid of bad ones. The bad ones are . . . very bad."

Huuq was struck by a few of the man's words. Once again, he dropped his anger.

"There have been Its in camp?" he asked. "You saw them? When?"

"Well, they're not a problem now," said Aki, looking uncomfortable, as though he had said too much. "As long as Inhabitants and Its respect each other, there's no problem. When one or both lose their respect—"

"But I've never seen any Its," said Huuq.

"Yet," corrected Aki. "You haven't seen them yet. Most never get seen at all, because they can make themselves thin as breath. Slippery as water. Subtle as shadow. Not all Its are the same. I wonder if we should stop talking about this now."

"Is that why people bring you gifts?" demanded Huuq. "Are they thanking you for getting rid of Its?"

"Something like that," Aki answered, looking irritated. "Talk about different stuff, now."

Huuq's grin was triumphant. "So," he said. "Paa is right. You are the Monster Man. Can I give you a gift, too?"

Aki smiled back, but he shifted nervously. "I don't need gifts from you," he said.

"But I want you to have it," said Huuq. As he spoke, he reached back and fiddled with his wide hood. From its folds, he retrieved a knife. It was a *pana*: a special tool used to shape the blocks of snow from which a snow house was made. The blade was of sharpened caribou antler. It was just a bit shorter than Huuq's forearm.

Still smiling, Huuq stood and placed it on the seat next to Aki. Then he sat back down. Looking pleased.

Aki sat very still. He eyed the knife, but did not reach out to touch it.

"Where did you get that?" the man asked.

"From Father," answered Huuq. "He's the one with the broken head. He didn't even see when I took it."

As Huuq spoke, Aki's features grew stony. Slowly, he grabbed the edge of the hide on which Huuq had placed the blade. He raised the edge of the hide slightly, turning it, until the knife slid off and tumbled onto the floor.

"Take it back," Aki said.

For a moment, Huuq said nothing. He sat puzzled. Then he stood and, once again, picked up the knife.

"But . . . it's yours," he told Aki. "It's a gift. Like your name. Gift. I gave it to you."

"No, you didn't," Aki answered. "That knife is needed by somebody else. By your father. Doesn't he use it to make and maintain a house for you and your family? It wasn't up to you to decide who should have it, Little Tooth. You cannot give something that was never yours. Take it back."

Aki's words felt like a barb in Huuq's heart. He had expected the man to laugh along with him. To congratulate him for a clever theft.

Then Huuq's hurt turned to rage.

"It's yours!" he yelled.

It was the first time that Huuq had ever hollered at an adult. But he could feel the odd thrill of it, the sense of sudden freedom, vibrating throughout his lean frame. Again, his voice had assumed the same tone as Father's; though, disappointingly, it was without the animal quality that had made his encounter with Paa so satisfying.

Despite being hollered at, Aki's face was calm. He stared at Huuq, keeping his eyes level. Unblinking.

(The red iris was again on the left.)

"We are going to stay friends, Little Tooth," Aki told Huuq. "We are. But you have to listen carefully. Where there is respect between equals, some say, there is trade. Your father might have chosen to give me his knife. Someday. But he will not be able to. Because you stole it. You have taken away his free will. This is a fine thing for a monster to do. But for you as you are now . . . ?"

Aki let his words trail off. Huuq stared at the man for a long moment, while Qipik cringed nearby. It was as though the dog could understand something in this exchange.

Huuq's feelings seemed to clamber about, like lemmings, inside his rib cage.

Huuq dropped the knife.

Then he kicked it aside.

"I have no friends," he said.

Huuq fell to his hands and knees, and crawled out of Aki's snow house.

The Push

"At least you're still my friend," Huuq told Qipik. The words sounded lame. Of course the dog was his friend. Dogs had no minds of their own. They were nicest to those nice to them.

Huuq stood outside of Aki's snow house, squinting as a gust whipped up dry snow to sting his face. He turned, watching Qipik race over low white hills. He thought about the other gift, the one he still carried in the folds of his hood. It was a comb, old and valuable, carved into exquisite detail from walrus ivory. Its body had been shaped to look like a fish, so that the teeth suggested a fish's spines. He had nipped the comb from Mother. His plan: if Aki had been amazed and thankful to receive the pana-knife, Huuq would have next produced the comb, gaining his friend's admiration for all time.

Now he was no longer sure that Aki was a friend.

"Only half a friend left," he muttered, watching Qipik. The dog was about a stone's throw distant, idiotically rolling in fresh snow, as though to clean herself off.

In visiting Aki, Huuq had come to the edge of camp. Now sour, he decided that he did not want to see any people for a while. He walked away from Aki's home, kicking at snow, wiping his nose from time to time. As he went, he grew calmer, his memory peppered with Aki's words.

Had Aki actually driven monsters out of camp?

Huuq looked up when he heard a distant laugh. Standing between camp and Aki's place were Paa and his followers. Huuq could see Paa pointing at him. Then the large boy turned to say something to his buddies, and they all laughed again.

Huuq walked up to the bullies and asked, "What's wrong with you now?"

"See?" Paa said to his friends, talking as though Huuq were not present. "He's learning how to talk to Its. Like the Monster Man. That's why he visits him."

"He wouldn't tell me how to talk to Its," Huuq told Paa in a matter-of-fact voice. "I asked, so that I could bring some Its into camp. I thought they might find you a pet falcon, Paa, since your dad never did get you one."

Paa's eyelids betrayed only the slightest twitch this time. Huuq realized that the boy was getting used to the barbs about falcons.

"Maybe if we're lucky," said Paa, "the Its will like you so much, they'll take you away. The Monster Man with you."

"Oh, I was only joking, Paa," said Huuq. "About the falcon, I mean. If I'd really brought some Its here, I'd have asked them to eat you."

Paa's face changed. His eyes looked at once alarmed and angry. Among the Inhabitants, it was bad enough to joke about Its—threatening someone with them was the worst thing one could do. The threat of men or women who made alliances with Its was very real. Such people were feared.

The bullies cast glances at each other, unsure of how to take Huuq's words.

Paa's eyes narrowed in fury. In three great strides, the tall boy came within arm's reach of the much shorter Huuq.

Out shot both of the boy's arms. Paa's open palms hit Huuq in the chest, knocking the wind out of him.

When Huuq's body hit the snowy ground, it filled his ears with a sound like:

FFUFF!

Huuq opened his eyes. He was lying on his back, in the snow. He saw Paa's face hovering over him.

"Got any other smart things to say, less-than-nothing?" growled Paa. But the big boy, mad as he was, still glanced around nervously, in case some adults had spotted what was going on. Bad as it was for Huuq to make threats, it was just as bad for one of the Inhabitants to strike another. Especially over mere words.

There must not have been any grown-ups around, because Paa redirected his flinty gaze at Huuq.

"Now you're in your proper position," the boy said. "At my feet. Like an animal. If you're lucky, maybe I'll make you my dog. Say anything else and you'll get a kick."

Huuq scrambled out from under Paa and stood up, brushing snow from his coat. He glanced around for Qipik, but the dog was nowhere in sight. Why did he not have a brave dog— just one decent ally to defend him? Huuq felt like giving Qipik back to Aki.

Huuq skipped backward, in case Paa tried to knock him down again. He caught his breath, then said to Paa, "Now I know why your dad takes you hunting."

Paa's face changed once again, the anger leaving his features. The boy puffed out his chest, perhaps believing that Huuq had complimented him.

"It's because your father," Huuq added, "keeps hoping to lose you out on the Land."

Paa snarled and dashed at Huuq, but Huuq, smaller, lighter, sidestepped and ran. While Paa went stumbling, Huuq ran toward Aki's snow house.

Huuq was almost at Aki's entrance, the bullies chasing, when Huuq suddenly realized how embarrassed he would feel to face Aki right now. He had just finished telling off his best friend. Telling him that he was not a friend. How could he face Aki, cowering and sheltering from some bullies, like a child who could not fight his own battles?

So Huuq ran in a half-circle around Aki's snow house, heading for the hills where he had last seen Qipik. He could hear the gasps of the bullies behind him, chuffing like bears, still determined to catch him. Only one of the bullies, lurching, managed to claw at the hem of Huuq's coat. The bully failed to get enough of a grip, however, and Huuq darted away from him. For just a moment, though, Huuq wished that he himself had been a bear—just so that he could whirl around and swat at the bully with a black-clawed paw.

None of them would have been so quick to chase someone who could fight back.

No doubt, Paa had some humiliating punishment in mind for what Huuq had said to him. But Huuq was sick of feeling humiliated. His father had shamed him. Aki had shamed him. Paa, as usual, had wanted to fight—no, just someone to pick on. Paa and his pals never really wanted to fight, but only to make small kids feel smaller.

There was no way that Huuq was going to be caught. The day had already been filled with too much shame. He was not about to let some huge boy sit on him, spit on him, or worse, make him feel the sting of having his face rubbed in snow while the bullies did some more laughing.

He would not be caught!

Up into the hills, dashing knees on ice-cradled stones, gnashing teeth whenever he fell into troughs filled with loose snow, Huuq struggled without a backward glance. As he stumbled and regained his footing again and again, feeling muscles burn, he imagined . . . .

He imagined that he was a *caribou*.

For a few precious heartbeats, he did not envision himself as a boy, but as a tall bull caribou. Triumphant as it outraced wolves. He managed to see his feet as hooves. In his imagination, his legs were long. Dense with power.

Huuq lost track of time. The caribou fantasy had fled from his mind, so that he collapsed, sliding back down the hill a bit. His legs were cramped. Almost useless. Not those of a caribou. More like trousers full of jellyfish.

For a few minutes, he lay unable to think about anything but pain. The bullies could have packed snow over him and left him to suffocate, and he would hardly have cared.

Some dim awareness grew in him that the bullies would, should, pounce at any minute. But time passed. Wind and snow lashed at him.

The pain eased off.

Where were the bullies?

Huuq heard a scratching noise. He looked up, spitting snow from his lips. He spotted Qipik nearby, clawing at some jumbled rocks and ice, hunting for lemmings that the dog never caught.

Useless thing, thought Huuq.

Qipik stopped and glanced at Huuq, as though she had heard the thought. Though he knew that the dog had merely noticed his eyes on her, the idea that the mutt had sensed his anger made Huuq feel a bit better.

Maybe Father was right, thought Huuq. *Why did I fight for a dog who won't even help me?*

Qipik's pointed ears seemed to wilt.

Then Huuq was distracted by cramps in his legs. He gasped, reflexively keeping his voice low, even though he was pretty sure that the bullies had stopped following him.

With difficulty, Huuq stood up, realizing that he had climbed most of the way up the slope. The camp was in a wide valley below. There was no sign of the bullies.

A gust of cold air attacked Huuq's cheeks. He brushed snow from himself, balancing so as not to trip and tumble down the slope. If he fell here, he would not roll like some typical ball of snow. This would be a serious tumble, since huge, bone-shattering stones were scattered all over the slope.

Below him, he could see the larger rocks sticking up, white-capped, lending the slope an irregular look. Like an animal with mismatched patches of fur. He shuddered at the sight. Had he fought his way up past all of that? No wonder his legs were cramped. How had he made it at all?

A storm was coming in. Snowfall was making things hazy. Maybe that was why the bullies had turned back.

So, thought Huuq: Paa and his friends were fierce and brave when it was five against one. When they were home and confident. But they would not even brave a storm, or climb a harsh slope, to get the one they were after. It made Huuq even angrier, somehow, to think that their inner power did not match their outer strength.

Huuq's heart, his inner strength, was much greater than those of the bullies. He was sure of that. Yet they could still master him with size. Numbers. Viciousness.

If things had been right, he would have possessed strength. It was Huuq who should have been given teeth, not his cowardly dog. He would have given anything to bite back at the bullies. To scatter them. To horrify them. To make them feel, tenfold, the fear they liked to inflict on Huuq. He would have given every last drop of his own blood to see one drop of Paa's. Just to leave a couple of puncture marks in his skin. Scars that others would shudder at forever after!

Yet it seemed that nature had intended Huuq to possess nothing of his own. No strength. No speed. No respect. What was he, then, if only the victim of others? For the first time in his life, Huuq felt out of balance. He had rarely thought of himself as happy, but he had always felt that, despite the dull, foggy fear of camp life, he had held a place. If normal life had been winter, Huuq's humour had been the sweet tang of a summer berry. If ordinary existence had been darkness, Huuq's pranks had been the Many Players, chasing each other across the night Sky.

Yet, what if Huuq had finally stepped into reality? What if the Land was in fact cruel? With no room for humour? For mischief? What if life meant pitting strength against strength until one fell and a victor bared claws, stamped feet, gnashed teeth—stood howling while a victim lay in blood?

Helpless, hating his weakness, hating even himself, Huuq stood on the hillside. He squeezed his eyelids together. Shivering. Trying to embrace rage instead of sorrow.

Anger, he figured, was at least strong.

Sorrow was weak.

The tears came anyway.

The Egg

Huuq's chest was tight with anger as he stood watching his camp, his "home," to which he did not wish to return. In time, snow came more heavily, until he could barely see the collection of little snow houses below. Huuq's emotions throbbed, ebbed, like dying embers in the wind. He glanced at Qipik, who ran in and out of sight among the boulders on the slope. She was agile, and the slope's steepness did not seem to tire her.

Huuq stood glancing back and forth between the camp and the top of the slope. He was so close to the summit. He knew the danger of a snowstorm, as did all Inhabitants. But as wracked and pained as he felt, he had never quite known this sense of freedom. He had outraced the bullies. He had wandered further than ever from camp. Without an adult's supervision.

Would Father have thought him so empty now, having seen what Huuq had accomplished on his own?

Would Mother have found him so broken?

What was at the top of this hill, anyway?

Huuq decided that, since it was a short distance, he would continue upward. It was steep here, and he started out thinking that the climb was an easy one. But Qipik came bounding out of the snowfall, tail wagging, tongue waggling, wanting to play.

Huuq pushed her away, snarling, "Oh, so now you're so loyal to me?"

Then Huuq teetered, trying to regain his balance. A mitt slid from his hand, becoming lost in the snow between some jagged rocks. On shoving Qipik, Huuq had nearly sent himself tumbling back down the slope.

Such uncontrolled falls were known to kill people. Huuq's alarm emerged as anger toward his dog.

"Get away!" Huuq yelled at Qipik, finding his balance again.

Ears wilting a bit, the dog backed away from him. Then she turned and began, in her dog-like way, to wind around random boulders. Huuq let out a chuff of frustration. Then he ignored her and continued upward.

By the time Huuq finally reached the top, he was gasping worse than when he had outraced the bullies. The snowfall was still not too bad, so Huuq could see a wide field stretching out for some distance. If there were more hills beyond the snowy field, Huuq was unable to see them.

He wished, suddenly, that he possessed his father's Land knowledge—what grown folk admiringly called being *pisiti*. Like any hunter, his father would have been able to tell if the storm was getting worse.

Huuq stood for a few minutes, blinking snowflakes away from his eyelashes, his bare left hand jammed up the right sleeve of his parka, to keep it warm. He squinted into the distance.

Were there shapes ahead?

It seemed as though, far out in the field, there were a few dark, rounded figures. He counted three of them.

Huuq's eyes grew wide and the breath caught in his throat.

Were they bears? Huuq had forgotten about the constant threat of bears. In this season, they were hungry, and would be more than happy to stop for a quick meal of Stupid Boy.

Huuq hunched low, retreating back to the slope so as not to be seen. It was probably a futile move. He imagined himself standing next to a bear, then running away from it for several hours. The hypothetical bear would still have been able to smell him. They could smell flesh, dead or alive, through several feet of snow.

But if the distant shapes were bears, wouldn't Qipik have smelled them and started to go crazy? She was a coward, but she was at least a dog, and there had never been a time when the Inhabitants had not relied on dogs to warn them of bears.

And where was Qipik now? The dog was out of sight.

Once again, she had let him down.

Still not going to let Father breed her, thought Huuq. *Though I won't have a choice if bears eat me.*

But Huuq was already beginning to wonder if he was really seeing bears. The dark figures were not moving. The field was one big, white sheet, so it was impossible to tell how large the shapes really were. Or how far away.

After some minutes of staring, Huuq became sure that he had given in to his own imagination. He was probably looking at rocks. Tall. Standing. Like so many people. But the shapes were still interesting against the whiteness of the field. So Huuq still wanted a closer look.

As Huuq trudged through the snow, nearing the stones, he was pleased to find that the ground was pretty level. He was tired of stumbling over ice-encrusted rocks. The cramps were only now letting go of his leg muscles, but they still burned.

Qipik soon joined him, bounding out of nowhere. Huuq made a face at the dog, even though he was secretly happy to see her. Qipik ran circles around him, goofing and yipping, stopping to assume a play position from time to time, as Huuq approached the standing stones.

By the time Huuq was within thirty paces of the stones, he could count a total of nine. He had not been able to see all of them when he'd been positioned so far away. They were different sizes and shapes, though all stood higher than his own head. Such boulders were not unusual on the stone-covered Land—though these were odd, because they were the only rocks on the field. They were also bizarre in that they almost formed a complete circle. The "opening" of the ring faced Huuq.

Huuq cast his gaze about the field, squinting in the unnecessary way that people do when searching. But he could not spot any other standing stones past the thickening snowfall. Qipik bounded in wide circles around him, her outline sometimes hazy through the veil of white.

Huuq's eyes were drawn to a lump of snow that lay amid the standing stones. This, too, was a stone. But it was covered in fresh snow and only came as high as Huuq's knee. It struck him that it looked *placed*. Small as it was compared to the larger stones, it was too big for any lone man to lift. Yet it seemed that someone had wanted it at the ring's centre.

On the Land, where there were no trees but as many stones as one might want, Inhabitants had endless uses for rocks of different sizes and shapes. There were round ones, smooth as an egg. There were rectangular ones. Square ones. Flat ones. Tiny, shiny ones. Gargantuan black ones. There were stones that could be used to build a little summer house. There were those for building traps to catch fish or other animals. There were rocks that could border a fire, so that one might boil some eggs or have a nice bit of fireweed tea. There were stones to sit on, to work on, to shelter oneself from the wind, or simply to hold down the edges of a tent. There were rocks that one piled over the dead. And for hunting or navigating, there were *inuksuit*: stones assembled to look like an Inhabitant.

Yet, with all these uses for rocks, Huuq had never seen anything quite like what he saw now. It was not that the sight was shocking. It was simply that there was no reason for Inhabitants to place a rock in the middle of a bunch of standing stones.

Qipik suddenly stopped in front of Huuq, with her back to him.

She was staring at the low, snow-covered stone, the one amid all the others. She emitted low, worried whines. From time to time, she gave Huuq a quick glance, before her amber eyes returned to the stone.

Huuq walked up and bent over the rock, noticing that a crack ran down its centre. Very little snow had settled in the crack, and it seemed that some object lay at its middle. Huuq frowned, then removed his bare left hand from his sleeve. He reached into the crack, not quite to his elbow, and fished out the object.

Whatever he had retrieved, it was smooth but surprisingly warm. It fit perfectly into his palm.

While Qipik whined by his side, Huuq turned the object about in his hand. It reminded him of a goose egg, because of its

size, though it was more rounded than most bird eggs. Like all Inhabitants, Huuq had grown up eating every kind of egg. Seagull eggs were fishy. The yolk of a tern egg possessed an amazing golden colour. Yet he had never seen an egg like this one (if it really was an egg). If Huuq did not look at it directly, its spots and lines grew brownish or rusty in colour, so that it resembled a kind of stone. But if he stared at it directly, odd patterns and tones jumped out at him. If he concentrated on one spot, he could even see colours—not unlike those of the Many Players.

Suddenly, the colours seemed to move, shifting in a gentle, sinuous way. The sight made Huuq smile in awe, but it also made him feel crawly, so that goosebumps stood up on his neck and arms. A wild thought rose in him: that he must not touch this object too much. Before he could seize the thought and weigh it in his mind, an impulse seemed to course out of his brain and down his arm. Like a weasel made of lightning. The feeling flashed into his fingertips. Straightened his fingers as it went.

His hand opened.

The object fell.

It did not have a hard landing. It landed in the snow at Huuq's feet. He jumped back, startled.

That was when Huuq learned that it really was an egg: for the shell had cracked open.

There, in the middle of the opened eggshell, lay a tiny white form. Huuq had only a moment to glimpse it. But it did not look like a chick. It did not seem to resemble a bird at all, but was wholly covered in clean, dry, perfect fur. There was not even a trace of fluid, as one might see with a newly hatched chick. The little creature shone as though each of its hairs was made of pure moonlight. Its body was curled in what looked like sleep . . . .

Huuq found himself knocked back as Qipik barged her way in front of him. She hunched over the silvery creature from the egg, her back to him.

A surge of horror: his dog was gobbling the little animal up.

"No!" he hollered. "No!"

He did not know why it seemed so important to keep

Qipik from devouring the egg's contents, but reflexes nevertheless kicked in. Roaring at his dog, Huuq grabbed her by the shoulders and tried to tear her away from the egg. Qipik was amazingly strong, though, and by the time Huuq got a hold of her neck fur and yanked with all his inconsiderable might, she was already licking her lips.

There were no more than empty pieces of shell lying in the snow, their contents now in Qipik's stomach.

"Less-than-nothing!" Huuq roared at his dog. "Now how do I know what that thing was?"

Something at Huuq's core seemed to ripple, like the agitated surface of a pool. The creature in the egg had seemed important. There was no reason why.

Qipik ignored him. She raced away into the snowfall.

"Stay lost this time!" Huuq called after her.

He did not really mean the words, and he immediately regretted them. Huuq suddenly feared that his relationship with Qipik was eroding, just as his relationship with Aki had. The wind had risen in only the last few seconds, so that Huuq had to turn his hooded head away from the lashing snow. The snowfall was now so thick that he was barely able to see.

"Blanket?" he called.

I'm sorry, he thought. He thought it to Qipik, and at once to Aki. Even to his parents.

Huuq was sure that he could find camp by remembering what types of standing stones lay closest or farthest from where he had come. As long as he made a roughly straight line from the stones, he would probably be able to find the slope. But he shuddered to think of what the downhill climb would be like.

Suddenly, he did not like this place. There was a feeling here. It was as if the stones were watching him. Judging.

Was it his imagination, or was the wind unusually cold?

Huuq glanced back at where the shell pieces lay, now almost invisible beneath new snowfall. He wondered if he should grab a bit of shell, take it back with him, perhaps ask an adult to tell him what kind of creature had laid the egg. Before he could reach down, though, he shuddered once again.

There was a new sense of dread in this place.

Huuq stood for several minutes, trying to make sure that he was facing the right direction to get himself home.

Forget the shell, he told himself.

He took a step, then stopped.

Had he heard a voice behind him?

Huuq turned at the sound of someone's low, grumbling voice, and saw the outline of a hunter through the snowfall. The man was a silhouette only, hood pulled tight, so that Huuq could not see his features.

Huuq sighed with relief. Here was a grown-up, returning home on the heels of the storm. This was someone who could get him safely back to camp. But where was the man's equipment? He had no spear or bow or any other tool in hand. Where was his dog team?

The man let out a low grumble once again. Huuq still could not discern any words.

Then Huuq noticed two more hunters nearby, standing almost out of sight behind the closest man. Like the first hunter, they held nothing in hand.

In a traditional Inhabitant greeting, Huuq raised his hands and smiled. The hunters did not respond.

Huuq gasped as one of the men took a step. Though it was but a step, the action raised goosebumps across Huuq's entire body. The forward leg seemed to lengthen with the step, pulling the hunter an impossible distance. When the figure stood still again, Huuq's eyes stayed locked on the man's knees. It seemed as though, on each leg, he had more than one knee—multiple joints that writhed under his pants.

Huuq felt a new flush of horror as the other hunters stepped likewise. All three made crazily long strides. Within seconds, they had moved around the furthest stones, brushing shoulders against the rock as they went, like a dog brushing past a friend in greeting. At all times, they stayed bent, leading with their hoods, the dark openings of which were turned toward Huuq. Like normal folk, the ruffs of their hoods were encircled with fur. But the tones and textures of the ruffs, long guard hairs jutting from mangy patches, even bits looking almost like dark feathers, were like nothing that Huuq had ever witnessed.

Then they were inside the circle, sliding into their own sort of circle around Huuq. They began to move faster, clothes bulging then collapsing in spots, as though they were stuffed with raging weasels. They continued to hunch, making guttural, gargling noises. It was as though they were grumbling. Muttering. Sometimes, even chanting. Or trying to sound past obstacles lodged deep in their throats.

At once, as though they had somehow agreed upon the action, all three removed their hoods.

The three were now close enough that Huuq could see each of them clearly, even through the snow.

Their hoods did not reveal heads.

At least, not Inhabitant heads.

There was a kind of rippled fungus that grew on the Land. It was dull black in colour. It clung to rocks, snuggling up to the more colourful lichens of red and orange. Unlike most things on the Land, the stuff was ugly and made stone look as if it had been infected with a disease. Huuq had never known anyone to use the fungus for anything, and he'd always avoided touching it.

The "head" of the figure standing directly in front of Huuq reminded him of that black fungus. The mass beneath the hood turned out to be little more than tarry folds, without ears or nose or mouth. At first, Huuq assumed that it at least possessed eyes. Yet, what he had thought were eyes, he realized, were two separate creatures crawling in and out of the folds. They were like mites, clusters of stubby legs around bodies the size of eyeballs. The mites pulsed, generating their own dim light: violet from one, orange from the other. Among the folds, Huuq could see others of their kind. Smaller. All different colours. Hiding as though shy.

The figure to Huuq's right looked nothing like the first. Its head resembled the skull of a seagull, yellow bone slick with stuff that might have been grease or slime. The lower part of the beak hung open. Out of it fell a great, pink tongue, like that of an exhausted dog. The tongue was almost as long as Huuq's arm. Its surface was covered in what might have been tattoos, except that their multi-hued patterns never ceased to shift and swirl. In the figure's right eye socket, there shone a golden pebble of light. Like a miniature sun. The left socket looked like a patch of night Sky. Complete with stars.

The final figure, on Huuq's left, possessed a head that resembled the body of a brine shrimp. Brine shrimp (or *kinguit*, as Huuq's folk called them) were usually tiny, grey, buggy things that infested the Sea and lakes, picking clean any dead flesh placed in the water. Leaving bones for the shrimp was a good way to clean them. In the summer, a bored Huuq had often watched the creatures squiggling their way through

the water. On their endless search for death.

It looked as if someone had stuck a head-sized brine shrimp onto the shoulders of this being. The grey bulk curved down toward Huuq, multiple legs working in rhythm, as when an impatient person thrums their fingers. The way the legs framed the head might have made Huuq think of a beard, except that the ends of those legs were tipped with tiny hands. They were complete, four digits plus a thumb. The flesh of them was swollen. Pink. Pudgy. But for their small size, they reminded Huuq of a baby's hands.

Huuq stood rigid. Breathless. Terror seemed to surround him like an actual substance. It was no ordinary fear, but a new and nameless emotion.

He stood as though in invisible ice. Held in solid fear.

Some dim part of Huuq remembered his fight with Aki. He had wanted to bring Its to camp. He had thought that the idea of getting Its to frighten everyone would make the greatest fun. He had even threatened to send Its against Paa. In many ways, Huuq had "wished" (as Aki had put it) for Its.

Now, with three Its staring him down, Huuq thought that they seemed worlds away from anything fun.

They had nothing to do with fun.

The Its

All at once, the Its stopped moving.

The It directly in front of Huuq leaned closer. The mites ceased to crawl among its fungal folds. Huuq realized that there were tiny eyes on the orange and violet mites. They were watching him.

The It made more of its guttural sounds. From where, Huuq could not tell. There was no evidence of a mouth, though the black fungus of the It's head seemed to quiver as it spoke. He noticed that the It emitted no steam of breath on the cold air.

Still struggling for his own breath, Huuq fell to his knees. He could not understand whatever the creature was saying. But as the It gargled over and over again, Huuq began to make out a word.

"Why?"

The It repeated the word, until the others joined in.

"Why?"

"Why?"

"Why?"

Some flutter of an idea told him that they were calling him by name.

"Yes?" he managed to squeak.

Yet the Its kept asking:

"Why?"

"Why?"

"Why?"

Huuq at last decided that they were asking a question.

"Please . . . please tell me what you mean," he said.

"Why . . . take?" the fungal It asked.

The It's words still meant nothing to Huuq. But he saw the being turn, for a moment, to where the egg had fallen. He thought that he understood.

"Why . . . take?" repeated the It.

"Why . . . take?" echoed the others at once.

"You mean the thing in the egg?" asked Huuq. "The animal inside?"

The Its seemed to exchange glances, before refocusing on Huuq.

"So," groaned the It with the fungus face, "the Egg . . . it has . . . become."

"What?" demanded the It whose head resembled a seagull skull (somehow it talked, despite its lolling tongue). "What . . . did it become?"

Huuq hugged himself against the cold. "I still don't understand what you're saying," he told them.

"The animal," said the It, looking like a talking brine shrimp. Its grey, plated form curled and uncurled as it gargled out words. The tiny baby fingers wiggled. "What . . . animal . . . was hatched?"

Huuq thought for a moment. "I don't know," he finally told them. "It had silver fur. It looked like it was made of moonlight. It looked asleep."

He did not bother to add that his dog had eaten the creature. But he flushed with horror when the fungus-faced It said,

"You must . . . give it to us."

Huuq had never bothered to keep count of the things he had stolen. If he had ever made the attempt, he would have lost track of such a number by now. But thefts were never simple matters. Since Huuq had already established himself as a figure of suspicion among the families of camp, he had come to rely upon misdirection. Most thefts were framed with lies: the carefully crafted ones that set up the initial nip, followed by the casual, improvised fibs, flying like sparks from his tongue, that kept the fun going.

He had never tried lying to an It.

"I can't give it to you," said a truthful part of Huuq. Then the spontaneous Liar stepped in before he could stop it, blurting, "That's because I'm keeping it safe."

"Where?"

"Where?"

"Where?"

"Never mind where," said Huuq. Lies were now flowing, dancing out of his mouth like a tiny waterfall. "You weren't around," he added. "I found it. That's fair. What do you expect if you're just going to leave something on the ground? And near a camp?" This was going surprisingly well. Lying, stealing, deceiving: these skills had all served him well in growing up. They would save him now.

The Its turned to regard each other. In their guttural voices, they chattered away. Oddly, the more Huuq listened to them, the more he seemed to understand. It was as though their sounds meant nothing, but the noises were nonetheless *heavy*. In Huuq's imagination, the meanings behind those sounds seeped out of the creatures. Then the meanings sank down below Huuq's feet. Into the Land. From there, Huuq's own brain somehow pulled them up again. It seemed, by some trick of suchness, that the creatures' thoughts became Huuq's.

He could tell, for instance, that the Its feared something. In fact, they were terrified. And that gave Huuq some confidence. He could discern, amid the shifting of their weighty, drippy thoughts, that they were even less smart than the camp folk from whom he typically stole. More importantly: he could tell that they believed the things he told them.

"Return," the fungal It demanded of Huuq.

"Return."

"Return."

Huuq immediately knew that they were not demanding that he return to camp. They wanted the contents of the Egg. That reminded Huuq of Aki, insisting that he return the pana-knife taken from his father. Now, as then, Huuq grew furious.

He stood up, and the fungal It took a step back.

Huuq grinned, despite feeling rather unfriendly.

"What will you trade," Huuq demanded, "for whatever was in that Egg?"

(After all, hadn't Aki said: "Where there is respect between equals, there is trade"?)

The Its seemed taken aback. They turned to one another, talking so fast that their meanings became a gooey tangle of ideas to Huuq's mind. When they were done, the fungal It turned back to Huuq and gargled,

"Whatever . . . your most . . . recent wishes. That is . . . the trade. Most recent wishes . . . granted."

Huuq's eyes grew wide. Was this actually possible? He had three Its at his beck and call. Finally, life had become fair again!

"Well, I think the first thing I'd wish for is—"

The It raised its hands, cutting Huuq off. Huuq noticed, now, that those hands were just as monstrous as the rest of the creature. One resembled a gnarled root covered in hairs. Like those of a spider. The other was a slender, feminine hand. It would have been quite normal, were it not made of green and black stone.

"No need," gurgled the It, "to . . . speak of wishes. Strength . . . of the Land . . . hears . . . your heart's . . . screams."

"Things . . . you wish," gargled the It with the head like a seagull skull, "are part of . . . you. Not us."

"But," protested Huuq, "that doesn't make any sense. Even *I'm* not sure what I want yet. Let's discuss what you can give me."

"Already," gurgled the third It, the one whose head was a giant brine shrimp, "done. Your wishes . . . were always part of . . . you. So they . . . remain."

"Such . . . is wishing," added the fungus-faced It, and Huuq could not tell if its thoughts were tinted with humour or pity. "No different . . . from being. Skin . . . outside. Fur inside. Being is . . . a matter of understanding. There is no . . . difference."

The Its chatted some more between each other, while Huuq grew increasingly angry. Nothing they said made sense.

Huuq thought about some of the stories that Aki had told him. None had described beings such as these. Were Its typically crazy, or was it just these three?

Then the thoughts of the Its shifted.

Huuq could sense the sudden turn. This impacted on Huuq's mind like the feeling of a boulder, pushed too far, finally rolling from an edge. There were new thoughts now, even heavier than those that had come before. They were not feelings of fear.

Wrath.

Wrath.

Wrath!

He could sense the emotions churning in whatever the Its used for souls.

Once again, Huuq's chest grew tight with fear. He suddenly realized that his demands had been foolish. He should have run from these Its. He should have at least explained. He should have begged and told them the truth instead of making stupid demands . . . .

"Fine, fine," said Huuq, trying to steady his voice. He swallowed. "I'll just go home now. I'll bring the little Egg animal to you tomorrow," he lied.

Before he could babble further, the fungal It groaned,

"No. Not yet. We . . . must have . . . a promise."

"Yes!" cried Huuq. "I promise! I definitely promise to bring—"

"Not . . . words," interrupted the It.

"Sounds," said the seagull skull, "cannot . . . make promises."

"Only . . . you . . . can promise," added the brine shrimp It, nodding. "Only you . . . can give."

"Oh, but I do give you my promise!" insisted Huuq. "I'm very reliable. Ask anyone. You have as many of my promises as you need. Yes? Let me go home now. Please? I'll bring back your pet!"

He just wanted to get away from the Its, was willing to say anything to escape. The feelings roiling off of these creatures made him nauseated. He could sense that their boggy thoughts had turned for the worse.

They did not mean him well.

"And . . . so," said Fungus Face, "I will take . . . these."

Huuq, beginning to tear up from sheer terror, did not manage to beg further before the It reached out a rootlike hand, tendrils writhing. Lights of violet and orange, like streams of fiery blood, seemed to run through the appendage. There was a surge that touched the air itself. That felt as if it were grabbing the very substance of whatever lay close to Huuq. More alarmingly, it seized whatever he was *made* of. It was as though a tide, a secret Sea inside the Land, had reached up from under Huuq's feet. The effect was like being pushed by the bully, Paa, only this time from the inside out.

Suddenly, he was falling.

Huuq landed hard on his side, crying out. But he truly screamed when he looked toward his legs.

They were gone.

His legs had not been cut off; they simply were *no longer there.*

He did not experience any pain. He was not bleeding. It was just that Huuq's legs had disappeared below the pelvis. His empty boots had rolled away from the pant legs, which lay in folds. Huuq could see the material blowing slightly in the wind.

Huuq could only stare.

And think nothing.

Do nothing.

But stare.

Then, like Fungus Face, Seagull Skull reached out a hand. Its fingers were the feathers of different birds, tipped with tiny snarls of lightning instead of nails.

When Huuq saw the gesture, he began to scream. To plead in as many ways as he could imagine.

Yet, once again, there was that violent tug. Huuq's left arm, the one whose hand lacked a mitt, was wrenched from his shoulder. This time, Huuq turned in time to see the limb disappear into the field itself. It was as though a toothless mouth, lips made only of frost and stone, had opened in the Land. The earth parted to suck down Huuq's arm, before snapping shut in a puff of windblown snow.

Though there was no pain, Huuq could not stop screaming.

He turned to see the shrimp-headed It. Its many crab-like legs no longer resembled a beard. The creature hovered very close. Miniature baby hands, each tipping a leg, flared tiny fingers out toward Huuq.

"I," gurgled Brine Beard, "will . . . take what I . . . see now."

A new feeling, like great palms clamping over his entire head, made Huuq's body spasm.

He went suddenly blind and deaf. He tried to cry out, but he was unsure of whether he still had a voice. He could feel through his skin. He could breathe. But along with sight and hearing, his sense of smell had disappeared.

An animal voice still wailed in the cavern of his being: the Its were the truest thieves. Not he.

Without shedding a drop of blood, they had taken everything from him.

6

The Blanket

uuq could still feel the cold. But without sight or hearing, he had no idea how long the Its remained, watching his new, wretched state.

Why had they done this?

They had believed him. He had felt that, somehow, through the wild way in which their thoughts seemed to go down into the Land, then back up into his own head. The Its had believed that he could retrieve the Egg's contents for them (even though the contents were long gone, now in Qipik's digestive tract).

Yet, assuming they *had* believed him, why would they have maimed him like this?

He had one arm left. He could feel that. He used the limb to shuffle himself around, turn most of his exposed flesh away from the wind. Then he felt his features.

Everything was gone. His eyes were smooth, fleshy sockets. His nose was a nub with two tiny holes in it. Huuq's mouth was a slit. His ears were shallow pits. They had even taken his long, blue-black hair.

Without tears, with sobs that somehow went inward instead of out, Huuq began to cry.

Time passed. Wind howled. Huuq grew numb. Even the despair, burning like a star within him, went cold. Dim. Like a forgotten campfire. He eventually realized that the storm would blow on and on, whether he was healthy or maimed. Why would the Land care if he had offended some monsters?

He was dying in the cold.

And no one cared.

After a time, Huuq was surprised by an odd sensation. It was warm, at once slick and rough. He could feel something rubbing at where his face had been. There was another such sensation. Then another.

Qipik.

Qipik, he realized, had come back. She was greeting him. Licking.

Huuq had forgotten all of his earlier anger at the dog. He was just glad to have a friend. He hooked his only arm around her frame, pulled her close.

Somehow, Qipik seemed to understand that Huuq was cold. She leaned into him. She rolled, until she was mostly on top of him. Normally, Huuq hated it when she did that. But this time, she was earning her name.

She was his Blanket.

Hours passed. A thick layer of snow settled over boy and dog. But Qipik kept herself between Huuq and the freezing wind. Another soul might have walked past the two of them lying there, unable to tell them from a mound of snow.

And Qipik never moved.

Not even once.

However much snow piled over her and Huuq, she was as still as stone.

But warm.

The Replacements

In time, Huuq was startled awake. Even though his last memories included having no ears, he was sure that someone had called his name:

"Hhhhhhuuq . . . ?"

Huuq sat up, and found that he could see. He was under caribou hide blankets—good ones, with thick fur and no thinned-out patches. He was comfortable. He lay on a sleeping platform at one side of a small snow house. Someone had removed his coat and lighter, inner top.

Nearby, there was a tiny soapstone lamp. It was roughly hewn. The lamp let off light from an uneven row of little orange flames, burning seal oil. Like all Inhabitants, Huuq knew that women kept such soapstone lamps for their families. His mother had a wonderful one, of greenish, striped stone, that even Huuq dared not steal. She was skilled in its use and her flames were never uneven.

Huuq knew of only one man who kept a lamp, and such an ugly one at that.

He was obviously in Aki's snow house.

But who had brought him here?

"Me," said a low voice. It was like a silky whisper.

Huuq looked around, but there was no one in sight.

Then, just behind him, he spotted Qipik. She was lying on the floor to Huuq's left. Her tail was wagging. But she did not rise to greet him.

Forgetting that monsters had taken his left arm, Huuq reached out for his dog, and stifled a scream. But it was not because his arm was gone.

From the shoulder down, Huuq's arm was white with fur. At first, it looked as if his own bear-fur pants had been wrapped tight about the limb.

Yet it *was* his limb. His arm. And his own fur. He knew that in an instant, as though it had been a fact borne in his mind since birth.

His arm was actually a leg: the leg of a white bear.

For a long moment, Huuq sat rigid with shock, unsure of what he was seeing. But no matter how much time he invested in staring, the arm was still there: thick and muscled, covered in silvery-white fur. His fingers and thumb were now a bear's digits, tipped with heavy black claws.

Huuq moved his arm about, feeling it. The deadly points of his claws frightened him—then made him excited. He bared them. He took a moment to rake the air.

His bear limb was fast.

So fast!

But how far up did this arm go? Huuq started feeling about his shoulder, and realized that the fur, the heavy muscle, went right to his spine. Right to the base of his neck.

Then he paused, feeling a bit alarmed.

There was fur on his neck.

This was a different kind of fur. Not bear. He was sure of it. From the time they were born, Inhabitants had chances to feel all kinds of fur, and this was not bear hair he was feeling. He plucked at some of it, pinched around his neck, until he caught a couple of strands between thumb and forefinger.

The hairs were dark, orange and black. Like wolverine fur.

What was going on?

Huuq's heart generated feelings like the World generating weather; as on the Land itself, small gusts of emotion came together into storms. Huuq started out confused. But he was also thrilled. And his confusion made him curious. His thrills made him startled. Together, the emotions clashed and spiralled into a column of fear in his breast. And that column climbed, widening, until his heart began to race and he felt almost as scared as when the Its had turned against him.

Huuq felt all around his face. It was completely distorted, elongated into a snout with heavy jaws and brow. It did not feel Inhabitant at all. But at least it was not like before, when the Its had taken his entire face away.

He could see.

Hear.

Smell.

The smells! The scents in this little snow house were far richer than he remembered. Again, he glanced at Qipik. She smelled like dirty, wet dog, along with several other scents that he could not identify. Even at arm's length, he could smell her last meal—frozen fish—lingering on her breath.

Disoriented, fighting the need to vomit, Huuq rolled off the sleeping platform and stood.

He toppled. Fell.

There, lying on the floor of Aki's snow house, Huuq got a chance to see his legs.

This time, he really did scream.

His legs were those of a caribou. It was as simple as that. There were the hooves. There were the long, sinewy legs, covered in the same kind of hide Huuq had just been using for blankets. But this was *his* hide. It was him. Alive. Part of his body. Huuq moved the legs about, kicking at the air as he lay on the floor of Aki's home, as though motion could somehow cast them off like boots.

Huuq was not breathing very evenly. He writhed in panic for a few moments, breath sticking in his chest until he began to see stars.

The stars gave way to blackness.

The Monster

uuq next awoke to Qipik licking his face. He was still on the floor of Aki's snow house. He guessed that he had passed out from shock. His last memories were of overwhelming nausea and panic at seeing . . . .

He forced himself to look down along his body.

There they were again. Caribou legs. He stared at them for some time, the wind moaning as it polished the snow house's exterior.

At last, Huuq gave a kick at the air with one hoof. Well, the new legs were not exactly uncomfortable. In fact, moving them felt pretty good.

His bear arm was also there. He used it to push himself up from the floor. The arm, as it turned out, was so strong that he could lift his own body like a feather. Out of sheer curiosity, Huuq did not try to stand upright. Not right away. Instead, he balanced on the silvery bear arm, thinking. He tried doing a few one-armed push-ups with it. He did many of them, eventually losing count. The arm never tired and Huuq stopped only after he got bored.

Wobbling, Huuq managed to balance himself on his new legs. Within little time, he found that awkwardness was not a problem—the legs were pretty easy to balance on. But they were almost as strong as the bear arm. Strangest of all, they were *springy*. He had to move very lightly to keep from launching himself through one of the snow house walls.

Huuq glanced at Qipik, who hunched low, whining. He tried to smile at his dog, and his mouth moved strangely. Qipik

actually shuffled back a bit, looking displeased at the sight of him grinning. It was an odd reaction, but then, the whole World had become strange.

Huuq desperately wished that Aki were here to advise him. How had he even arrived back at Aki's place? And where was the so-called Monster Man?

Huuq started to voice his frustration, but was shocked by the sounds coming from his own throat. They were garbled, guttural, not unlike the gargling noises the three Its had made. He tried to force himself to speak properly—and the result was that he bit his tongue.

Wait: why were his teeth so sharp?

With great care, Huuq reached his sole Inhabitant hand up to his mouth. He felt around. His lips were covered in fur. His teeth were quite long. Pointed. Like those of a wolf or fox or bear.

Or a wolverine. Yes, definitely a wolverine. Wide. Flat. Blunt, with heavy bones. But not a wolverine's small head size. This was a wolverine head larger than a dog's; as large as his own head had been.

As with those drippy It-thoughts fished up from the Land, sudden truths came to occupy Huuq's mind: the Its had not simply stolen his arms, legs, and face. They had replaced them. The Its had remade him. Then the heavy thoughts, veil-like, trembled in his being, so that the exact words of the Its returned to his memory:

"Things . . . you wish . . . are part of . . . you."

"Your wishes . . . were always part of . . . you."

"Such . . . is wishing. No different . . . from being. Skin . . . outside. Fur inside. Being is . . . a matter of understanding. There is no . . . difference."

For a long while, Huuq stood thinking. Remembering. When Paa and the bullies had chased him, when they had almost caught him, had he not experienced a special moment? Had he not wished that he could turn, swatting at one of them with the claws of a bear?

And when he had been struggling up the hillside, legs

burning, had he not wished for the powerful limbs of a caribou?

And when he had stood at the top of the hill, trying to rage because that was better than crying, had he not thought about a wolverine's terrible jaws? Had his heart not cried out to the World, to the very suchness of things, wishing that he had been born with the strength to defend himself?

The fullness of the situation at last came to mind.

Something in his World had moved. Shifted. Somehow, the Its had made outward reality of his own anger. His terror. His despair. The monsters had brushed against his heart, so that even his mind was slightly different now. It was as though Huuq could *see* his own thoughts, with an eye inside his brain. The things that he knew now sat like objects in the dark of his being. They were like coloured reflections in water. But rippled.

Huuq was different now. More an It than a person.

Had he become a monster?

While he stood thinking, he also recalled that the Its had taken his Inhabitant limbs and face. They still held them. He could sense that. They wanted him to bring back whatever had been in that Egg. In return for his original limbs and face?

Huuq had not told them his dog had eaten the Egg's contents. How would he get his Inhabitant parts back?

And would he want them?

Part Two
HUUQ THE MONSTER

The Prey

He had to find Aki. Only the Monster Man could explain exactly what had happened. What it meant to have changed in this way. Huuq was confused. Experiencing mixed fear and excitement. He was not sure how he felt. But he at least knew that he needed information.

Or the presence of a friend.

Huuq fumbled about the snow house until he found his clothes. Someone had neatly set them to one side. Had Aki already tended to him while he was passed out? Everything was there, except for his mitts and boots. Huuq remembered losing the mitt from his left hand—the one that was now a bear's paw—on his way up the hillside. As for boots, when he had last seen them, they'd been lying in the snow, without legs to fit them.

It was good to have legs again, even if they were a caribou's. Huuq doubted that boots would stay on them, anyway.

There was some struggling—a couple of falls—involved in getting his pants on. Putting on his light inner coat and outer parka were easier. But Huuq noted that the bear paw was not great for grabbing things. The claws tended to catch on whatever material they touched. He soon learned to keep his "paw" (it was still hard to think of it as such) away from his clothes. He dressed himself one-handed.

Huuq went through some more awkwardness in figuring out how to get down on his hands and knees. His new limbs moved at somewhat different angles from Inhabitant ones.

Huuq started to crawl out of Aki's snow house. He made it about halfway when he heard a voice behind him say,

"Ssssstay!"

It was that low, silky voice that he had earlier heard.

Huuq paused, looking behind him. But there was no one else in the snow house. Only Qipik was there.

Huuq shrugged and crawled out of the snow house. It was snowing more heavily than ever. Winds roared over the camp like the wings of giants, but Huuq found that his new limbs did not even feel cold.

Huuq could see a few of the community's snow houses through the blizzard. Now used to his caribou legs, he strode toward his parents' home. The legs were so springy that they were ready to leap with every twitch. It occurred to him that they might be even more powerful than a normal caribou's limbs. He would look forward to testing them later.

Huuq made a few more strides, then stopped, thinking.

Had he gone crazy? What would his parents say when they saw him? Huuq was basically a monster. He could not just walk up to camp folk. People who knew him well might recognize his clothes. But when they saw his face . . .

A few figures, moving from one snow house to another, caught Huuq's attention. Heartbeats passed, until the wind at last blew in a useful direction. It pushed a scent toward Huuq, and he instantly recognized it.

Paa.

Huuq was at once startled and delighted.

It seemed impossible to think

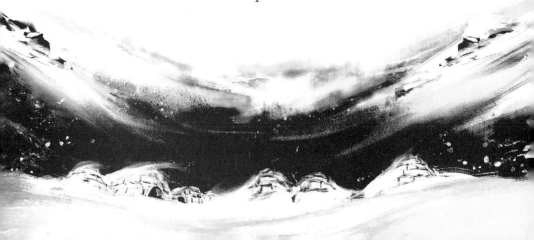

that he could actually *smell* the tall boy. He guessed that it was his wolverine nose. He snuffled at the air, then realized that he could smell all of Paa's bully pack. He could even tell one boy from another. He had no idea why he was able to discern scents; he had no memory of ever noting the personal smells of the bullies. He could even tell that a couple had recently snacked. One had had caribou marrow. Another had been chewing on char salmon skin.

Not wanting to be seen in this state, Huuq cringed, looking around for someplace to hide. The last thing he needed right now was to endure Paa: his insults, his challenges, his humiliating attacks. The bully already hated Huuq as it was. How bad would things get now that there was really something to pick on?

Then Huuq thought for a moment. His wolverine eyes narrowed.

He had a bear's claws. He possessed jaws. Hooves.

Things had changed, but not necessarily for the worse. In the struggle of Huuq versus Paa, who would feel the terror this time?

Huuq smiled, showing the points of all his nice new yellow teeth. He pulled his hood up over his head. He hunched, not unlike the Its that had taken his limbs and head.

"P . . . P-P . . . !" His new lips were not managing a "p" sound very well.

After some struggling, he called out, "P-Paa!"

The name did not come out well. It sounded like a roar.

"Paa!" Huuq repeated.

It took a few heartbeats, but Huuq at last saw Paa standing straight, staring in his direction. The bullies huddled for a moment, then walked toward Huuq. Huuq's new ears were also pretty good. He could hear the bullies giggling to each other. Tittering that the Land had "returned" Huuq to them. Maybe they had recognized him by his clothing.

Their evil laughter seemed to set Huuq's blood on fire. His anger seemed especially jagged, somehow—edged in a way that he had never before experienced. He took a few more strides forward. Then stopped. His new legs would give him away.

Especially if he did too much walking on them. He did not want to frighten off the bullies.

Not yet.

"Is that you, Huuq?" called Paa. The tall boy continued to approach, followers at his heels. Luckily, the snowfall was thick. Concealing. It had already piled to the point where Huuq's bizarre caribou legs sank down, hidden from view.

When Paa called again, Huuq simply nodded. He kept his hood up, bear paw out of sight.

Paa and his cronies stopped at just over an arm's length. Their own hoods were up, covered with accumulating snow. Yet all the bullies were strangely still. Quiet. Maybe Paa had noticed Huuq's height difference. Maybe the boy was trying to figure out what felt wrong about this encounter.

"That you, Huuq?" Paa asked once again.

The tall boy's voice was harsh. Confident, as always. But Huuq knew that Paa was afraid. Somehow, he could sense it. Then he realized that it was the boy's smell. There was an actual smell to fear. Paa was letting off trails of the invisible stuff. To Huuq, the fear was like smoke coiling on the wind.

This fulfilled a greater wish than the Its could ever have realized. And the monsters had thought that they had taken his Inhabitant parts hostage! Paa's fear was a greater gift than Huuq might ever have dreamed.

Huuq's sheer joy began to make him laugh. But the sounds were inhuman ones. Guttural. Horrid. Noises that Inhabitant vocal cords would never have managed.

A few of the bullies took a step back. Paa's eyes widened in fear, though he stood his ground. Then the bully gulped, gaze becoming flinty again, as though he were trying to regain his courage.

Huuq could smell Paa's fear beginning to ebb.

"So," Paa told Huuq, "you didn't get lost in the storm, like I hoped. But here you are. You think I forgot what you said to me earlier? There's a lot of new snow now. So I think I'll make you eat some. Think I'll push your face in it for a while. Until you know why you should watch your mouth."

It was the usual garbage that Paa threatened Huuq with.

Bullies, Huuq thought to himself, *never think of anything new.* It was always sitting on you. Or spitting. Or rubbing your face in something gross. But Huuq, new face hidden in the depths of his hood, let Paa talk on and on. And when the bully got no reaction, and his voice eventually trailed off . . .

Huuq removed his hood.

The reaction from the bullies was mixed. There were only a couple of girls among the pack that was made up mainly of boys. Neither of them made a sound, but they stared, whites of their eyes starker than snow. It was their bodies that seemed comical. Frozen. Rigid. As though they had become life-sized dolls carved from driftwood.

But Huuq got screams from three boys. True screeches of horror. Their voices were high in pitch, bothering Huuq's new ears. He winced at the sounds.

The last two of Paa's followers contorted their faces in a way that almost made Huuq want to laugh. "No! No! No! No! No!" was all they kept repeating.

It was fascinating to note the different ways people expressed fear. It was . . .

Tasty, Huuq thought.

As for Paa, the tall boy's face changed in a way that made him seem as though he had tasted something intensely bitter. Perhaps on reflex, he struck out with both arms, flailing at Huuq in a mad, desperate flurry. Huuq was startled by the reaction, so much so that he leapt backward. His mind no longer on keeping his legs disciplined, he released some of the strength coiled in his new sinews; the jump positioned him about twenty paces from the bullies, landing in a great puff of dry snow.

All of the bullies, Paa included, ran as though a white bear had appeared in camp. The fact of their cowardice did not sit well with Huuq, especially after they had so cheerfully pursued him out of camp. At least, he thought, after all of Paa's bragging and threatening, the tall boy could have tried to fight.

The sight of his tormentors running filled Huuq with a sudden hatred far deeper than that which he had experienced up by the standing stones. The emotion was founded in disgust. These bullies were not strong. They were no more mighty than seagulls picking at some poor shellfish, washed up onto a rock. What were they, after all, if they ran at the first sight of an equal?

An inner voice, tighter and colder than the winds that swirled around him, rose from Huuq's core:

Prey, it told him. *These beings are prey.*

That was when Huuq knew that his face, his legs, his arms, were the least of the new features he had acquired from the Its. He had gained a new soul. It hunched and flexed within him, licking at the droplets of fear the bullies left as they fled.

He wanted more.

Laughing with a noise that was like the roar of mingled beasts, Huuq bounded after the bullies. They lurched. Zigzagged. All were screaming now. Among the snow houses. Huuq could somehow sense their hopes and fears as they went, each wondering if they could escape by staying out of sight until one of their friends was eaten.

That was what they all thought: that Huuq would actually eat them.

(And there was a shadowed, bristly voice, somewhere in the new mix of his tastes, that muttered, "Why not?")

Huuq spent a few seconds playing with the bullies. He leapt past several of them, blocking them and enjoying the way they veered left or right. If he felt like seeing someone recoil, he loosed an especially ugly roar. But, delicious as the game was, he did not waste too much time with it.

After all, he did not want to neglect his main target.

Paa.

Now, where was Paa?

Huuq stopped and sniffed the air, challenged by the terrible winds. It took him only a few heartbeats, however, to locate the tall boy. He left the latest bully that he had cornered, left him quivering and pleading in the snow, so that he could set off after his most hated enemy. Three leaps took him around a series of snow houses—followed by a great bound that brought him over the roof of his own home, near the centre of camp.

Paa screamed, his nearly adult voice warbling, as Huuq came down within paces of him. Huuq raised his bear limb high in the air, black claws stabbing at the winds themselves. He was not trying to frighten Paa. The game was over. He was now a living pillar of wrath—all the righteousness of the Land itself. His wolverine jaws fell open, pink tongue licking at the storm. His eyes were like polished black stones, seeing only Paa. He could feel the lips curling back from his fangs, not in any attempt to threaten, but simply because the hatred snarled like lightning through his skin.

Paa fell to his knees. His cheeks were iced, tears having turned to frost in the cold winds. The boy's mouth was moving, throat producing sounds, but Huuq could not make out any actual words. He sniffed at Paa, realized that the bully's mind was about to snap like an icicle. Paa was going mad.

Go mad, he thought at Paa. *Crumble and go crazy. It's what you did to me. You hunted me. And now I'm in this crazy dream . . . .*

Huuq lowered his paw, growing furious in a different sort of way. This was his moment, and Paa was ruining it by giving up. By submitting himself. By acknowledging that he was prey.

Stop it! thought Huuq. *Push me like you did before! Quit crying and fight!*

Yet Paa stared up at the black marbles of Huuq's eyes, looking through him and past him. As though he were trapped in a nightmare that must be waited out until the rescue of wakefulness. He continued to kneel in the snow. And babble.

Huuq tried to yell at Paa that he was not being fair, that going mad was not a reasonable way to escape justice. Yet Huuq was so furious that the words came out badly, in a series of mingled sounds that were somehow uglier than his earlier roaring.

Huuq's voice fell silent as something shoved him.

He was startled, looking toward his bear shoulder, where he had felt a violent push. He was even more startled to see an arrow sticking out of his parka: there, still quivering a bit, was the long shaft, carved from driftwood as with most Inhabitant arrows, eider duck feathers used for fletching. Huuq was amazed that the arrow did not hurt, and he rotated his arm as though to make sure that it was not his imagination, that there really was evidence of having been shot.

He stopped rotating his arm when he heard an adult's voice cry,

"Monster!"

Another arrow thumped into him.

10

The Better

Huuq turned to see the camp. Not the camp as it was laid out with its snow homes. He turned to see the camp, with almost all of its Inhabitants. Those who were not pointing held bows. It seemed that, to the tune of Huuq's roaring and the wails of the bullies, the adults had finally emerged.

Huuq, fixated on levelling matters with Paa and his pack, had completely forgotten about the grown-ups.

Huuq did not even manage to raise his arms before several more arrows struck him. He was puzzled that the missiles merely seemed *uncomfortable*. They itched terribly, made him feel somehow out of sorts—as with the beginnings of a cramp—in the spots where they stuck from his flesh. Even the Inhabitant parts of him did not register any actual pain.

He tried to think, but another couple of arrows staggered him. He was becoming messy with shafts and fletching sticking from almost every part of him. What could he say to stop the attacks? He could barely speak. Certainly not in his own voice.

Huuq raised his Inhabitant arm to block an arrow that almost met his eye. Pain, he realized, was not the only issue here: he did not want to end up blind. The arrow thumped into his elbow, freezing the arm in a half-bent position. Panic flashed. Were these arrows barbed? How could he get barbed arrows out of his flesh?

Huuq tried to enunciate some words, but it seemed that, as with rage, panic damaged his ability to speak. All he could think to do, for long moments, was to hold up his arms. He raised his head but barely, trying to guard eyes and nose.

Peeking, he spotted Mother and Father.

Mother's expression was no different from those of the faces around her. There was terror. Disgust. Hatred. Huuq's heart sank further as he realized that, for all the times she had treated him as someone whose head was "broken," she had at least never loathed him. Mother clutched Huuq's baby sister tight, as though she hoped to pack the child back into her own body. Her eyes burned with the wish for Huuq's death.

Father was pure focus. The skinny little man's face was grim. Determined. His features, as he drew back the string of his bow, were of someone determined to protect his family with his own flesh, attacking until he himself fell.

Father, Huuq realized, was the archer who had been going for the eyes. Huuq lowered his head again, feeling the arrow thump into him, bringing sadness with its touch. He wondered if this was one of the arrows that Father had asked for Huuq's help in fletching. He wondered if the arrowhead was one that the man had tried to teach Huuq to carve.

Huuq knew that his parents did not recognize him. To them, he was a monster. He was an It. Still, each blow of an arrow felt more like a harsh word than a physical attack. He felt punished. Dimly, he realized that he might jump away. He might use his unnaturally powerful legs to flee this place. But in being here, wilting under the storm of arrows, punishment began to feel . . . deserved.

He had always known that the camp did not like him. His parents, perhaps, loved him—because that is what parents did with children. They had never actually liked him. They had judged him to be broken. Empty. Yet they had tolerated his presence, ever emitting the sense that he might correct himself one day, that he might grow into the dull, foggy fear that defined normal existence.

Yet this scenario was at least honest. Now the camp no longer had to pretend that Huuq was one of them. He had always been the monster. Perhaps he had always been trying to prove it to them. To at least get some truth.

Could they kill him? He knew that he should have died

long ago, under the first few arrows. Now he was feathered like a great, ugly bird, pinions quivering in the storm winds.

Without his realizing it, a caribou leg had collapsed under him. He was lying, tilted at an odd angle in the snow, arms wrapped about his face.

Yet, there in the dark of his thoughts, an urge emerged. Will forced strength into his legs, so that he rose. He hunched, turning away from his attackers, so that arrows decorated his back. Quickly, he used his Inhabitant hand to fish about in the depths of his hood.

Huuq at last seized and withdrew the comb, the fine tool whose teeth resembled fish spines. With it in hand and without looking, he turned until he was oriented toward Mother.

He jumped.

Snow flew as he landed, but he could immediately smell the personal scents of family: the intensity of Father, the desperate concern of Mother, the confused terror of his little sister. It was as though, through his mock wolverine senses, the smells of his family were bathed in sudden sunlight. It was as though he had perceived them but dimly for all of his life, only to have their true essences revealed through aroma.

Now, so near to them, he could smell all of their emotions. The sheer complexity of them. He had never known that they were more than Mother. Father. Sister.

He risked a peek, only to find an arrow pointed at him. It was Father's arrow, tip no more than three paces distant. It was ready to find a home in Huuq's right eye.

Huuq lowered his head and held out the comb.

A long moment passed, in which no further arrows struck. Huuq could hear muttering. It was Mother, saying,

"Don't shoot, don't shoot . . . . "

"Why?" asked Father. "Why?"

Then, after a long moment, Huuq looked up at them. He still held the comb outstretched, offering back what he had stolen. Yet his parents merely stared at him. It took him a few heartbeats to realize that they had not been asking questions of each other. They had been calling him by name.

"Why? Is that you?"

While his little sister wailed in confusion, Mother and Father watched Huuq with wide eyes. There was still terror in them. Huuq did not need to see their faces, for he could smell the emotion. He could smell so many, churning, taking turns in coming to the forefront of their hearts. Huuq's strange new nose identified and assessed each sentiment as he took it in: the sickly sweet tinge of bafflement; panic streaking like salty blood; a fresh and airy hint of awe; an earthy, slightly fungal sense of curiosity . . . .

And then love.

It had no scent at all, but it was more strongly *there* than any other emotion. Love was beyond smell. It was an un-aroma. Cleansing his awareness of all others.

He realized, in love's little rise from Mother and Father both, that they knew him. And he realized, in the same tiny beat of Sky Time, that he had been wrong. It was always better to be loved than liked.

It was always better.

Then the dogs were upon him. Huuq had forgotten about the camp's dogs, and Mother loosed a scream as the bear-hunting canines ringed round Huuq's body.

In moments, they had him to the ground, teeth on every part of his flesh and clothing. They savaged, pulling him in half-circles, so that for several heartbeats he saw nothing but the flash of grey and rusty fur—and teeth. His world was filled with teeth. He could hear the sound of wood snapping all around him, and realized that, in their eagerness to kill him, the dogs were grabbing even the arrows that stood out from his body. The snaps were the sounds of shafts breaking in their jaws.

Then the dogs organized themselves. As one, they formed a perfect circle outside of arm's length.

Huuq knew how this worked. This was bear hunting. The dogs would treat him the same as they treated any predator that wandered into camp. Whatever dogs he faced would taunt him, while the ones at his back bit over and over, until he was at last crippled.

Huuq's odd flavour of anger—an inhuman gift given by the Its—rose in him. He knew that, even bristling with arrows, he could hurt these dogs.

He could kill every one.

But they were friends. Family. And of all the living things in camp, they had always been among the least offensive. The Inhabitants bred their dogs to be remorseless with predators, especially the white bears that preyed on all flesh across the wide Land; yet these same dogs would allow small children to poke them in the ears.

Huuq would not allow his new nature to harm the dogs, so he braced himself for a great leap. Perhaps, with enough jumping, he could get . . .

"*Fear!*" cried a voice.

It was a man's voice. It sounded all about the camp, as though rising from the stone and ice. Despite his current concerns, the odd shiver of the word made Huuq want to scratch at his ears.

Huuq winced, but when he again looked about him, he realized that nothing in camp was moving. At least, not of its own volition.

He could see hair and dog fur and feather fletching stirred by the winds. But every one of the camp folk stood rigid. Even the dogs. They seemed to stare at nothing, some with heads cocked, as though to a familiar tune.

Huuq turned to see Aki. The Monster Man was striding toward him, past men and women and children and dogs who did not acknowledge his presence. As he walked, he sang:

*"Blind eyes with black fire
touched by an animal heart.
These lice turn up, down, in
every direction, their terror
licking soul till it is whiter
than ancient bone. And so,
may it bind them in a flame
that scorches only mind!"*

As Huuq watched, the people and animals of the camp began to shiver violently. Their eyes were wide. Distant. Unseeing. The tails of the dogs were between their legs. To Huuq, every Inhabitant face around him, including those of his parents, resembled that of a child suffering from night terrors.

Except for Aki. The Monster Man's features were grim, steps steady, eyes unblinking. He stopped singing long enough to cry:

"Hunger!"

Then his song continued.

> *"What laughter there is to be*
> *taken from the animal joy*
> *others take from their taking*
> *from others. So I sing to this*
> *spectacle of hunger choking*
> *on its own feast. Eat the flesh*
> *of the senses! Drink the blood*
> *of wit! Man given to animal."*

Huuq continued to cast his gaze about his surroundings. People and animals, all had ceased in their disturbing shivering. As one, they bared their teeth—even the small children. Their eyes became wild, though unfixed on any particular sight. The faces around Huuq had become sheer rage. Somehow, their features had been less disturbing when they had actually seen Huuq and been attacking him.

Faces, thought Huuq, *like masks . . . like animal masks . . . .*

Still, Aki marched toward Huuq. The man was close enough now that Huuq could see his irises. The red one was on the left.

"Wrath!" cried Aki, and Huuq shuddered. Despite the wind and snow, Aki would not blink.

He sang:

> *"They see nothing of the one*
> *snarling amid flame and chill,*

*whose poison dreams rake the
wakeful mind. So may terror
freeze! May appetite scorch!
 Never see our monster rearing
its whip, fed fat and fastened
by a left eye of fear and right of
hunger. Wrath's coiling grip!"*

Huuq was overcome by a lurching sensation that gripped his entire body like a tide. It reminded him of those tugs of invisible power called upon by the Its. He had felt such a pull, as though the Land itself had snatched at him, each time a body part had been taken. This tug was as sudden, but much more powerful, and it gripped Huuq to his core.

He panicked for a moment, so that when the tug passed, he checked himself over, expecting to find that new things had disappeared. But he seemed whole. Somehow, he knew that the power of Aki's song—or at least, the power that it had called upon—had passed over him. His body had refused to accept it, somehow, just as a stone resists water.

The camp, however: that was different.

All around Huuq, people and dogs fell to the ground. They curled like small children (or pups) in slumber. Their flesh turned red. Their hair turned crimson. Within moments, every life in the camp lost the appearance of life. Instead, each person and animal, old and young, seemed carved from stone. Stone that was blood-red and streaked with black bands.

Huuq could not smell them anymore.

He turned to his family and cried out. Like everyone else in the camp, his mother and father, his little sister, lay like carvings of dead, red rock.

Yet as Huuq stared, he began to spot a gauzy shape hovering over each body. Huuq gazed about the camp. Similar bubbles hovered over every reddened person. Every animal. Some were larger than others, but they seemed to average at the size of a man's fist. They shimmered like river water on a sunny day. They ran with bands of varying colours, reminding Huuq of the Many Players. If he focused on any one of the spheres, he could make out more or less colour than others, and it took him seconds to realize that they were connected to their individual owners by the slimmest of smoky tendrils . . . .

"Little Tooth, what a mess you look."

It was Aki. The Monster Man had stopped within arm's length, shaking his head at the dozens of arrows decorating Huuq.

"You killed them!" cried Huuq. "You murdered everyone! My family! You—"

"No one's dead," interrupted Aki with a wave of his hand. "I've simply moved their souls to the outside of their bodies. You must be able to see them. Try."

Huuq blinked, growing a bit calmer. "Are those the bubbles?" he asked.

Aki said *yes* with his face. "The open air is not a healthy place for the soul," he explained. "Souls are made up of parts. It's the body that keeps them bound together. Once they're outside of flesh, like when someone is sick, they tend to want to fly off somewhere. Annoying things."

"So you made them sick?" asked Huuq, outrage returning.

Aki blinked, looking surprised. "Did you think I had a choice?" he asked. "You are an It now, Little Tooth. Even your mind has become like that of an It. Look at how you hunted down Paa and his friends. Do not tell me that you didn't enjoy the taste of that experience. But you revealed yourself. Went out in the open. The camp would not have stopped till they'd killed you. Presenting the comb was clever, though."

"I wasn't trying to be clever," Huuq said. "I just wanted . . . I didn't want my parents to hate me . . . ."

"This is all pointless," said Aki, waving his hand once again. "Come to my home now. We must hurry. The camp folk are safe for the moment. Hunger, thirst, cold, discomfort—they'll feel nothing. But it is unsafe to leave them in this state for too long. We must act, before I'm forced to release them."

Aki wheeled and began to trudge toward his snow house.

"Aki?" called Huuq.

The Monster Man paused and turned, waiting for Huuq to speak.

"How come you can understand me?" asked Huuq. "Why can I talk now?"

The man smiled, red iris on the right.

"Because, Little Tooth," he answered, "you're no longer trying to speak in Inuktitut, as the Inhabitants do. You may not hear yourself, but your words are in *Tarriumak*—the Shaded Tongue. You speak in the way of the Its now, rich in the Strength of the Land."

"How do you know this?" asked Huuq. Could it be true that he was speaking a different language? Without even knowing? How was that possible?

Aki's smile grew wider. "Because," he said, "the Shaded Tongue is not only known by the Its. My kind can speak it, as well. Me and mine. The shamans."

The Creature

Aki looked Huuq up and down, shaking his head at the number of arrows protruding from his body.

"This is not good," muttered the man.

"They don't hurt," said Huuq.

"I know that," answered Aki. "I'm thinking about my home. The way in is not very big. How am I going to get you inside?"

The two of them were standing outside the doorway to Aki's snow house. Huuq could feel the wind tugging at him every time it caught the majority of arrow fletchings. He supposed that the Monster Man was right. Life would become even more difficult if he could not get these arrows out. But how? He had already tugged at a couple on the way to the snow house. They were barbed.

"Try to get rid of them," said Aki.

Huuq laughed without humour. "Where do I start?" he asked the man. He held up his Inhabitant arm, the one that an arrow had locked at the elbow. "Should I keep pulling? Or you?"

Aki made a sour face. His red iris was on the left. "You still think like an Inhabitant," he said. "At least, mostly. That's good, because the It nature has not driven you mad. The drawback is, you know nothing of being a proper It. You shouldn't have to pull on the arrows, Little Tooth. You can simply eat them."

Huuq wondered if he had misheard. He blinked, staring at Aki for a long moment. "Eat an arrow?" he finally asked. He turned his eyes to one of the shafts, wondering how it would feel in his teeth.

"No, no, not in the way you're thinking," said Aki. He sighed. "Keep your eyes on the arrows, Little Tooth. Like you're doing now."

Instead, Huuq looked up at Aki, who frowned. He turned his eyes back to the arrows.

"Now what?" asked Huuq.

"Now remember what you felt when you were chasing Paa," said Aki. His voice became lower. "Accept the memory with your It self. Pull the stuff of that moment up between your eyes. Your despair had become rage. Your fear had turned to joy. Like your body, your heart had transformed in that moment. There was blinding hunger . . . ."

Huuq was startled by the Monster Man's words. How could Aki have known what he had been feeling? But the man was right. Every emotion that he spoke of echoed in Huuq's memory, so that those feelings returned to him. They flashed like a black spark inside his brow.

There was a surge—as when the Its had taken his body parts. As when Aki had sung his terrible song.

The arrows were sucked into Huuq's body. He saw the shafts slide into him without emerging on any other side. Fletching and all, the arrows disappeared into Huuq.

He had eaten them.

And he was just fine. Huuq moved his limbs about, testing them. There were no holes, except in his clothes. No sign that arrows had ever touched his flesh.

"Where are they?" he asked Aki. He was stilled by his own awe.

"Later," said the Monster Man. The man fell to his knees and began to crawl into his snow house.

Once Huuq was also inside, Qipik danced up to greet him. She shivered with enthusiasm. Stepped from foot to foot. Licked his hand. She even licked his bear paw, leaving saliva all over the comb that he now held between his black-clawed digits (he wondered: did these count as fingers or as toes?). Qipik leaned against his side until he almost tottered on his stilt-like caribou legs. Huuq scratched at her ears. His impulse was to smile, but he knew that that would only look like a wolverine baring its fangs.

Huuq finally looked up at Aki, who was standing nearby, waiting for him to finish greeting the dog.

Then Huuq looked over at Aki, who was sitting, chewing on dried meat.

Huuq straightened, startled, looking back and forth between the two Monster Men.

"What is this?" he demanded. "There are two of you!"

The dual Aki figures smiled simultaneously. "No," they said in tandem, "just one . . . ."

By the time the statement trailed off, the standing Aki began to fade. The figure became translucent, outlined in a bluish-black aura. Then it disappeared.

"I was never outside my home," said Aki. "At least, not in the sense you know. Qipik called me, told me you were in trouble. So I sent my . . . image. To see if you were all right."

Huuq did not bother to ask how Qipik could have called Aki. He said, "But I was here. When I woke up. I didn't see you."

"I was here, Little Tooth," said Aki. "I was here and asleep."

That seemed impossible. But it had been a strange time. So many questions jostled in Huuq's head. He was unable to know what to ask.

Aki sighed, offering Huuq some meat, which he refused. "As I told you, Little Tooth," said the Monster Man in between chews, "you're an It now. My kind and yours, we have abilities. Powers. You'll find, in time, that you can do many things that seemed odd in your Inhabitant life."

"I don't want to find anything in time," asserted Huuq. "And I'm still an Inhabitant." He sat as he said this, struggling against the fact that his caribou legs disliked the sitting position, and he stared defiantly at Aki.

The Monster Man did not speak again until he was finished eating. Then he wiped his hands on his pants, saying, "Qipik told me some of what happened on the hill. But she did not see everything. I want to hear the rest from you."

"You speak the language of Its," asked Huuq, "and dogs?"

"Just tell me," Aki insisted.

Huuq sighed in frustration. Then he spoke of the bullies. The Monster Man was silent, blinking rarely, as Huuq described the way he had been chased up the hill. Huuq told of his exhaustion. Terror. Pain and shame and outrage.

Then, choosing cooler words, he spoke about the standing stones. He felt compelled to describe them in great detail, before mentioning the much shorter boulder that sat at the centre of the stone ring. He described it, crack and all, before adding, "There was an Egg."

Aki leaned closer. "What do you mean, egg?" he asked. "A bird's egg?"

Huuq tried to say *no* with his wolverine face, but managed only a snarl.

"No," he said. "No. This was like the Many Players, when they come out across the Sky. All the colours. All moving across the shell." Huuq sighed. "But I dropped it. It cracked open."

"And there was something inside," said Aki.

"Yes," Huuq answered. "A . . . creature. An animal."

"What did it look like, Little Tooth? This is most important. You must remember."

Yet Huuq's eyes had wandered to his dog, who was lying nearby. Qipik stared up at him with irises of amber. The dog was utterly still, unblinking. Then she glanced, once, quickly, at what lay under her paw. It was Father's pana-knife. Apparently, Aki had not bothered to move it from where it had fallen earlier.

Huuq was struck by the oddest feeling: he did not want to talk anymore. He was tired. Sad. He knew that it was his imagination, but Qipik's eyes seemed to plead with him, to beg him to rest.

"I don't remember," Huuq mumbled.

"You must!" hissed Aki. His red iris was on the left. Huuq had never before seen rage on the man's face, but it was there now. After a heartbeat, it passed. Aki rubbed at his brow.

"I'm sorry, Little Tooth," said the Monster Man. "I know you're tired. So am I. But our work begins. Your misadventure has put the camp—your entire family—in danger. I need to know what kind of animal you found in the Egg. It had brown fur, did it not?"

"Yes," said Huuq. It was a sudden, spontaneous lie, emerging like a hiccup. Perhaps it was born of the fact that Aki had snapped at him.

Silver, he thought to himself. He would never forget the silver of that little, unknown animal: a colour as of stolen moonlight.

Aki fell silent for a moment, before demanding that Huuq tell the rest.

Huuq went on about the arrival of the Its, describing each monster in detail. He believed that he recalled their alternately drippy and grinding words fairly well. He told of how he had tried to trick them.

His best memories, of course, were of having the pieces of his flesh taken, sucked into the Land itself. And then he spoke of lying there, like an exposed maggot on the open Land—his greatest return to the fear and powerlessness that generally scarred his life.

(Oh, and there was Qipik. He spoke of her, covering and protecting him, and his heart grew warm again.)

Once he was done, Aki grunted, scratching his pointed beard. The man seemed to stare at something far in the distance.

"You're sure there is nothing else you want to tell me?" Aki asked after a while. "You've given me every detail, Little Tooth?"

"Of course," Huuq lied. He was sure that his untruth about the Egg-animal's colour meant nothing.

"What you found, Little Tooth," explained the Monster Man, "is a *Nunaup Manninga*."

Aki's words sounded a bit like "noo" and "nowp," added to "muhn" and "nih" and "nguh." To Huuq's ears, the man said, "Land's Egg."

Huuq stared for a long moment, uncomprehending. Then he scratched at the back of one ear (the thick fur was impossible— he was not sure how wolverines could stand it) and asked, "What are you talking about now?"

Aki grinned, showing wide yellow teeth. "On the Land," he explained, "you can find every kind of egg. Most of us have eaten most eggs. But birds are not the only things that lay them. The Land lays its own Eggs, Little Tooth. This is what you found."

"But that doesn't make any sense," argued Huuq. "The Land is the Land. It doesn't have babies. Why would it want to lay an Egg? To do what?"

Aki shook his head. "Don't think of it that way," said Aki. "A Land's Egg isn't the kind that results in a baby Land."

Again, the Monster Man shook his head. "How to put it simply?" he asked, seemingly to himself. Then he rubbed his rough hands together, ending with a soft clap.

"Little Tooth," said Aki. "You must understand a few things before I can help you. We do not have much time, and there are matters here that may take lifetimes to understand. Even among the immortals, there is no one with perfect understanding of the Land, Sea, and Sky."

Aki drew in a great breath. His red iris was on the left. "Many beings," he said, "believe that they dwell on something that is dead. Dead sand. Dead rock. Dead hills. They are wrong. For they dwell on something alive, and that is the Land. The Land doesn't have a mind. Nor does it have organs of the body, like you or I. But it does possess Strength. The Strength of the Land is the source of most powers in the World."

Aki gestured up and down Huuq's body. "These new features of yours," he said, "are made of such Strength. When I called upon power earlier, with my song, that was Strength. And the Its of the World, of whom there are infinite numbers, they are born from such Strength."

Huuq raised his bear's paw before his eyes, staring as though to see the Strength of which Aki spoke. He did not expect to see anything. But after only a moment, his vision seemed to penetrate the limb. In a flash, it became translucent as wet ice. And within it he could veins of fire running like tiny rivers of azure, orange, silver, and violet.

Huuq lowered his arm. His eyes were closed. His heart thundered in panic.

When he looked again, the paw-hand was opaque, shining with creamy, silver fur.

Aki nodded. "Yes," said the Monster Man, "you will find that you have the senses of an It. The Strength of the Land is more obvious to you. When you wish to see it."

Tears streamed from Huuq's wolverine eyes. "Please, Aki," he begged, "cure me of this. I'm sorry I ever wanted to have anything to do with Its. I . . . I'm sorry I stole my father's knife. My mother's comb. Just make it right. Use your powers or something."

Yet Aki shook his head. "Don't you think I'd have done so already, Little Tooth," he asked, "if I could? No, you've offended the Its, you see. In the worst possible way. You've stolen the Land's Egg they were guarding . . . ."

"But I didn't!" cried Huuq. "Blanket—she ate it! I mean, I told the Its that I had their Egg, but that was to save myself. I had to lie!"

"And you see how well that worked out," murmured Aki.

"All I did was drop it," Huuq went on. "I didn't mean to. Then Blanket lunged and—what am I going to do now, Aki? I can't return whatever was in the Egg. It's long dead."

Aki held up a hand for silence. "You have not understood everything you saw, Little Tooth." For the first time, the man turned his eyes to Qipik. "The creature from the Egg is still alive. Qipik merely sensed that you were in danger. The Egg cracked open, and the creature within would surely have died in the cold. Then the Its would have taken full vengeance upon you. Qipik, here, stepped in to save you."

Huuq was more confused than ever. "What do you mean?" he asked. "She saved me by making a meal of the thing? How is that saving anybody?"

Yet Aki was waving a hand. "No, no," said the Monster Man. "The creature is still alive *inside* Qipik."

There was long silence as Huuq stared at his dog. It did seem that her belly was a bit larger, perhaps even moving ever so slightly. Then his It eyes looked into the dog.

Suddenly, the husky became a whorl of rainbow light, at

the centre of which burned a silver flame. The effect was like seeing a lamp burning within a lamp, and Huuq sensed that he was seeing two lives. Qipik, aglow with her own fires, was carrying the moonlight creature within her.

Huuq closed his eyes. When they opened again, there was just a dog. Qipik whined expectantly.

"Did you see it just now?" asked Aki. The man's eyes narrowed in curiosity.

"Yes," said Huuq, "I saw it."

Dimly, he wondered: why could Aki not see the colour of the creature?

The Departure

"Your dog is carrying the Egg creature," said Aki, "and it is quite alive. So you see, Little Tooth, you did not entirely lie to the Its. You did steal the Egg's contents. In a way."

"Then how do I return the thing?" demanded Huuq.

Is it as simple as getting Qipik to throw the thing up? Huuq wondered.

Or worse . . . .

"We," said the Monster Man, "are simply going to have to get you to do something that runs against your nature. We are going to get you to be honest, Little Tooth. You must bring the Egg creature back to the Its. Until you do so, they will hold your true limbs, your true face, hostage. And they will send endless storms to bury this camp in snow. A Land's Egg is among the rarest of things. The creature within it is a . . . child of the Land. That's the best way to understand it, I think. More important, it's a concentration of Strength. Many Its will die to guard such a being. They will never forget you. Never forgive. Not until you have returned with the animal. As promised."

"Then I'll go now!" cried Huuq, jumping to his hooves. "If the thing's alive, why are we talking? Can you get it out of Blanket?"

"Wait, wait," said Aki. "Did you think the Its would simply wait for you at the top of the hill? No, Little Tooth, they are long gone. And you must now find them. You must take Qipik with you. She alone shields the Land's creature against the elements. She will continue to bear it for you."

"But . . . how do I find the Its?" asked Huuq. "How far

away are they?"

Aki simply shrugged. "No telling," said the Monster Man. "They are beyond the ring of stones, where you first found the Egg. That's all I know for certain. It is possible that, if you walk far and long enough, they will seek you out."

Huuq wilted, feeling very small and lost. Earlier, enjoying his new body, he had felt like purest power. Now he was fragile as a fledgling bird.

"Don't look so sad, Little Tooth," said Aki. His red iris was on the right. He grinned from where he sat. "You have many new abilities. New senses. They will lead you as you go. Perhaps finding the Its will take no more than a few years."

"Years?" The very word made Huuq's blood run cold.

Aki said *yes* with his face. "The Its," he said, "will come when they come."

"But . . . what about the camp folk?" Huuq asked. "What about my family?"

Aki nodded. "My song cannot hold this many people," he said. "Not for long. I will have to release them soon after you go. However . . . ."

Huuq was silent, his heart twisted like a rag within him, waiting for the Monster Man to finish.

"If you wish," said Aki, "I can make your family forget you. So that they do not remember this day. So that they do not suffer, wondering what became of you. I can sing a song that will do that. My final gift to you, Little Tooth. But this song, if you ask me to sing it, will be fragile. If you ever return to this camp, if you ever seek it out, it will break. Then the full horror of what has happened here will come back to your parents. They may even call you monster—refuse to ever see you again."

"You mean," asked Huuq in a small voice, "I can never come back?"

"Never," Aki told him. "Not without jeopardizing everything you hold dear." Aki's features seemed strained. Sad. "I'm sorry, Little Tooth. I can at least promise one thing: the camp will be safe afterward. If I sing my song. If I waken the camp. If you return the Egg's contents. If you never return. If those four conditions are met, your people—your *family*—will live in peace and never remember the horror of this day."

Huuq nodded, though his head was hung low. His heart felt like something cold. Dry. Like an old bone forgotten on the Land.

The wind blew while Aki waited for Huuq's reply.

"Sing your song, then," he told the Monster Man. "I'll return the thing from the Egg. And I won't come back."

Huuq began to leave Aki's home, when the Monster Man stopped him. "Little Tooth," he said, pointing to Father's pana-knife, "you should take that with you. As with your mother's comb. You never know what power the belonging of a loved one might carry."

Huuq stared at the bone blade for a long moment. Qipik stepped away from it, whining. Then Huuq at last answered, "No. You bring it back to Father, will you, Aki? I'm . . . not sure I'd like to carry it. Stealing it seemed like such fun, but . . ."

Huuq turned his mother's comb about in hand, before tucking it into his large hood. There was a fold in the hood, a favourite rumple that was good for holding stolen items. Back when he'd owned ten fingers, he had personally added stitches to it, shaping the fold into something like a pocket.

At least he had tried to give the comb back. It no longer felt like a true theft. The object would help to remind him of his family.

Aki tried to argue, but Huuq wordlessly turned and left the snow home.

Out in the open, he sniffed the air. The camp somehow smelled lifeless. Under the power of Aki's song, the people and dogs slept in their peculiar way, and they smelled little different from stones.

Huuq walked toward the camp's centre, until he spotted the soul-bubbles hovering over his parents and little sister. They were still, like life-sized carvings of crimson stone, curled as though sleeping (or in pain), but were now mostly covered over with snow.

With a sad groan, Huuq called his sister's name. "Mother,"

he added, "Father, I'm so sorry . . . ."

"They can't hear you." It was the voice of Aki, standing nearby.

Startled, Huuq nearly jumped, until he realized that the man had no scent. "Is this really you?" Huuq asked. "Or an image, like before?"

"Like before," said Aki's image. His red iris was on the right. "You had best go now, Little Tooth. I will sing my song, and it will take some time before it's finished. Then I'll waken everyone, and you will be remembered only as a dream."

"Thank you, Aki. You're a good friend."

"You're welcome, Little Tooth. Take care of yourself."

Huuq started to leave in the direction of the standing stones. He was, after all, looking for Its: the stones were the first and last place where Huuq had seen such beings.

"Little Tooth!" called Aki. "Don't bother with the standing stones. I suggest leaving by the mouth of this valley. Less climbing. Besides, the Its will not be where you last saw them."

Huuq was a bit puzzled. If Aki didn't know exactly where the Its would be, how was it that he could say where they would *not* be? But the Monster Man knew more about such matters than Huuq. So, Huuq turned around and made his way past the snow houses, past even the house of his parents, until he neared the valley's mouth. There, he paused for a deep breath.

The Land: Huuq knew little about it, except that it was endless. He was not even a hunter. There were no landmarks. No familiar grounds or coasts that might make for a meaningful journey.

Only now did he appreciate the fact that he was deliberately wandering.

It was like getting lost on purpose.

The craziness of this act froze his legs for a moment. He looked back, but the camp's snow houses were now little more than vague shapes as seen through the snowfall. Wind stung his eyes for a moment, and the shapes were lost.

"Blanket!" he called.

His dog had to come with him. Aki had said as much, and Huuq was glad of having a companion.

But where was she?

Huuq's ears were sharper than his eyes, and he at last heard a low whine carried on the wind. He wheeled toward the sound, to see Qipik standing at the outer edge of the community.

"Blanket!"

The dog began to make her way up the nearest slope. Huuq called again and again. At first, she seemed to ignore him. Yet he saw her turn several times, fixing her gaze on him, each time higher above the camp than the last.

Finally, Huuq's temper flared. He leapt forward with a snarl, intent on grabbing the dog. She could not outrace him now. Not with these legs.

With only a few bounds, he was partway up the slope. Even when his shanks scratched across the rocks, dislodging ice, he felt nothing that he could call actual pain.

Qipik was not far above him. She continued with her pattern: run and pause, run and pause. With each pause, she would turn to regard him, as though teasing. Always, she made her way upward.

Huuq called on the full power of his caribou legs. He surged upward, as much leaping as stepping, zigzagging his way past icy boulders on the slope. His yellow fangs were bared in anger. Seizing his ridiculous dog by the scruff of her neck: it became his lone thought.

Before he realized it, Huuq was at the top of the slope.

Once again, he stood over the community, which was now hard to see at all through the blizzard. Before, he had been deafened by the sounds of his own heartbeat. His own panting. Now there was just wind. Only . . . .

His new ears could barely detect a tune. It seemed to meld with the storm itself, too faint for words to be gleaned.

Aki's song.

This, Huuq knew, would be the song that would make everyone in camp, even Huuq's parents and sister, forget his existence.

Provided that he never returned.

With his wolverine eyes remaining defiant, black and tearless, Huuq's heart wept.

Huuq became unaware of passing time, until he was startled by a low, silken voice.

"Fool," it said. "How long are you going to stand there?"

Huuq turned all around, but he only saw Qipik lying nearby. She was curled, in the way of huskies, into a kind of ball against the snow. Her tail was over her nose, protecting it from the wind. Snow lay across her back. She resembled the stone from which Huuq had pulled the Egg.

"Someone there?" called Huuq, speaking only to the wind.

There was no reply, so Huuq hopped over to Qipik. The dog looked up at him with her amber eyes.

"I'm glad you're back," he told her, while scratching one of her ears. "I swear I heard a voice. Don't run off like that again, all right?"

She continued to stare while he sighed in mingled sadness and frustration. "I was hoping," he told the dog, "that I was hearing an It. That would make things easier. Except, even if we do find an It, how do we get that animal out of you? This is all so crazy."

Huuq turned, sniffing at the wind, trying to get his bearings.

"Where do we even go?" he muttered.

"First of all," said Qipik, "you *were* hearing an It. And, to answer your last question, we go to the Standing Stones."

The Stones

Taken aback, Huuq stood for some time. He stared at his dog, who returned his gaze with confident eyes that rarely blinked. When she seemed to have given him enough time, Qipik told him,

"Power has less of a hold on me right now. It's like that with Strength. More you do one thing, less you can do of another. At least I can talk now. Only a matter of time before the Strength binds me again, though."

"You *can* talk!" cried Huuq. "Like when Aki—"

"Like when he said he talked to me," said Qipik. "Fast as ever, Huuq. Amazing. You believed everything else. The Its you saw. Shape-changing. Aki's powers. But you never thought I could talk."

"Yes, but you're a dog!" said Huuq. He could not stop staring. When Qipik "spoke," he heard the words in his head, as when the Its had spoken to him. Her voice, however, was smooth and pleasant. It was a bit sibilant, like wind in summer sedge.

"You've never had a dog, cherished boy," she told him. "Use your insight. Use this great gift the Land has given you. Do you really see only a dog?"

Huuq started to argue, but instead snapped his jaws shut. A dim thought shaped itself in his mind: the notion that, just this one time, it might be fun to try listening instead of talking. So, he did as Qipik said. He understood what she wanted him to do, just as he had come to understand "eating" the arrows that had earlier covered his body. He drew in a great breath and felt the

Land murmur beneath his hooves.

Then, sure as he knew his own name, he snatched a fact out of the Land. It was a fact about Qipik.

"That was your voice I heard!" he said. "Back in Aki's house. That was you."

"Very good," said Qipik. She sounded proud, her eyes sparkling with some inner fire. "And what else?" she pressed.

Huuq furrowed his brow, concentrating.

"It's better to relax when you're doing that," said Qipik.

Reflexively, Huuq shook himself, not unlike an animal. He tried to relax, but it was difficult. Huuq was a colourful dreamer: many times in the past, he had dreamed of Qipik talking to him. He had always awakened unable to recall what they had talked about. Now that he was actually looking at his dog, knowing that they were exchanging real words, the experience was unsettling.

"I don't have much time," said Qipik. "Try harder."

Huuq heaved a great sigh and closed his eyes. It was odd, but he could feel the part of himself that was resisting relaxation. Concentration. Somehow, he was able to set it aside. Being able to do so seemed as odd as talking to Qipik.

But at least the Land again murmured.

"You're an It," he said.

"I am," Qipik answered, standing and shaking the snow from herself. "And we have wasted time in which I might have better explained myself. We need the Standing Stones, cherished boy. Now."

Before Huuq could ask why, she bounded off along the valley's edge. Huuq stood for a moment, baffled, watching her move gradually further out across the snowy plain. Then he heard her yell, "Come!"

Huuq jumped, startled at the Strength that laced her voice (and at being commanded by a dog). But he shook off his daze and, with great bounds, caught up with her.

Soon, the two of them were at the Stones.

"Aki told me not to come here," Huuq said. "You can still hear me, can't you? I didn't just imagine you spoke?"

Qipik made a disgruntled noise and turned her back,

approaching one of the tall Stones that formed a partial ring around where Huuq had found the Land's Egg. As Huuq watched, she brushed her side across the base of the Stone. As a dog might do in greeting. She moved to another Stone. Then another. Within little time, she had rubbed herself on every Stone but for the squat one—the Egg's rock—at the centre.

Looking a bit tired, eyes half-lidded, Qipik walked slowly over to Huuq. He could see that her belly had become larger since they had left camp. She was holding the Egg animal inside of her. Supposedly safe.

For the first time, Huuq wondered, *Is this really okay for her? Is carrying the living creature somehow harmful?*

Qipik sat at his side, panting lightly.

"All right, so you're an It," Huuq told her at last. "Why didn't you speak to me before?" A thought occurred to him. "Why didn't Aki tell me about you? Aki gave you to me as a pup. Did he know you were an It? He would have had to know, right?"

Qipik merely stared up at him, amber eyes conveying something like exhaustion. She was silent.

"Don't make me feel like I'm going crazier," Huuq told her. His temper, flashing yellow teeth in his soul, rose suddenly. "You can't just talk and then not!" he exploded.

He began to swear in Father's colourful manner.

"Why are we here?" Huuq roared. "What did you just do? Why bring me here?"

The yelling seemed to make Qipik wilt a bit. Her eyes seemed almost pitying, like an Inhabitant gaze, and they somehow filled Huuq with more rage than ever before.

"What a monstrous person you are," said a low, rumbling voice. The sound was almost like listening to hard objects clacking and grinding against each other. The voice pulled at Huuq's consciousness. Somehow, he knew instantly that he was hearing an It.

Huuq wheeled, turning in all directions. He saw nothing.

"Is that an It?" he shouted. "I heard somebody!"

"You did, indeed, you monstrous person," said the voice.

"And I awoke for this? To watch you abuse some innocent animal?"

It took Huuq a moment to realize what the voice was referring to. "She's not an animal," he argued. "Blanket's an It. And you're an It, too, aren't you? So you should know what she is. Whoever you are. Wherever you are. Where are you?"

"Where, on the Land, did all the wise folk go?" asked the voice. "Where are those of grand Sky? Of the high wisdom? I remember the days before Inhabitants went blind. Of course your companion is an It. Of course she is a dog, too. Do you think that, just because I'm a Stone, that keeps me from being an It? Why do Inhabitants now think that everything must be one thing or another?"

Huuq's eyes at last settled on the Stones. Reaching into the Strength, as he was getting used to doing, he let the Land's life fill his eyes. He squinted as one of the tallest Stones before him flared, whorls of silver and gold burning all around it, before finally settling into an aura that made the Stone stand out like a dark wick at the centre of a flame.

Huuq squeezed his eyes shut, and the tug of the Land receded. When he looked again, the Standing Stone was normal, no different from the others—but he could feel the life in it. For that matter, he could sense life in all the Standing Stones. The lives of the other Stones were sedate, diminished, as though they were merely lingering heat emitted by coals that had ceased to glow. But the Stone to which Huuq was speaking— that one burned.

"I'm sorry," Huuq said in a calmer voice. "I'm still getting used to being an It. I'm not very good at it yet."

"What makes you think that you are an It, you monstrous person?" asked the Standing Stone. "No matter. You are offensive and have made me regret awakening. I am going back to sleep now."

Qipik whined at Huuq's side, gaze now urgent.

"Wait!" cried Huuq. "Please! Don't sleep yet. I'm very, very, very sorry. I can do better. Me and Blanket . . . I think she wanted your help or something. I think that's why she woke you up."

"Did she?" asked the Standing Stone. "Then why does she

not ask me herself?"

"I'm not sure," said Huuq. "I don't think she can talk."

"Then how did you know she wanted my help?"

"A guess," said Huuq with a shrug. Inwardly, he was not so sure that his answer was true. Might some part of him, awakening to Strength, still be providing him with insight?

"I mean," Huuq went on, "she *was* able to talk. For a bit. Then she went quiet. She seemed upset about it, like she knew she'd end up not being able to. Talk, that is. Then she brought me here."

The Stone did not answer, but Huuq knew that it was far from inactive. He could feel a tug of Strength, as though he were situated above the centre of a gentle whirlpool deep in the Land.

Then the Stone said, "I have examined your friend. Did you know that she is partly under the control of another will? A very Strong will. Your friend struggles, but she is no match. Have you not noticed her exhaustion?"

Huuq was startled by the Stone's words, and wondered if every rock provided answers mixed with so many questions. Before he could ask anything of his own, the Stone added, "I am not an expert in these matters, of course. But it seems that, when I See into your friend, I am looking at two beings instead of one. Your friend blankets the other, so that I cannot say what I am perceiving. Yet you already should know this. You are of the kind to know such things."

"Like I said," muttered Huuq, feeling quite lame. "I haven't been an It for very long."

"You keep saying that," said the Stone. "Is that supposed to be a riddle? Or a joke? Be aware that we Stones enjoy neither."

Huuq shrugged helplessly. "I'm so sorry," he said, "but I don't understand anything. Not anything. I wish Aki had come along. Maybe he would know how to talk properly to a rock."

"And this Aki is another friend of yours?" asked the Stone. "I hope that you do not abuse him like your silent friend, here."

"No," said Huuq, thinking. "At least, I never thought I did."

I don't abuse Blanket, he thought. *Do I?*

Do I abuse her?

He suddenly remembered how he had stormed out on the Monster Man, who had been displeased with Huuq's "gift." He also thought about the thefts from his parents. He thought of how he had overdone his vengeance against Paa and the bullies.

All they had done was tease him. Shove him. Yet he had wanted to punish them threefold. He had been ready to do them extreme harm.

How had that seemed so right?

So delicious?

"I wonder," whispered Huuq, almost to himself, "how many people I've abused. Aki and I are friends, but we haven't been getting along lately."

At his side, Qipik whined.

"I guess we never will again," Huuq added. "I guess I just don't get along with people at all. Maybe. Maybe I always should have been an It."

"You are no It," asserted the Stone.

"Oh, I wasn't at first," Huuq explained. "Some Its made me into one. That was right here."

Huuq stamped a hoof to make his point.

"But I guess you were sleeping, so you didn't see."

"That has nothing to do with it, you monstrous person," argued the Stone. "You simply cannot be an It."

Leaning against Huuq, Qipik whined once again. Some dim part of him, a spark at his core, wondered what she was trying to say. But the Stone's words were distracting. Angering. He was tired of being negated. Controlled. Told that, no matter what he did, he was always wrong.

Why couldn't someone, Inhabitant or not, just agree with him for once?

"I am an It," Huuq insisted. His body was rigid in anger. But he inwardly vowed to be polite. "Aki told me, and he knows."

"Aki?" asked the Stone. "An odd word. It means 'barb,' in the Inhabitant speak. Yes?"

"Yes," Huuq agreed, "and it means 'gift,' too. He's the Monster Man. At least, that's what Paa and his friends call him. But he's a shaman. He speaks the Shaded Tongue and deals with

Its all the time."

"You are from the camp below?" asked the Stone. "Nonsense. My brother and sisters and I would know if there was such a person."

Qipik shoved against Huuq. It was annoying.

"Stop that!" Huuq snapped. His peculiar It rage, red, snapping, emerged on its own. He regretted his tone.

"I'm . . . sorry, my Blanket," Huuq told his dog, taking a deep breath. "What's bothering you?"

"Why don't you ask that one, behind you?" asked the Stone.

Huuq peered over his shoulder and spotted movement. With his inhuman reflexes, he wheeled in half a heartbeat. He was unsure of how to judge what he saw. If he had still been an Inhabitant, he might not have been fast enough to see it at all.

Huuq spotted a human-shaped shadow. It was a clot of pure blackness. Like a man standing upright. Huuq could even see edges that indicated a coat and boots. The image was utterly still.

Then the shadow-form darted, trying once again to get behind Huuq and out of his field of vision. But Huuq was too fast. Again, he turned, keeping his eyes on the black figure.

The figure hunched, seemed to look left and right, as though seeking cover.

"Who are you?" Huuq demanded. "Are you one of the Its? Are you here to get the Egg creature? I have it! Blanket has it! Maybe she can . . . barf it out or something. Are you listening to me?"

Suddenly, the shadow-form stood with legs far apart. It stretched its arms out to the sides. As Huuq watched, it fell forward, distorting, until it became no different from a shadow that might be cast from one of the Stones, or Qipik, or Huuq himself.

Then it faded.

And it was gone.

Huuq waited. "Hello?" he eventually called. "Are you still around?" He did not understand. Why did the shadowy

It suddenly disappear? He had assumed that the shadow had appeared to reclaim the Egg. Now Huuq had no idea what was going on.

"Where did it go?" Huuq asked aloud. He looked to Qipik. To the Standing Stone. "What does this mean? I thought the Its wanted their Egg creature back."

Huuq shook with frustration, curling bear paw and hand into fists.

"Come and get your creature!" Huuq roared, turning in circles.

He leapt more than twice his own height, leaving a crater in the snow with his landing.

"I don't want the thing! Take it back!"

"I am still here, monstrous person," said the Standing Stone.

"I wasn't talking to you!" Huuq snarled. "I was talking to the other It. The shadow. I want to get this Egg creature back to the Its! How do I return the thing if they disappear like that? And where are the original Its? The ones who took my legs? My arm? My face?"

"Let us talk about this Egg of yours," said the Standing Stone. Its feel had changed. Waves seemed to lap at Huuq, like dark waters, with each word the Stone uttered.

Qipik jumped up on Huuq, then off again, still whining. He ignored her.

Huuq turned to the Stone. "I don't have an Egg. I have the creature that was inside it. Or Blanket does, anyway. It's still alive."

Huuq looked at Qipik, whose ears were pulled back against her head. Her tail was between her legs.

"You can get it out of yourself, can't you?" he asked the dog. "Barf it up or something?"

"So, you have the Egg . . . creature," said the Standing Stone. It seemed to be weighing its own words.

"Yes!" cried Huuq. "We can leave it with you. Can't we? If the other Its want it, they can find the thing here. Why couldn't we leave it here? You could take care of it, right?"

While speaking, he glanced at Qipik, but she was utterly still. A sense of alarm grew in Huuq.

The Stone had gone silent. A different kind of power seemed to radiate from it. A different life. Somehow, Huuq could feel the Standing Stone reaching into the Land, delving for power. For a word.

For a scream.

"THIEF!"

The cry was a super-sound. A reverberation that ran up through Huuq's leg bones and into his mind, making him hunch and shiver.

"THIEF!"

Its voice sounded like wet shale shattering in a campfire.

"MONSTER!"

Huuq took a step back.

"Monstrous! Monstrous person!" called the Stone. "My siblings and I slept. And you stole what was most beautiful from this place! Your deeds have left prints. Etched in the Land! And you almost tricked me into *helping* you!"

Qipik was running now. She ran some distance while the Stone ranted, turning only to bark once at Huuq, who stood horrified. Dumbstruck.

Huuq glanced at Qipik. Then at the Stone.

And he ran.

He followed Qipik beyond the Standing Stones, across the icy plain that led deep into the blizzard's embrace. He did not question Qipik. The Stone's tone, its angry Strength, still plucked at his nerves and lent him speed.

Behind him, the Stone was still screaming. He could hear it crying,

"Awake, brothers! Awake, sisters! We have failed watching

the Egg! *Wake!*"

Huuq's loping run had turned to great leaps, which carried him far. He caught up with Qipik, who continued to run. But after a while, with the wind skirling in his ears, he thought:

No need for this. How can a chunk of rock catch anyone?

He stopped, calling to Qipik. Maybe, if he was lucky, she could talk again. He needed information. He needed to make sense of this insanity.

Suddenly, it all seemed a bit funny. Here he was, running from a rock. As though it were a bear. Or the bullies from back home. He started to laugh. The sounds emerged from his throat as a succession of huffs and chuffs.

Qipik was now ahead of him again. When he called, she stopped and turned. Huuq waved. She began to bark. Frantically.

Huuq went to take a step toward her, but found that he could not move his leg.

More puzzled than alarmed, he reflexively went to step again, and almost fell down. That was how he discovered that his other leg was fixed, as well.

He looked down to see that he was held by a pair of hands. They were massive. Made entirely of stone. Except for their shape, they looked like the stuff of any ordinary rock or boulder or ridge or cliff that one might see on the Land. Here and there, he noted regular dots and bands of mineral texture. Rough red. Porous beige. They even had spots of orange lichen.

The hands were of unmoving stone.

And Huuq was their prisoner.

The Hands

uuq teetered, but remained upright. He realized that, had the stone hands not held him so firmly, he would already have fallen. He wondered how they had grabbed him with such stealth.

Panic flashed through his brain. His black wolverine eyes focused automatically. Their Strong vision pierced the ordinary appearance of the World around Huuq. Their sight delved deep into the Land. In a blink, Huuq found himself looking at the roots of the Strength that moved these stone hands. They were like long veins or arteries, running in all directions through the earth—but they pulsed with a special power linked to the Standing Stones.

Huuq found his lips pulling back, fangs bared. He wished that he could have put his head into the Land itself, through the rock, like a man dipping his head into lake water. If he had been able, he would have bit at the Strong cords tying these hands to the will of the Stones. Instead, he found himself growling like an infuriated animal.

Huuq's normal vision returned. He tried to force calm on himself. *Calm. Calm*, he thought. He looked up to see Qipik racing back toward him.

"Are you able to talk yet?" he called to her. "I really could use some advice now . . . ."

Instead, Qipik loosed a pained yip. Before Huuq's eyes, a third hand sprang from the Land. Its fingertips were pointed. Clawed. Qipik was in full gallop when the digits seemed to grope for one of her front legs. Instead, they merely tripped her, so that she rolled forward in a tangle of scrambling limbs.

"Blanket!" Huuq roared. "Move back! Don't come near me!"

Qipik regained her footing, but only in time for a fourth hand to emerge and seize her tail. She turned, snarling, but hand after hand exploded from the Land to seize every one of her legs. Between the blizzard and whatever snow the hands sent flying in their upward thrust, Qipik was momentarily concealed by a white cloud. Once the wind had blown much of the whiteness away, Huuq could see that Qipik was held by a total of six hands.

One was on her throat.

Before Huuq could say anything further, he felt pressure on his legs. He still could not feel true pain, but the sensation was far from comfortable.

The hands were squeezing.

A panicked thought came to him.

Are they doing the same to Qipik?

Without proper thought to form them, wild words took control of Huuq's throat. He was still snarling, growling, at the stone hands. But over his animal noises, the guttural sounds of Shaded Tongue emerged. In a voice not quite his own—and at once more *himself* than he had ever felt before—he told the hands:

"No. You will not do this. Not with Blanket. Not with me. I deny you Strength against us. To get any harm you wish to be . . . ."

As the last word was uttered, Huuq's vision altered. He again saw the veins of Strength connecting hands to the Standing Stones. Yellow, azure, violet, and silver: these were the colours that Huuq saw clearly, winding round and round like tangled roots.

Huuq pulled in a spontaneous breath. He became draped in calm. He was tense, but no longer furious. As his chest expanded, he saw the roots of Strength extend from the stony hands into himself. He sensed that they were also coming to him directly from the Land below his hooves. They shot through his body, making it feel light as a feather.

Then he himself felt like one great root. He was no longer trapped. He knew that. He was simply part of the Land.

(How could its touch possibly harm him?)

Huuq blinked and felt strong. Even better, he felt Strong. His vision had returned to normal. He looked down at the stone hands, still trying to shatter his caribou legs in their grip.

Disdain.

Scorn.

Disgust.

These were the feelings that arose in him.

He snarled and pulled one of his legs upward. There was a monstrous crack, and Huuq found that his leg could move again. The stone hand still gripped him. But he had snapped it off at the wrist.

Huuq stamped down with his hoof and the hand shattered, leaving his leg unfettered. Quickly, he gave a wrench with the other leg, shattering the hand that held it.

He had to move fast. Qipik was much worse off than himself.

Huuq took a moment to regain his balance. He stepped lightly, expecting more hands to shoot out of the ground and grope for him.

Then he looked at the field. For as far as his inhuman eyes could see, through the blowing snow, the field was nothing but hands. The stone claws snatched at open air, as though waiting for legs to fall into their grasp.

They were everywhere.

Huuq spared only a few heartbeats to take in the sight. The hands were close enough together that, wherever he sprang to, something might catch him. He knew that he would probably be able to free himself again, should a pair get a new grip on him. But he didn't want to keep stopping to fight the claws with Strength. The Land's power had its uses. But Strength was not easy to wield. As with anything useful, it was difficult. As with anything difficult, it was time-consuming.

With a hoof, Huuq lashed out at the nearest stony hand. He struck downward diagonally, so that his kick struck the hand at its wrist.

The hand broke off. As it did so, some bizarre reflex caused the digits to curl into a fist. This sent the whole hand rolling, like an ordinary stone.

The sight was startling. Like watching a limb go dead.

It is cut off, thought Huuq, *from the Land.*

And that gave him an idea.

Huuq kicked at another hand. Like the first, it clenched.

Snap. Clench. Tumble.

Once the hands were broken, they automatically seemed to make fists. After that, they lay "dead."

Scooping with his bear limb, Huuq snatched up the two fallen fists.

Once he had them, each about the size of a man's head, Huuq threw one of the fists. His bear arm was fast. Powerful. It shot forward like a diving falcon.

And, Huuq was pleased to find, the limb was *accurate.*

The huge stone fist struck the claws gripping Qipik's throat. Fist and hand both shattered, sending out a spray of tiny, blade-like fragments. Qipik's head was freed. She shook as though relieved.

Without pausing, Huuq hurled the other fist. It shattered a hand groping close to Qipik's side. This left a small spot free of claws.

With all the Strength that his legs could manage, Huuq leapt over to Qipik. One hoof landed in the spot free of claws. The other landed too close to another groping hand. The sharp stone fingertips raked fur from Huuq's shank. Scraped across his hoof. But he managed to get his leg away before it was seized. In doing so, his arms flailed, so that another hand caught the sleeve of his bear arm. Huuq pulled back with terrific force. His sleeve, already torn in places due to the size of his great bear arm, was ripped away at the shoulder.

With the same hoof that had just been raked by stone claws, Huuq lashed out. The claws that had taken his sleeve exploded into lifeless fragments.

Huuq now had just enough room to stand beside Qipik. His furred arm began a series of downward swats, cracking fingers and thumbs off of the hands that held Qipik. After a total of seven blows, Qipik was able to shake herself completely free.

She saw the field, as had Huuq, and looked up at him. Her tail was between her legs.

"I know," said Huuq. "So many. But I think this is all of them. The Standing Stones sent them, somehow. To catch us. I saw their Strength. Don't know how, but I . . . feel like they're done. They can't send any more."

Qipik whined, staying close to Huuq's side.

"I could probably fight my way out," Huuq mumbled. "But that doesn't help you, does it?"

Huuq's eyes narrowed as he spotted a nearby hand. Loathing for the thing filled him as he watched it blindly snatch: north, south, east, west, upward once in a while, in the hopes of catching any body part that might brush up against it. Out of sheer spite, his leg snapped outward and down. Broke the hand off at the wrist. Like all others, the claws closed into a fist. The hand fell dead. Lay like one more rock on the Land.

Huuq let out a guttural laugh.

He suddenly knew how to get himself and Qipik out of this field.

Huuq began a process. He was methodical. Focused. The first step in the series was always a kick. Aimed at whatever wrist lay nearest. The next step was a grab. He scooped up the fist as it fell. Then he threw that hand to shatter others.

With this process repeated until his mind grew numb, Huuq forged a steady path toward the edge of the grasping field. Qipik shadowed Huuq perfectly, staying behind him. As for Huuq's kicks, he sometimes aimed poorly, shattering a hand instead of breaking it off at the wrist. At other times, he had to pause; not for breath, but because he had to gauge the best hands to collect, as opposed to those he would shatter. But he did make progress. The wind continued to howl, snow snaking, raking at Huuq and Qipik, as they bowled their way free.

Some time later, Huuq and Qipik stood outside the fields of hands: a groping, twitching assembly that separated them from the Standing Stones.

112

Huuq sighed with relief. Then again with frustration.

After a time, he thought about his circumstances and asked, "Why did that Stone get angry?"

He sensed that Qipik could probably not answer. "It called me a thief," he added. Then after a moment, he said, "Well, I am sort of a thief. But I tried to give the Egg creature back. Doesn't count as stealing if you try to give something back. Does it?"

He thought some more.

"You're the only It," he told Qipik, "who hasn't ended up mad at me."

"Not true," Qipik whispered. "I've been pretty angry with you. But thanks for saving me."

Huuq was startled to hear her voice.

"I thought you couldn't talk anymore," he said.

"Hard," said the dog. "Hard enough since carrying the Egg creature. Now I have to use my Strength for healing. The Land-claws. They hurt me."

Huuq stepped closer to her, alarmed.

"But you're not bleeding," he said. "What can I do? Maybe there's something I can do?"

"No," said Qipik. "I'll survive. But I have to tell you things. While I have enough Strength. You wondered why the Standing Stone was angered."

She shivered in the wind.

"I woke that Stone so it could lend me something. Something I need."

"What do you need?" interrupted Huuq. "Maybe I can get it for you!"

"Time for ears, precious boy," said the dog. "Not mouth. Soon, I will go quiet again. Like a beast. I woke the Stone in hopes of borrowing some of what has been . . . stolen from me. If I'd been able, I'd have told you not to mention the Egg creature."

"Why?" asked Huuq. He clamped his jaws shut, trying to stem a flood of further questions.

"Because the Stones were guarding it," answered Qipik. "And it was best not to let them know they'd failed. Stones don't react well to disturbances. They're brittle. They panic."

"Why were they guarding it? What from?" pressed Huuq. He *had* to ask questions. Simply listening, amid all this madness, was impossible. "And what was that shadow? Was it an It? Why did it appear and disappear? Why didn't it answer me? Why didn't it want the Egg creature? Why didn't the Stone?"

Qipik stared, her ears pulled back, until Huuq's river of questions ran dry. She opened her mouth, seemed about to answer. But the dog suddenly snapped her teeth together. Her eyes closed. She flinched as though struck.

"Blanket!" cried Huuq. "What is it now?"

"Pinched," wheezed the dog.

"How? What do you mean? What's pinching you?"

"Enemy," she gasped.

Before Huuq could absorb her answer, Qipik seemed to relax, letting out a relieved breath on the frigid air. Her eyes reopened.

She looked up at Huuq, giving the slightest wag of her tail.

Huuq simply stared, waiting for his Blanket to explain what had just happened. But her eyes locked onto his own, unblinking, and no words came. It was then that he knew: she had gone mute again. Whatever it was that she needed, whatever had been stolen from her, its loss had left her too weak for speech.

At least her tail kept wagging. That would have to be good enough.

15

The She-Stone

uuq had nothing to do other than continue on his interrupted journey. So he walked. And walked. And walked. The snow never quit and he was quite blind at times. All he knew, after what might have been a full day's hike, was that he was gradually moving downhill. In time, the Land seemed to level out. Through the storm, Huuq could sometimes spot hulking, hazy shapes. He supposed that they were snowy mounds or boulders.

At his side, Qipik let out something like a sneeze. The heavy snow was obviously bothering her. Now that Huuq had a snout of his own, he could appreciate how uncomfortable it was, having it pile on the bridge of one's nose. At least he had limbs with which he could wipe himself—but he had to remember to use the Inhabitant one only. He tried, once only, with the bear paw. It turned out to be alarming to have black claws swishing close to his eyes.

Huuq kept expecting fatigue. Or hunger. Or thirst. But, as with pain, his new body felt nothing other than a peculiar discomfort. He wondered, as his hooves plunged through the snow and his thoughts drifted, if pain might be linked to things like sleeping or eating or drinking. Maybe, in the end, need was need. And all need was the same as pain.

The Inhabitants were a people comfortable with silence, respecting the stillness of stark hills and mirrored waters, of drifting snow and open Sky. For the first time, however, Huuq found himself wanting idle conversation. He began to eye Qipik, whose steps were a bit laboured. Her torso, he noticed, had lost its sleekness. She seemed heavy. More than ever, he wished that she could talk. He no longer craved words of explanation. Oddly, he just wanted to regain the feeling of . . . chatting.

"This doesn't feel right," Huuq groaned. "Why won't the Its come and take their Egg creature? Nobody just walks and walks. We could walk right off a cliff."

As usual, Qipik said nothing. Huuq glanced at her, concerned over the way she seemed to trudge ever on, head bowed.

Was she in pain?

A great deal more time passed. Huuq's worries and discontent gnawed and bit at him, until a roar of frustration began to coil within him. The storm made him feel somehow captive, more surely than if he had been tied with a hundred knots.

How far from camp am I, now? he thought to himself. *Too far to see it. Even on a clear day. That's for certain.*

If only Qipik would say something . . . .

"When do you think we'll leave this storm behind?" he asked, dimly hoping that she had regained her voice.

"You won't," said another voice.

Huuq left the ground. His startled leap took him to about the height of a man. He landed in a blinding puff of snow.

The wind swept the snow away almost instantly, and Huuq could see that Qipik's hackles were up. She was snarling, making a wide circle around a spot on the ground.

As Huuq watched, the snow bulged. The bulge rose higher. Then higher. Like the cap of a vast mushroom, it left the ground.

As Huuq watched, a Standing Stone emerged out of the very Land.

In six or seven heartbeats, the Stone loomed over Huuq and Qipik.

"Not again," hissed Huuq. "I thought we left you behind."

The wind blew, and the looming Stone said nothing. The edges of its cap of snow and ice fell away. In the haze, it looked like a white-tufted giant.

Something about the Standing Stone felt different. The

dark, almost tidal, sense of wrath was no longer present. While he was intimidated by its height, by the very fact of a Stone that had just emerged from the Land in front of him, the great rock felt completely neutral. It radiated no emotion at all.

Huuq backed away. Waited. He glanced at Qipik, who had done the same. The dog was still, eyes on the Stone.

"What do you want?" Huuq asked after a time.

"Your attention," said the Standing Stone in its rattling voice.

"That's easy," Huuq answered. At once, he braced for an attack. "Got that already. My attention."

"You will not succeed," said the Stone.

"I'm not trying to succeed at anything," Huuq argued. "Except giving the Egg creature back. But nobody wants it. I was going to leave it with you. But you went crazy."

"No. I did not."

"Yes, you started yelling."

"No."

"Yes. Then you sent those hands after us. And that was really creepy. How can you do that, anyway? What did me and Blanket do to deserve that?"

The Standing Stone was silent for a moment, as though taken aback at being scolded.

"The others," the Stone eventually said, "called upon the Land-claws. My brothers and sisters. I am their youngest sibling, and am not in agreement with them. Please forgive my family for attacking you. As I am part of them, I, too, beg your forgiveness."

Huuq stood wordless, startled by the Stone's politeness. He liked politeness. It was good that, if he had to talk to a rock, she was at least treating him decently.

Then he realized something.

She?

He thought of the Stone as female, though he wasn't sure why. Maybe it was because she had mentioned family. Brothers. Sisters.

The She-Stone seemed to wait, while Huuq tried to gather his thoughts. They buzzed at him like summer flies. When he made no reply, she asked, "Is something wrong? Are you well?"

"I'm fine," Huuq muttered, "I guess. Considering I'm talking to another big stone. I was just . . ."

He struggled to get the question out, since it seemed ridiculous.

"Are you a girl?" he asked.

"No," said the She-Stone. "I am a stone."

"But you don't feel like it. Not exactly."

"Your feelings," said the Stone. "They race too far ahead of you. As a result, they stand between us as we speak. You see through them to see me. They colour your perception. Maybe there is something about me that you wish was female. But that comes from you. When you master your impulses, steady them like rock, you will know."

"What?" asked Huuq.

"The basis, of course," said the Stone. "Of feeling."

Huuq squinted, trying hard to understand. Finding meaning in the Stone's statement was like trying to keep his eyes on a lone snowflake in a storm. But, for the merest heartbeat, her words seemed to make sense.

Then he remembered Qipik. The hands. Grabbing at her from every side.

"So you're a nice rock?" he snarled. "Then why didn't you stop those Land-claw things? Where were your apologies back there?"

With his bear limb, Huuq raked at the air, gesturing toward the field of hands.

"I could do nothing!" insisted the She-Stone. "My family commanded them! I already asked you. Forgive us."

"And then there's the name-calling," said Huuq. He had to look away from the Stone in order to calm himself. "Like 'monstrous person' and that. I don't like it too much."

"Pardon us all," said the She-Stone. "Please. And I will assist you."

Huuq thought it over for a long moment. "Not sure I want to pardon anybody," he said at last. "Your brothers and sisters tried to kill me. And Blanket. They would have killed us, if I hadn't been Stronger."

Huuq found it tasty to brag about his Strength. Even if it was to a rock.

The She-Stone seemed to be weighing Huuq's words. After some time, she answered, "Perhaps my siblings would have tried to kill you. There is no saying. They were panicked. That is all I know. We were all frightened for the fate of the Egg. For what it carried. It is precious beyond imagination."

"If you love it so much," asked Huuq, "why won't you take the creature back?"

"Impossible!" said the She-Stone. "The Egg is not ours. It can belong to no one."

Huuq shook his head, turned to Qipik. "You see?" he told his dog. "Try to ask questions, and you get something new to ask questions about. Its never explain anything."

The She-Stone laughed. It was a sound like a small landslide of pebbles.

"*Explain*," she said, echoing Huuq. "That is a good joke. As well to explain the Sky . . . ."

Huuq did not bother to mention that he hadn't been joking. Instead, he said, "I thought rocks disliked jokes."

The She-Stone sighed. "I am not my siblings," she said. "Perhaps I am more porous. But I thought that at least pretending to enjoy your Inhabitant joke would make you feel forgiving. Have I failed?"

Huuq shook his head. Sighed. "All right," he answered. "I give up. You're forgiven. I don't understand half of what you're talking about, anyway. Can I go now?"

"You must stay," cautioned the She-Stone. "You must listen."

"Everyone wants me to listen," growled Huuq. "No one wants to hear *me*."

"I do not understand," said the Stone.

"Now you know how it feels," said Huuq. "I might have become an It, but I still don't know how to talk to them. This," he added, appreciating the full craziness of his words, "is exactly . . . why I have to get my dog talking again."

"She is bound," said the She-Stone. "She will say nothing until her knots are allowed to slip. As each one loosens, she will be free to exercise her own will. To say as she wishes."

Huuq glanced at Qipik, who gave a couple of slow tail wags. He was proud, at least, that he could comprehend that the Stone was talking about matters of Strength. He stared at Qipik for a moment.

Then he looked at the dog with his Stronger gaze.

"I don't see anything," said Huuq. "How is she bound?"

"She is bound by theft," said the She-Stone. "By what has been taken from her. My siblings and I have discussed her condition. She has been weakened by a loss of *inua*."

The Stone uttered sounds much like "ih" attached to "noo" and "uh." Huuq recognized the word as the root of what the Inhabitants called themselves: Inuit. But he also recognized the term as one that Aki had mentioned. The Monster Man had used it in a special sense. If only Huuq could recall what the man had said.

"But you do not need knowledge," said the She-Stone. "Not yet. Your insight is far more important. Has no one explained how to use it?"

"My insight . . . as an It?" asked Huuq. "I think Blanket tried. So did another friend. But . . ."

He gestured toward Qipik, reminding the Stone that his dog had gone silent.

Could the Stone see her? For that matter, how could a rock see anything? Where were its eyes? Huuq decided not to ask.

"Not insight as an It," the She-Stone answered. "I meant an insight far greater." The Stone made a discontented noise. Some more snow tumbled from its top.

"But," the Stone added, "if no one has taught you about your nature, I must try. For the moment, at least."

Huuq expected more. Yet the She-Stone went silent.

Snow raked.

Wind skirled.

Huuq began to walk in impatient circles.

Just as Huuq was thinking about whether or not to abandon the mad Stone, it spoke again. This time, its voice was softer. On the outside, where there was cold and storm, Huuq's ears picked up words as the barest whisper. But on the inside of himself, in some place where he had never before expected to know another voice, he heard the Stone with perfect clarity:

"Look with the back of your eyes, Inhabitant. Do not snap up sensation, as the fish does the worm. Remain steady. Resolved. Like the Land. Then you will find that you are already gripping truth, as a falcon does its prey. Then you will find that your very being is knowledge. Knowing itself."

In the span of a heartbeat, insight seemed to drape itself around Huuq. He could feel it, almost like a solid object.

Like a cloak made of summer wind.

Huuq's insight told him to be still. To wait for more.

The Stone provided more, saying, "I can feel you waking. A bit. Perhaps you can now understand your dog's loss. This loss of inua: it is a loss of what your folk might say it means to be human. Inhabitant. It is the aware power. Deep as Strength. It is the power of the self to know itself as a self among other selves."

"I . . . get that, somehow," said Huuq, wondering if he really did. He shook his head, trying to clear it. For a moment, it had almost seemed that he'd been talking to himself, rather than the Stone.

"But how was her inua stolen?" he asked. Huuq had nipped many things in his life, but he could not imagine stealing a piece of someone's . . . selfhood. Where was the self in a person, anyway? A person never put their selfhood aside, where a hand might reach it. It could not be grabbed, like a knife or comb. And where would a thief hide such self?

"And why would losing that keep Blanket from talking?" he added aloud.

The She-Stone was silent for a moment, before saying,

"Those are questions deeper even than Land. The theft of inua was probably to keep her under control. The less inua she possesses, the more like a simple animal she becomes. As for who stole it, I would look to the evil of your camp."

Huuq was taken aback. "I didn't understand that last part," he said after a moment. "My camp? Something about my camp? This happened in camp?"

"Yes," said the She-Stone, as though such notions were the most obvious of facts. "Your camp. It is utterly evil. And must be purged. All of the Its know this."

When Huuq made no reply, the Stone said,

"I am sorry. Did you not know? That is the sole reason why the Egg was placed there."

Part Three

HUUQ THE WAKENED

The Evil

"**B**ut," said Huuq to the She-Stone, "you don't understand. There can't be . . . what you say there is. Not in *my* camp."

Not exactly evil, he thought as he spoke. He had never been happy in camp. He had never liked the people.

(Nor, it seemed, had they liked him.)

But evil?

"Really?" asked the She-Stone. "Why do you say this?"

"I . . . think someone would have told me." Huuq stared at his hooves while speaking, trying to force his thoughts to catch up with the Stone's words. "They'd have told me. Wouldn't they?"

"I know very little about Inhabitant camps," said the She-Stone. "I have some relatives who eavesdrop when people are near. Most of us rocks prefer our sleep, though. Sometimes, I wonder if we pay enough attention to the Land. It makes me wonder why we were assigned to guard the Egg."

Huuq turned to Qipik. He found that, once again, the dog's amber eyes were fixed on him. As Huuq watched, though, her eyelids seemed to droop for a moment. Her head bobbed. It was clear that she was unwell. But what could Huuq do? He had no way to find out what was bothering her.

"My Blanket," said Huuq. The dog gave a slight wag of her tail.

"Can you find a way to tell me?" he begged her. "Tell me if this Stone's words are true?"

126

Qipik closed her eyes. She swayed in the wind. Huuq could feel a touch of Strength on the move, and realized that Qipik was moving it. The feeling soon passed.

"I'm sorry, precious boy," the dog whispered. Her eyes were still squeezed shut, as though she forced her words past great agony. "So hard to talk. Hard to carry the Egg creature. Keep it alive. All the Stone says is true. Trust in what she tells you. Please stay with me. You're all I have left."

Eyes still closed, Qipik fell over on her side.

Huuq loosed a cry of alarm. He tried to kneel with his caribou legs, then fell on all fours next to Qipik. He stroked the fur of her head. Scratched behind an ear.

Her eyes opened a bit, but they seemed to gaze at nothing.

"What happened to her?" Huuq asked the She-Stone.

"I think she tried to find her voice," said the Stone. "But she is too weak. It is that one's doing."

It took Huuq a moment to realize what the She-Stone meant by "that one." But then he turned. There, not far behind him, stood the shadow-figure that he had earlier confronted.

"That's the It," Huuq muttered. "The one by the Stones. Who I tried to return the Egg creature to . . . ."

"As I said," the She-Stone told him, "you cannot return the Egg. And certainly not to *that* one. You behold, now, the source of your friend's affliction."

"Why are you doing this?" Huuq demanded of the shadow-being. When it made no reply, Huuq roared, "This is my dog! Stop hurting her!"

The shadow-figure's only response was to raise one arm.

The result was that Qipik started to shiver. Violently.

Huuq's It rage caught him up suddenly. In a spray of snow, one liquid movement, Huuq whirled into a standing position and sprang. He hurled himself onto the shadow-being.

Only to find himself landing on more snow.

Startled, Huuq took a step backward. He stood face to non-face with the shadow. The figure was featureless—only the outline of a person. It did not flinch.

The figure gestured again.

Behind him, Qipik loosed a pained yowl.

Without a thought, Huuq's wolverine teeth flashed. His open jaws shot forward. They snapped together in blackness. Huuq pulled back again.

It was truly as if he had tried to bite a shadow.

No effect.

"The evil is not here," advised the She-Stone. "Not in the sense you know. It is still back at your camp. This is but an image. As it dreams evil thoughts, it can bundle such blackness together. Make strands of it. Tangles expressed in Strength. It sends them forth. Winding. Streaming. Walking. Acting."

Again, the figure gestured.

Qipik's throat emitted a strange, warbling noise, before she yowled again. For a moment, the sheer horror of the sounds made Huuq stand frozen.

"Why is it here?" Huuq cried to the Stone. "How do I stop it?"

"That was what the Egg was for," answered the She-Stone. "It was to tie this evil down. I am surprised that the Enemy has sent a dream-strider only. It should be free. Much, much Stronger. But, without my siblings, I have little power to help your friend."

"Then call your family! Do it now!"

"That time has passed," said the Stone with a trace of sadness. "Your friend tried to wake them for help. Regretfully, one of my brothers panicked before the others could convene. They will remain locked in bitter argument, now."

"How long?" pressed Huuq.

"As it's a simple issue," said the She-Stone, "only about a year or so."

Huuq snarled at the Stone.

Then his face went blank.

He was struck by a flash of insight.

One of the She-Stone's chosen words—"tie"—returned to echo in his head.

. . . *tie this evil down . . . .*

After a moment, Huuq turned his gaze to the Land below the shadow's feet. The Strength of his sight penetrated snow.

Ice.

Sand.

Old roots.

Rock.

He gazed into the quick of the Land.

Instantly, Huuq could see tendrils of Strength. They ran out of the shadow-figure, fanning in all directions. Some of them, entangled like a root bundle, wound through the Land and up into Qipik. Huuq could see their colours: pulsing shades of violet closest to the shadow; dirty yellows and oranges closer to Qipik. The colours waxed and waned like shallow breaths.

Huuq could feel the life in them.

He turned his gaze to the great bear arm attached to his upper body. He thought nothing as he held it up—felt only the urgency that led his Strength—and began to see colours playing through the limb. From shoulder to claw tips, Huuq visualized tiny rivers of azure and silver, glittering as they wound around muscle and bone. It was as though another *version* of his mind had risen within him. Overtaken his body.

Huuq focused all of his own Strength on the limb. Within a few heartbeats, it spangled in sheer power.

With a grunt, he thrust his arm into the Land.

There was no resistance. Respecting his Strength, which was also its own, the Land seemed to permit Huuq to move through it. The rock became like water to his touch, allowing him to reach deep.

It took him only a moment to hook his paw under the root bundle linking the shadow to Qipik.

Huuq gave a great tug, reassured by the memory of how his arm had performed against the stone claws. Now, however, there was resistance. His own tug nearly pulled Huuq off balance.

He staggered, trying to keep a hold of the root bundle.

"Don't just touch," advised the She-Stone. "Hold. Know that it is yours."

"My prey," Huuq added in a whisper, almost to himself.

His eyes were closed. He could already sense the shadow-figure struggling against him, trying to will the Strong roots to squirm out of his grasp. Again, then again, he hooked his paw under the thickest part of the bundle. He could sense, then, what emotions their life pulses carried:

Fear.

Hunger.

Wrath.

Over all arched the sense that such urges, together, were delicious. Sheerest animal life, the most wild (and at once, somehow beautiful) part of that force, lay below him.

Throbbing and mad, the Strong sensations caught up his mind.

Suddenly, Huuq did not want to disturb the root bundle. He wanted to stay with it. Blend with its power. He wished to savour that terror, a fear which seemed to sweep like ocean tide. He wanted to chase with it, learn of all which this power craved. And he wanted to rage, to tear at the very stuff of existence.

He wanted to feel his teeth set in the World's flesh.

Then insight, that steady cloak, draped over him again.

Insight anchored him. Gave him mastery over the Strength. Made him steady.

And his mind was not washed away.

His heart jumped, told him to pull.

So he pulled.

Again, there was resistance. But not like before. The bundle began to move. Tendrils tore, spilling their bloody intent out into the earth. Huuq could feel the Land gobbling them up, as though any single emotion, an intent of any kind, were no more than a tasty drop of gravy.

Wolverine teeth flashed. Bear sinews worked. Hooves were set firm.

Roaring, Huuq tore the root bundle out of the Land. There was no disturbance in the rock or ice. Not so much as a puff of snow. His arm, he knew, had switched away from the material World.

(Or at least, it had become a different kind of material for a time.)

He was made, now, of a Strong material.

To touch Strength.

Huuq had only a moment to watch the Strong roots, torn and with their violet-orange ends wriggling between his claws, as they melted like snowflakes. He was distracted by a terrible sound.

He wheeled to see the shadow-figure. It was hunching. Its edges had frayed. Its limbs were distorted. Where a face should have been, there was a great ember. That light flickered and burned even without Huuq's Strong gaze, streaming red fire into the frigid air.

The sound, though: the shadow seemed to emit the loudest, most resounding retch that Huuq had ever heard. He knew, somehow, that it was a kind of scream.

Huuq roared back at the figure.

As he watched, storm winds seemed to whip at the shadow's burning face. The light guttered, like a crimson flame, then went out.

The figure collapsed, writhing, becoming something more like the shadow of a massive worm, thrown on the white snow.

With its sounds levelling into a series of croaks, the shadow shot off at amazing speed, stretching and wriggling its way into the veil of snowfall.

The Strong insight was no longer upon him, and Huuq instead felt draped in nausea. Though he'd walked for what had seemed like days, without food, water, or rest, he only now experienced something like fatigue. He shuddered, filled with memories of the shadow's soul. It was one thing to know of an enemy. It was far worse, however, to have the *flavour* of that enemy filling one's selfhood. He wanted to vomit, though there was nothing in his stomach. He wanted the enemy's taste out of his being.

Huuq shuddered violently, before his head cleared.

He turned to Qipik.

She was not moving at all.

"Blanket!" he cried.

"She still lives," said the She-Stone. "In a way."

"Blanket's dying," whispered Huuq, falling by his dog's

side. "Did I do something wrong?"

"Far from it," said the Stone. "You performed admirably. Simply, the Enemy has stolen much from her. Their relationship must have been old, indeed, for its evil to have had such power over her."

"Garbage," snarled Huuq. "Stop guessing at things you know nothing about. She's always been my dog. Even from a pup."

"A pup? This one could never have been a pup. Maybe the seeming of one—"

"Shut up," snapped Huuq. He brushed at Qipik lightly, with his Inhabitant fingertips, as though a touch might cause her to crumble like packed snow.

"Sorry," he told the Stone, phantom tears drifting somewhere behind his dry monster eyes. "I'm sorry. I know you're trying to help. I just can't think very well, right now. My dog's in trouble. My Blanket. So, just, please be kind."

We need some kindness, he thought, brushing at Qipik. *This is too much. Somewhere, there has to be some kindness . . . .*

The She-Stone sighed. She stood quietly for a time, as Huuq went numb. All he could think to do, with despair blackening his soul, was to keep snow off of Qipik.

"The worst possible outcome," said the Stone at last. "Such a disaster, all of this. Shameful. I will return to my brothers and sisters. Tell them the news. I do not relish the experience. Stones feel the deepest shame, and we have all earned it well."

Huuq shook his head. "There you go, again," he muttered. "Always about your family. You said you'd help. But what have you really done?"

"I told you," said the She-Stone, "I have no power over the one who did this. I meant to advise . . . ."

"And what good is that?" snarled Huuq. "Look at Blanket!"

The She-Stone made a discontented noise. "You speak," she said, "as though matters of Strength mean nothing to you."

"They don't," said Huuq. "Because I don't understand them. Or you. Blanket said to listen to you. But how? All you say is the Egg's important. My camp's 'evil.' You're ashamed . . . ."

"Yes!" blurted the Stone. "Ashamed! Of course I am ashamed. We have failed to guard the Egg. Its contents have entered your 'dog.' Now she is dying. With her dies the Egg. And that which would have undone the Enemy."

Though Huuq had already feared it to be true, the Stone's declaration that Qipik was dying struck him like a blow. He placed his Inhabitant hand over her eyes.

"She didn't mean to eat the Egg," he muttered. "I think she thought that might shelter . . . whatever the creature was. She was probably trying to keep it warm. Alive."

Huuq was shocked by the She-Stone's stark reply.

"Do not be absurd," said the Stone. "She was ordered to eat it. And with it, she was intended to die."

The Path

Huuq stared at the She-Stone for a long moment, shocked into stillness by what she'd said about the Egg and Qipik.

"She was ordered to eat it. And with it, she was intended to die."

For a moment, his lips opened to ask his usual questions. To demand meaning. To beg for some sanity.

Then he shook his head. Sighed.

Slowly, he stood up on his hooves. He leaned over to brush the snow from Qipik. With great care, he picked her up. His Inhabitant arm felt her weight; the bear arm, nothing at all.

He turned away from the She-Stone. Toward the great, white veil, and in no particular direction, he walked.

"Where are you going?" asked the Stone.

Huuq ignored her.

No point, he thought to himself, *talking to Its. All crazy.*

There was a rumbling sound at his back.

Ten paces ahead of him, snow and icy rocks sprayed upward. The She-Stone rose up, blocking his path.

Huuq stopped and stared at the Stone. His eyes narrowed in thought.

"You need my help," said the She-Stone.

Huuq placed Qipik on the snow.

"Get out of my way," he growled, "or I'll fight you." His caribou legs tensed to spring.

"You are like no other being," said the Stone. "Utterly confusing. Are my words so empty?"

"Yes," said Huuq. "You talk and talk. Your family. The

shadow. The Egg. Now about how Qipik was supposed to eat it. And die. I think you just make things up. Maybe to play with me. I haven't met an It who hasn't tried to make me feel crazy."

Huuq kicked snow at the Stone.

"Get out of my way," he repeated. "Or I'll break you. It might take longer than with Land-claws. But I know I can crack stone."

The She-Stone said nothing. Huuq waited while the storm whipped at his fur.

"It is becoming clear," she said at last. "I do not know how this could be, given what you are, but you know absolutely nothing."

"Yes!" roared Huuq. He had never imagined feeling so pleased at being regarded as ignorant.

"Finally!" he went on. "I know nothing! I've been trying to tell you that all along. But you're dense as a . . ."

He paused as the word met his lips.

"And I am no teacher," added the She-Stone. "I admit this."

Huuq waited for more, but the Stone went silent.

After some time, he became aware of her Strength—or at least, of her mind reaching into the Strength around and beneath them. This was a different manipulation of Strength than Huuq had become used to. Up until now, he had encountered the Strength of the Land in concentrated form: as raw power, shaping physical events. As crude as one rock knocking into another.

Now, the She-Stone's Strength seemed to drift. The "scent" of such Strength (for that was how Huuq was beginning think of it) was mild, but cast like a wide net. He could even feel it lapping, like gentle water, at his own mind.

"What are you doing?" asked Huuq.

"Finding a teacher," said the Stone. "Hopefully. We are on the edge of a Water power. Your kind always did better with that sort of element. A good, rudimentary power for a good, though rudimentary, mind."

Huuq wondered if he had just been insulted. But his insight advised: if he could not say for sure, perhaps the rock was right to call him rudimentary, after all.

He waited, blinking away snow as it accumulated on his lashes. He could feel every subtle change in the winds, as they moved his fur. An odd impulse welled up in him. Something twitchy. Before he knew it, he had shaken exactly like a dog. Snow flew from him in all directions.

He stood worried, looking at the half-circle around him, where clumps of snow had fallen.

Was he becoming more animal-like? Was he somehow losing his inua, the human part of himself?

Like Qipik?

Heavier than ever, the snowstorm blew.

"So," said the She-Stone after some time. Her voice was sharp, assertive.

"You must walk to *there*."

Given that Huuq had been blinded by a snowstorm for what seemed like days, he opened his mouth to ask what "there" meant. Before he could utter a word, though, sharp pain—the first he had felt since becoming an It—stabbed at a spot between his eyes. It disappeared quickly, too fast for him to bother crying out.

He suddenly felt pulled.

Huuq turned in the direction of the tug.

He saw a new oddity. Nearby, various rocks had shot out of the snow. They had appeared without a sound. Not even his It ears had been able to hear them move. Dozens of the new stones trailed off into whiteness. There were sharp-edged boulders. Round ones. Vaguely triangular formations. A few of the rocks held familiar shapes, like those of animals or people. No stone was exactly like any other. None were higher than his hips.

Yet insight flooded Huuq's mind, and he knew what he was seeing.

A path, he thought.

"I promised that I would help you," said the She-Stone, "for I perceived that you had been misled. Whether accidentally or deliberately, I do not know. Follow these with good fortune and the best of my heart. They will lead to a power that may be able to fill your gaps. To mend the cracks in your knowledge."

Huuq looked all around him. Then at Qipik. He would have to carry her, and he did not like the idea of staggering around some rocks, perhaps even tripping, when she was so ill. But his latest flush of insight told him that he should follow the She-Stone's path. And a doubtful path, it seemed, was better than none at all.

"Maybe I should wait for the storm to die down?" he asked the Stone.

At once, Qipik's last words seemed to blow like soft winds in his mind.

Please stay with me.

"This storm can never die," the She-Stone answered. "This storm is the wrath of Sea, Sky, and Land. It centres around your camp. The Enemy's presence is an insult to the Way Things Should Be. We lesser powers cannot be surprised that the Sky Time does anything other than rebel against it."

Huuq thought for a moment. He had seen cruelty in camp. Greed. Pettiness. Envy. Many times, he had watched camp folk trying to snuff out the happiness of others. Simply to feel strong. Or important.

Was any of this exactly evil? Evil, to Huuq, was a monster. Especially a monster that threatened the things he loved. It had claws. Fangs, maybe. It was . . .

Like me? he suddenly wondered.

Am I evil?

As when he'd lived in camp—under the dull, foggy fear—he tried to put such thoughts away from himself.

He was left with a strange nausea.

"Evil," he said. "What would it look like?"

"Like whatever you feel it should not look like," said the Stone.

Huuq sighed. Maybe she was right to direct him to someone who could communicate a bit better.

"Does it at least have a name?" he pressed.

"Yes."

Yet Huuq was getting used to the way of Stones. He

immediately explained with, "By asking, I meant you should tell me what it is."

"Ah," said the Stone. "We just call it Enemy. That is its name. Enemy."

Huuq thought some more.

"Who is 'we'?" he asked.

"Those of us who were asked to watch," the She-Stone explained. "Until such time as the Egg might have hatched. There are powers who wished to see it manifest. More powers than those simply in the Land."

The She-Stone gave a sad sigh.

"Except," she added, "that my siblings and I fell asleep. Our shame will last into the next age. Such a simple matter, guarding one object. And we failed in this basic task. Now the Enemy should be free, though something still keeps it bound. At least, in part."

"What did the Egg actually do?" Huuq asked. "Tell me simply. If you can."

"Very little," said the She-Stone. "The Egg was only powerful because of the Child inside it. The Child who must die now. With Qipik."

Huuq winced.

"The Child's Strength," the Stone went on, "radiated through the Egg. Through Land. Through Sky. Into the Enemy. It poured light into those black dreams that sicken us all."

"This . . . Enemy," Huuq asked, "wasn't Strong enough to fight an Egg?"

When Huuq had reached into the Land, he had felt the shadow's power. And he had fought only a dream-image of the Enemy. How Strong, then, was the Enemy itself?

"How," he pressed, "did it attack Qipik, then?"

The She-Stone went silent for a long moment.

"Think," she said at last, "of a lamp. Its light shines into the darkness. But can the shadow fight back? No. For the darkness has no substance of its own. This, Inhabitant, is about what is real. The light is reality. Darkness is but a word for when our eyes are closed."

Again, Huuq wanted to ask how the Stone knew anything about eyes. But he said nothing.

The She-Stone sighed once more.

"I told you," she said, "I am a poor teacher."

"So, what would have happened," asked Huuq, "if the Egg had hatched?"

"The Child," said the Stone, "would have brought its power to the Land. The Enemy would have been killed."

Again, Huuq glanced at Qipik, taking in the full weight of how badly matters had turned out. If he had simply stood his ground, not allowed the bullies to chase him up the hill . . .

Yet, it seemed impossible: how had his dog come under the control of this Enemy? Qipik was no evil being. He would have sensed something, somehow, if she were bad.

Wouldn't he?

"I do not wish to confuse you further," said the She-Stone. "Follow the path I have made. Go to the power who can help you. That one is dangerous. Perhaps even murderous. But such a consultation promises much knowledge."

Huuq was not overjoyed to hear that word: "murderous." He shifted uncomfortably, then asked, "So, why don't you come along? Talk to this person for me?"

"I would," answered the Stone, "if I were able. Your new teacher is not really a person. Not as you know such. Do you not see what lies around you? You stand on the edge of the Sea ice."

Huuq was unsure of how, through this storm, anyone could know where anything lay. Around him, he could see only the vaguest hulking shapes. It was impossible to tell how large or distant they might be.

"What does Sea ice have to do with anything?" he asked.

The She-Stone chuckled with the sound of sliding shale.

"This time," she told him, "you truly did amuse me. The Land is my power. You venture toward a new power now. Too close to the Sea and I would be overwhelmed by its Strength. I would let it sing to me, as I do too often under the caress of wind. And I would dream its dreams, until the World turned, as it always will, and I awakened again."

"I'm really glad," said Huuq, "you don't want to confuse me further."

Again, he picked up Qipik.

She's so limp . . . .

"Best leave her to the snows," said the Stone with some sadness.

"No," snapped Huuq. "No."

"Then you will have to feel further anguish," said the She-Stone, "by watching her death. And you will know when a grand, beautiful being—the Child—dies with her."

Huuq glanced down at Qipik's fur, smoky grey and white, with streaks the colour of rusty rocks.

"She was ready to be with me," Huuq murmured, "when she probably thought I might die."

"Then may death," said the Stone, "at least bring both of you, one day, to a happier place."

The She-Stone was already sinking as she spoke. Huuq watched her recede into the Land, the reverse of the way she had emerged. Within moments, snowfall obscured even the area originally disturbed by her appearance.

Huuq turned his gaze toward the Sky. He wondered if, beyond the storm, there was a place where the Many Players still spangled in all their colours.

"If there is a happier place," he whispered.

The Maze

In walking, Huuq soon found himself depending on the trail of boulders for something other than guidance: he found that they kept the storm from driving him crazy.

Earlier, in his silent trudge with Qipik, he had come to feel like a captive of the cloistering whiteness. Now, at least, he had objects to look at. They were not wildly entertaining. But the rocks nevertheless differed from each other. He soon found himself playing a kind of game.

Each time he passed a particularly interesting rock, he would try to compare it to an object that he was familiar with. After a while, just to hear something other than the mad winds, he named them aloud. After a longer while, his mind began to fight the monotony. It became difficult to play his own game.

"Bear."

"Old man."

"Old man's bum."

"Dog."

"Dog poop."

"Cloud."

"Cloud."

"Rock."

"Another stupid rock . . . ."

More than once, he stumbled. Only once did he glance backward. The snowfall was so thick that it was dark grey, rather than white. Before, when he had been feeling so lost and desolate and without hope, the storm had barely bothered him. Now it was somehow terrifying. It was as though he were being stalked by a great, hazy wall.

Huuq tried to keep his gaze fixed to the ground. To the stone after stone that made up his only path.

"Um, baby bear."

"Duck egg."

"Pile of fish eggs."

"Pile of fish . . . ."

He was not sure whether to feel saddened or relieved when the rock trail finally ended. Huuq had followed them along a roughly flat plain for some time (at least there had been no smaller rocks to trip him). He had expected something at their end.

He saw nothing other than more storm. More whiteness.

What now? he thought.

He could think of nothing to do, other than to keep walking as though a trail still existed. He glanced back, to make sure that he was still moving in the same direction as his original path. But when he glanced back again, only a few heartbeats later, he could not see the rocks at all.

Huuq sighed, hoping that the She-Stone knew what she was doing.

He thought about her words:

A Sea power, she said.

What would a Sea power look like?

He walked.

Soon, dark shapes seemed to approach from the whiteness. Huuq paused, staring, blinking past falling flakes. He was not sure of what he was seeing: ice or rock, apparently, all in a jumble. But how big? How far away?

He took a step and stumbled.

Huuq managed to catch himself by springing away from the area of his misstep. On landing, he found himself teetering once again. It seemed that he stood on treacherous ground—an area riddled with icy fissures that tended to catch his caribou hooves.

Regaining his balance, Huuq took in a deep breath. He sniffed. He did not know why he had not become aware of it sooner, but the smell of brine filled his nostrils. He looked once again at the fissures around him.

Ice cracks.

He stared at the jumble of shapes that he had spotted earlier. He was closer now, and could see their jagged angles much better.

Shattered Sea ice.

Father had explained the ice to him, one time. As the Sea froze, older ice pushed in younger, breaking it up, piling and locking it in place along the shore, so that it sat throughout the winter: a great, frigid maze. The blocks were sculpted by constant winds, so that by winter's end, they were worn into a variety of tortured shapes.

He was at the Sea's edge. He guessed that he stood a stone's throw out from shore.

Huuq stood confused for a while. The She-Stone had told him that she would lead him to a Sea power. Whatever that meant. Here was the Sea.

Where was the power? Was it expecting him, or did he have to search a bit?

"Um, here I am!" he called. He was answered only by winds whistling and moaning past the icy blocks. He began to feel silly.

"I'm not supposed to walk through that, am I?" He phrased his question to Qipik, though he knew she could not hear him. Somehow, he was sure that she was not yet dead. She was not quite alive, either. But it made him feel better, directing words to a friend.

Huuq made sure that he had a good grip on Qipik. With great care, he began to step toward the ice-maze. He found the going difficult, since he had to peer past Qipik's bulk in order to see whether or not he was about to put a hoof in an ice crack. The Sea ice was laced with them, but many were obscured under snow. It was at least interesting to discover that his hooves, which he considered so monstrous, were useful here. On reflex alone, the parts of his hooves pinched together each time a foot came down. They somehow found whatever tiny, invisible edges the ice had to offer.

His step was steady. For now, at least, he was pleased to be walking on hooves rather than boots.

It was not long before Huuq was engulfed by the ice-maze. Piles of solid, shattered Sea loomed over him. Up close, he could see the vast, jagged edges, often dirtied by sand and silt, in between which were beautiful blue spots of especially dense ice.

He found his head moving often—left and right—to keep from bumping or grazing ice. Down, to avoid tripping. Up and ahead, to find his way through.

Often, Huuq found himself taking a course that he was sure would bring him through the maze, only to find it leading him to another jumble of blocks. Most often, there were dead ends. He began to dread these, since the way back never looked much like the way forward. Soon, he wandered without any particular plan.

In some ways, the great mass of broken Sea ice was worse than a maze, since there were no exact paths. He soon gave up hope that his nose could lead him. Fresh Sea air was whipped toward him by winds that curled and spiralled. They deceived him, sometimes leading him back toward the coast. Only once did Huuq try kicking at ice to clear it: the result was a small avalanche, making him nervous, mostly for Qipik's safety. The kick revealed more ice on the other side.

Huuq's wolverine lips were curled back much of the time. It seemed stupid to get mad at ice, but his patience was wearing thin.

Finally, Huuq stopped. The maze still loomed. The storm still blew.

Why had he not thought of this sooner?

Gently, he placed Qipik on the ice.

He leapt.

A great spring took him high, positioning him on the side of an angular heap. His hooves skidded, but he dug in with his bear claws. His Inhabitant hand was useful for steadying him.

Huuq gauged his surroundings, then spotted a slightly higher position.

A second leap took him there.

With another three jumps, and terrific care after some ice gave way under his weight, Huuq found himself balancing atop a triangular wedge of Sea ice—a shard as large as a hill.

His lungs pulled in the perfect air, and he looked out on the Sea.

It was a vast, white expanse, hazy through the storm, but at least visible. He could see shapes that were probably icebergs, small mountains of frozen water locked in the very Ocean that had birthed them. He thought he could even spot islands far in the distance. He sighed, wishing that Father were here. Father would have known what he was looking at.

Now, at least, Huuq knew where to find open air.

A single leap took him almost all the way down. A smaller bound brought him back to Qipik. He placed his hand on her head, indulging the sliver of hope that he might see eyelids flicker. At least her nose twitched a little. That was life.

Huuq picked her up, then tried to recall everything that he had seen from his perch. While above the maze, he had also spotted some areas that had given him ideas, notions of how he might work his way out.

The going was still slow, but Huuq eventually stepped over a last block of broken Sea, and looked toward the flatter Sea ahead.

He had escaped the maze. But there was still no Sea power. At least, none that he could recognize.

He stood, nose twitching, thoughts roiling.

Do I wait? he wondered.

Do I walk?

Some impulse drove him to turn his head Skyward. His eyes closed. He lost himself, for a few heartbeats, in the feel of flakes settling on his eyelashes.

Now, he thought, *I Walk.*

The thought had the force of a command. Of a whip-crack. Though he could no longer feel the Strength of the Land beneath his hooves, not in the way that he had before, he sensed that a special power had just brushed at his mind. Maybe, it had touched something deeper than his mind.

A wide thing.

A very deep thing.

That was what had come upon him: a power of width and depth. He could not understand it in any other way.

This power was nothing at all like that of the Land. The Land had felt alive and conscious, but with the feeling of a giant that always slumbered. Its thoughts were like accidents. Like dreams. Without will or purpose behind them.

This power, however . . .

It made the Land look dead by comparison. But its life was a roar. A surge. It neither thought nor dreamed. It was free of even a slumbering mentality. Fixed completely in the present.

Wakeful.

Vibrant.

Mindless.

Huuq found the power strangely alluring. Some part of him wanted to play in its depth. At once, a different part of his selfhood jerked back from this power. There was fear here. Tremendous fear. The very stuff of which that emotion was made.

He had to deal with this power, though. The Sea power. He knew it now. The Sea had come to him. And it held something for him.

Reward.

Threat.

And the Sea did not simply want him to walk.

It demanded that he Walk.

(Whatever that might mean.)

Yet Huuq wondered. How long could he walk on this open expanse before the Sea physically stopped him? He was an It now. But he had been born an Inhabitant. Like every Inhabitant, he knew that the cracks he had encountered up until now were tiny, trifling things. They were a bother. Little danger. The Ocean, however, was not entirely frozen. It was criss-rossed with yawning cracks that even his legs might not manage to jump—cracks that offered frigid darkness, without escape.

So far, as an It, he could not freeze. It seemed that he could not grow hungry. Or grow thirsty. Or tire.

Could he drown?

So, heaving a great sigh, Huuq obeyed.

And Walked.

In time, Huuq's trek took him far from the ice-maze. The Sea breeze was free of snow, yet its gusts, at times, were more powerful. In carrying Qipik, Huuq was top heavy. More than once, he paused, balancing so that a sudden gust did not bowl him over.

He looked back and gasped. From out on the white expanse, he could see the snowstorm behind him.

In past summers, Huuq had enjoyed outdoor fires. The Land was covered in low-growing, brown clumps of heather. There had been great relief from the boredom of camp life in throwing handfuls of this stuff into small, stone-enclosed fires. The heather burned fiercely, with hot orange flame. And smoke. Huuq had loved to toss it in and step back, watching the vast clouds of smoke wind upward to spread out on the winds.

From a distance, the storm now reminded him of a heather fire. Of the smoke, anyway. He could see the vague outlines of low hills, patchy with the light and dark of snow and rock. Over them loomed a series of interconnected clouds—clots of storm— all connected to the greater ashen Sky. The storm seemed to rake at the inland areas with twisted, claw-tipped fingers.

The sight made him shudder.

"Strange," Huuq muttered to Qipik. He sensed that she could not hear. But, somehow, he felt more alone than he ever had before. He needed to feel as though there were some companion for him. Somewhere.

"You'd think a snowstorm would look white," he went on. "But it just looks . . . mad."

If anger had a colour, he imagined, it would look like that storm.

He turned and trekked further out to Sea.

The Fisherman

Under the ashen Sky, Huuq passed icebergs. Some, from a distance, had at first seemed quite close to him. They were ice-mountains, caught in the frozen water, oftentimes with perfectly vertical sides that jutted from the Ocean's flatness. He wondered what they looked like up close, but it seemed to take forever to reach them. It always turned out that, by some trick of the Sea, they were never really where he expected.

It was as though, as he moved toward the icebergs, they moved, as well. Sometimes, it seemed as though they were circling him from afar.

Huuq began to avoid the icebergs. They were too creepy. His experience with them made him think of what Inhabitants sometimes claimed: that a few icebergs were Its in disguise. He tried to be more mindful of the lore of his folk. Advice like: don't whistle under the Many Players or they'll swoop down on you; don't take things from graves unless you leave something in return; don't mix things of the Land and Sea indiscriminately . . . .

Yet why could he never recall useful lore when he needed it?

Huuq was startled when he noticed a shape against the grey Sky. A raven flew by. It was the first animal he had seen since leaving camp. As his eyes tracked the bird, a patch of cloud broke to reveal night Sky. He could see a couple of stars. Colours.

The Many Players were there.

Huuq was not sure why, but he blew a sigh of relief. Somehow, the dancing lights comforted him.

The bird turned out to be a falcon, not a raven. The creature was easier to distinguish without cloud cover turning it into a black silhouette. After a moment, the falcon coasted past the starry patch. And before it did so, something seemed to loosen in Huuq's chest. For the merest heartbeat, he felt the pure air in his lungs, and he felt like an Inhabitant again. Not an It.

Then the clouds came together again, as though the Sky had closed the mouth of a bag. The patch disappeared.

Huuq returned to his grey, lonely World.

Some distance ahead, Huuq spotted a black figure on the ice.

The Enemy, he thought. But he was not sure. Any figure looked shadowy in this gloom.

There was nowhere to hide. No way to assume that the figure could not see him. So Huuq marched toward it.

He did not have to walk for long before he came near enough to make out details. The figure was fishing. In the way of Inhabitants, the dark being knelt by a narrow hole in the ice. It held a short stick, from which trailed a line.

The figure did not bother to look up, even when Huuq came quite close.

Huuq took a measured breath. He could now see that part of his suspicion had been correct: the figure was not an Inhabitant. Though it wore the coat of an adult male, a hunter, the being was no larger than a child of seven or eight years. Its hood was pulled back, revealing the head of *kanajuq*: a spiny sculpin fish. Huuq had caught small versions of this fish in summer streams. They were clever, with dark, spotted skin and the ability to blend in with surroundings, finding any available shadow in which to hide.

The Fisherman did not seem to notice Huuq. Huuq stopped about a stone's throw distant. But when he was still ignored, he edged closer.

The Fisherman kept one glassy eye on his hole. All the while, his slimy, mottled hand bobbed the stick. Its rhythm was steady, with only occasional interrupted beats. Like a silent song.

Huuq stared for some time, wondering how to—or whether he even should—introduce himself. He was looking for a Sea power. Was this it?

Huuq almost jumped when the Fisherman suddenly cried out.

"Uh-yai!"

The being threw its stick aside. Still focused on the hole, it began to reel the line in with a hand-over-hand motion.

After a moment, the Fisherman held up a small cod. It wriggled on the hook, but the Fisherman shook it until the fish was still. The being turned the fish until he was able to gaze into one of its bubble-eyes.

"So!" said the Fisherman in a croaking voice. "Just as I suspected. Didn't I warn you never to come into these waters again?"

Huuq stood dumbstruck as the being carefully released the fish from its hook. The creature struggled in the Fisherman's hand for a moment, before the being said, "Enough of your arguing! This is not a discussion."

Huuq watched as the Fisherman tossed the cod back into the hole. Then the small figure stood, shouting into the dark opening,

"Go straight home! And careful of seals! There's an overpopulation of them right now!"

The being coiled his line around the stick, tucked the tools into his wide hood. Then he walked toward Huuq. As though to an old friend, he said, "Why are you just standing there, Huuq? You didn't so much as greet me. You're not trying to be rude, are you?"

For a moment, Huuq simply blinked, confused.

"You know my name," he told the Fisherman.

The being looked up at Huuq, turning an eye so that it met one of Huuq's own. His broad fish mouth seemed to smile, which made the mouth look as if it were curving halfway around the Fisherman's spiny head.

"Did you tell me your name?" asked the being.

"N-no," said Huuq, a bit rattled. He had thought that, after his extreme experiences with Its, he could no longer be shocked.

"Smart of you," said the Fisherman. "Wise not to say

153

your name at first. But is Huuq your true name?"

"I, um, think so," said Huuq. He was pretty certain that, before camp folk had started calling him Why, they had called him something else. He had been a baby, back then. Maybe his parents could remember the name.

"If it were your true name," said the Fisherman, "it would not be smart to tell someone."

"People," Huuq explained, "call me Why because they don't like me. My head is broken. My heart is empty . . . ."

"Quite the self-analysis," said the being. "Who told you all that?"

Huuq made no answer for a long moment. At last, he said, "I used to steal. People hated me for that."

He thought some more, unsure of why he had told the being such a thing. Then he added, "I guess I never thought about stealing as wrong. Well, maybe I did."

"Then why did you do it, Why?" the Fisherman asked.

Huuq sighed. Then he shrugged, wordless.

"Or is it that you meant to say," asked the being, "that you *thought* it was wrong? But you *felt* it was right?"

Huuq's wolverine ears pricked up.

"Yes!" he barked. "That's exactly it. Felt. That's how it was. Felt. But it was wrong. I know that now. Because I got in so much trouble."

"Why?" pressed the Fisherman. "Did you harm someone through your thefts?"

"Well . . . no," Huuq answered. "But I made them mad."

"So, making someone mad is the measure of whether or not an action is wrong?"

Huuq stood confused. He began to wonder if this was really the Sea power he had been sent to see. To learn from.

And now that Huuq thought about it, he did not really want to learn. That had been the She-Stone's idea. What Huuq really wanted was help. He wanted to keep Qipik alive. He wanted his limbs and proper head back. To go back to being an Inhabitant. To live in a healthy community. Not one cursed by some kind of Enemy.

He wanted to un-become.

To stop being Why.

Why, the Thief.

Why, the hated.

He just wanted to live, now.

In safety.

"All I'm saying," Huuq told the Fisherman, "is that people hated me for a reason. That's why . . . my name."

"But I'm calling you Why. And I don't dislike you, Huuq."

"You don't know me yet. Even I hate myself."

Huuq had stabbed himself with the thought. He seemed to feel the concept, self-loathing, as his own words penetrated him. His soul had become a sudden stone, sinking in bottomless water.

Down, down, the thought travelled.

I hate myself.

The Fisherman chuckled in a way that made him sound as if he had a bad cold. "People don't call you Huuq," he explained, "because they hate you. Maybe they think they do, but it's not their place to ordain what you end up with for names. 'Why' is what the Land calls you, and folks just echo it. So, let's see, then."

Huuq stood, uncomprehending.

"See what?" he eventually asked.

"Let's see this Self of yours," said the being. "You said it's worth hating. Let's have a look."

Huuq shrugged.

"You mean," pressed the Fisherman, "you can't take it out? Turn it around? Look at it from every angle?"

Huuq stared for a long moment, then answered, "No."

"Then how can you know your Self is worth hating?" asked the being. "At least have a peek at the poor thing, first."

Huuq frowned. "I don't think I can do that," he answered. "At least, nobody ever told me that could be done."

Huuq wondered if the Fisherman was talking about some trick that Strong beings could do. Like when Aki had shown Huuq how to "eat" the arrows stuck in his body. Or when the She-Stone had helped him find the right expression of Strength to uproot the Enemy's shadow.

"Hmph," sounded the Fisherman. "Don't drive yourself crazy with why people say what they do, Huuq. Some words are tidal in power. Others are no more than foam. The forces of this World bully our feelings about all the time. Our minds are liquid, sloshing in a bag. The weak-minded person thinks his thoughts are his own. He doesn't feel the World acting on him. Answering a runaway brain."

"Are you talking about the Strength of the Land?" asked Huuq. "Or about the Sea? The Stone said to expect a Sea power. Is that what you are? Or are you talking about some kind of Strength in . . . ?"

Lacking words, Huuq gestured all around, indicating the entirety of the frozen Ocean.

The Fisherman waved a slender, webbed hand. "Strength is Strength, Huuq. Tell me, what's the difference between Water and Land? Water is the great Mover. The Doer. It saturates and shapes what you call Land. Land, though—that is the cradle of Water. Land is the Basis. The Measure. Over both Water and Land arches the Sky, whether blue or black of night, enfolding them both."

As the being spoke, Huuq felt a vibration building. It did not seem to come only from below him, as the power had when he had felt rooted in the Land. It came from all around, in coils, catching his very being up in a climbing shiver.

From bones to brain, the sensation rose within him. It came to seem that reality was a vast surface, churning a hundred times with each heartbeat. Faster. Faster. He himself was like a wave within its vastness. A whitecap. Rising. Falling. Forming a crest. Then falling back into mere water. Then forming again.

Odd thoughts climbed into and out of Huuq's awareness, spurred by the Fisherman's words. As Huuq heard "Water," he began to think of his own heart: of the dissatisfaction that had ripped and gnawed at him since . . . forever. As Huuq heard "Land," he thought of his mind: of the frustrated attempts to make sense of his own life. But with the word "Sky," boundless peace, fulfillment, seemed to flood his awareness.

What part of him did the Sky signify?

He fell into the Fisherman's words, wanting to know.

If only . . .

"Huuq!"

Huuq shuddered as he heard the Fisherman call to him.

"Huuq!"

Huuq looked down and remembered where he stood. He returned to awareness only with confusion, unable to tell whether he stood in a dream, or if the dream had occurred moments ago.

Then he realized something awful:

He had dropped Qipik.

He bent in alarm, but froze when the Fisherman said, "Leave her. She'll be fine. For now. You are the one who worries me, Huuq. You seemed to go adrift while I was talking. Like you'd been hit on the head. What just happened?"

"I . . . don't know," Huuq told the being. "Your words. They made me feel funny. Like I wasn't even here."

"You weren't," agreed the Fisherman. "At least, your soul wasn't exactly here. Your time is far overdue. I'm glad the Stone sent you to us. Bad thing about Stones: they're not very pliant in their thinking. Good thing: they're sensible."

"So you are the Sea power," Huuq asserted. Like an animal, he shook himself, trying to shed the last of his odd dream impressions. "You're the one the Stone sent me to see."

"No," answered the Fisherman. "That would be my Wife. She's the one who is so mad at your camp. She was mistreated by Inhabitants a while back. Born among them, you see. Prefers the company of Its, these days. Long story. Just know that She isn't one to let go of insults easily. So, when She gets wind of folks mistreating each other, it reminds Her of the old days. Then She gets a bit . . . extreme. For a while. She's not that bad, really. Best if you get to know Her before judging . . . ."

As he spoke, the Fisherman shot an anxious glance at the hole in the ice.

"You talk like your wife is an Inhabitant," said Huuq. "I thought I was being sent to talk to an It."

"She *was* an Inhabitant," explained the Fisherman. "She's

what you'd call an It, now."

Then the being, still staring into the hole, whispered, "Maybe She's beyond Inhabitant and It."

Once again, the being waved a fishy hand. "If you'd received proper training, Huuq," he said, "you'd know all this. I'm sorry. We're making up, here, for the fact that you've been cheated all your life. Just bear in mind: there's no such thing as an actual It. Don't get obsessed with words. Anyone can be an It. Anything. Saying 'It' is like saying 'Force' or 'Power' or 'Urge.'"

The Fisherman gestured at the ice below his little sealskin boots, at the icebergs looming in the distance.

"The Sea," he explained, "is a kind of It. Land, too. Sky. My Wife, as my fellow husbands and I are often reminded, could be called the Sea's wrath. The Sea's justice, as well. She's surrounded by Its who are drawn to what She represents. At her whim, She heals. At another, kills."

"Then She can heal Blanket!" cried Huuq. "I need to see Her."

"Don't be so hasty," advised the Fisherman. "I told you, She's not in the best of moods right now. And you're coming into this raw. Unconditioned."

"No, you don't understand," pressed Huuq. "Blanket, she's my dog. But she's an It, too."

"I know," said the Fisherman. "I've already examined you. And her. And what she carries. What did you think I was doing while you faded out, there?"

Huuq tried to control his temper. "Then you have to know," he said, "Blanket ate a Land's Egg. It's killing her. Or something is. Whoever made her eat the thing is killing her. Please, I need help."

The being shook his spiny head. "I'm very sorry," he told Huuq. "You're upset because of the gaps in your knowledge. Nothing can save your Qipik."

"But you just said your Wife—"

"I said my Wife, the Deep Mother, has power. Especially over Its. Yes, she does. But She is not the only power in the World. You would understand me better, Huuq, if you understood that you did not see what you saw. Your sight is untrained, so you were unable to See. You thought there was a dog. You thought there was an Egg. You thought the dog ate the Egg. Look at me now. But don't see me. Look at what I truly am. Can you See me?"

Huuq tried to calm himself. He did understand what the strange being was requesting.

So he closed his eyes.

He opened them again.

"The Strength!" cried Huuq. "I can't feel the Strength of the Land anymore!"

"Because you don't believe me," said the Fisherman. "You think you need to stand on the Land, because that's what you're used to. That's all that defines limits, you know: what we're used to. We live bound, under the tight knots of what we know."

Huuq laughed darkly.

"What's funny?" asked the Fisherman.

"It's just," said Huuq, "that's all easy for you to say. You're an It. You're used to not having limits. I've lived most of my life as an Inhabitant. We know nothing but limits. I haven't been in my life as an It very long. Everyone expects me to be used to this existence by now. Like I was born with claws! Fangs! Hooves! Could you please stop treating me like I know everything that Its do? I only became an It a little while ago!"

The Fisherman stood silent, staring.

After a long moment, Huuq grew worried. His voice had risen into a monstrous yowl as he'd spoken. He wondered if he had offended the Fisherman.

"Did I say something wrong?" Huuq eventually asked.

The small being did not answer at first. He brushed snow from one boot, scratched behind a gill. He looked at Huuq as though he were meeting him for the first time.

"Only everything," the Fisherman answered at last. "You said everything wrong."

Huuq sighed, exasperated.

"Because your point of view is wrong, Huuq," the Fisherman went on. "Wrong. Wrong. Wrong. You've been lied to, Huuq. You're no It, and never have been."

Huuq frowned. Lied to? But he had little time to think about this statement, as he was shocked by the Fisherman's next words:

"You're a shaman."

The Enemy

"You're crazy!" cried Huuq.

Now he knew that this strange being was either insane or a liar. Huuq knew very little about the Hidden World. But he had at least learned the difference between a shaman and an It.

"Look at me," the Fisherman repeated. "Try to See me."

"Didn't you hear?" asked Huuq. "I can't be a shaman. My friend Aki, he's a shaman. Can't you see what I look like? I've been turned into an It!"

"See me," repeated the Fisherman. There was an odd reverberation to his voice, as though he spoke from inside some cave or grotto.

Huuq blew a snort and made circles in frustration. When he looked back at the small being, the Fisherman was still staring. Waiting. Ignoring Huuq's fit.

"See me. Try."

It was difficult, since Huuq was far from calm, but he reached out to look for Strength. At first, the feeling was as before: like being unable to find any last scrap of meat on a bone. But then he remembered what the Fisherman had told him. Of how Strength was just a word. An idea. Strength was supposedly all around him.

It was laced into all the World.

He frowned, his thoughts becoming scrambled. Was he recalling the Fisherman's notions? Or his own?

In an instant, Strength flooded into Huuq's mind and heart. His bones seemed to swell, organs steeping, hairs quivering, all bathed in Strength. He realized, then, that it was impossible to "lose" Strength.

The World is a body.

Strength is its blood.

"Oh, that's wonderful," said the Fisherman. "I like the imagery. But try to do it with eyes open. Did you know you're prone to letting your thoughts wander?"

Huuq had not realized that his eyes had shut.

He opened them.

And he Saw the Fisherman.

Instead of a funny little man with a fish head, Huuq saw a massive waterspout. Spangling in opal and aquamarine, the spout spiralled up into the Sky. At its core, there were fiery bursts, gold that flashed and twisted upward along the spire's length. The spout seemed to have no exact source, but flowed from the very Sea ice.

The being whom Huuq had thought of as the Fisherman spoke again. This time, his voice was like a waterfall's roar:

"What do you See?"

"I . . . See the real you, I think," answered Huuq. His Strong eyes ranged up and down the spout. "You're like water," he added, "filled with light."

"Better," roared the being. "Still just another image. But close enough and certainly better than before. Quit now, so as not to give yourself a headache."

Huuq blinked, and the Fisherman form had returned.

"I think I hear what you're trying to say," said Huuq. "You—" he waved toward the being, unsure of how to put his words. "You, what I see there, it just . . . represents you. It isn't really you. Your look just stands for what you are."

"It stands for what *you* are," croaked the being, "since your mind dreams it up. But maybe you do understand. You live in a World of symbols now, Huuq. That is what it is to be a shaman."

"This . . . shaman thing," said Huuq. "I still don't think so."

"To be precise," said the Fisherman, "you are a potential shaman. Did you not have strange senses since your earliest memories? Did you not find yourself dissatisfied with ordinary life, as though you were foreign to your own folk? Did it not seem that others, around you, were seeing the World through one eye instead of two? You were a potential."

"I was a thief," said Huuq. "That was all. People hated me—my own family hated me—because I was a thief."

"No," said the Fisherman with great firmness. "Those were not true thefts. Your mind sees things in symbolic ways, Huuq. When you stole, it was because you sensed that something had been taken from you. You were struggling to get something back. But you never knew what it was. Think. Did you ever steal for profit? Out of envy? Out of malice?"

Huuq was stilled by the being's words, unable to escape the feeling that there was some truth to them. But he shook his head, saying, "This doesn't make sense. Aki is a shaman, and he would have told me. Wouldn't he? He said I was an It. I'm sure of that. He's a shaman, so—"

"Is he?" interrupted the Fisherman. "Is he a shaman? Think about his name, Huuq. Use your Strong insight. Aki. In the Inhabitant tongue, this can mean 'Gift.' Also 'Barb.' But where would you also hear it?"

Huuq worked hard to find something in the Fisherman's words. But every time he closed his eyes, concentrated, waited for insight to waft into him, he felt blocked.

Aki, he thought.

Sounds of "uh" connected to "kih."

As in . . .

"Uh."

"Kih."

"Ruk'h."

The last syllable tumbled from his tongue, so that the word finished itself:

"AKIRAQ."

"ENEMY."

It was then, as the word at last revealed itself, that the Strong insight soared across Huuq's awareness. He knew, in a heartbeat, that he had always owned the ability to understand matters of Its and their Strength. He had owned the power to See every aspect of himself.

Yet, something in him had wanted to remain ignorant. Blind. Simple. A part of him had insisted upon being an Inhabitant boy. A troublemaker. A thief.

His potential had been too wide.

It had been terrifying.

The Strength of the Land had always been there. From the time he'd been carried in his mother, that Strength had run like blood through his body. And, respecting his unspoken wishes, Huuq's Strength had remained quiet within him.

It had kept him from knowing all that there was to know.

Across Land.

Sea.

Sky.

Now, with no choice, Huuq had been plunged into Strength. No longer quiet, it roared, poured knowledge into his mind.

Huuq collapsed, falling to a sitting position on the ice. His eyes fixed on Qipik, a furry grey heap. Was she still alive?

How could I not know? he thought to himself. *Right in front of me. Aki . . . .*

His friend's name was the root word of "Enemy."

The Strong part of Huuq had blinded him to the fact.

But why?

Had he so badly wanted a friend?

Someone to accept him?

"And now you have it," said the Fisherman in a low voice.

"Yes," said Huuq. "I know everything. I think. At least, the parts connected to me. Aki is the evil in my camp. The Enemy. He pretended to be a shaman. He goaded me, somehow, into taking Blanket up the hill."

"Like I told you," said the Fisherman, "Strength can move people without them realizing it."

As though he had not heard the being, Huuq continued, muttering, "Aki knew the Egg was there. He knew if he allowed it to hatch, the Egg-Child would destroy him. Blanket was his Helper. He made sure she came with me, up that hill, because I had the ability to find the Egg. He must have known, somehow, that I would mess things up. That Blanket would have a chance to eat it. After that, he sent us out on the Land, with the Egg-Child. That way, it would be far away from him. Blanket would take it away. And die. The Egg-Child would die with her. He would be free."

Almost with the sound of wings, the Strong insight fluttered away from Huuq's awareness.

Feeling numb, Huuq looked up at the Fisherman.

"Aki must be really happy now," he told the being. "I'm such a fool. A stupid fool."

The Fisherman scratched at a fin along the side of his neck. "The Enemy might not be as happy as you think," he said. "Consider, Huuq: you've fought him. Yes, I know all about that, as with other matters. You fought his shadow. It was admittedly weak, but still Stronger than many Its. And you won."

The Fisherman stepped close to Huuq, coming eye to eye with him.

"Take heart," the being said, "in the fact that your Qipik fought the Enemy every step of the way. She tried to upset his plans. Oppressed by the Enemy, she was nevertheless *with* you."

"I know," said Huuq. He could feel tears welling in his core—his invisible, monstrous way of weeping.

"She tried to tell me, I think. I was too stupid to listen. But why didn't the Its just tell me everything when they took my limbs and face?"

The Fisherman took a step back. "Those particular Its are harder to comprehend," he said. "They are the original guardians of the Egg, the ones who set the Stones to watch over its hatching. They may answer calls, but they have no master. I saw your meeting with them, written on your heart. Wondered about it."

"They were angry," said Huuq.

"Maybe," answered the Fisherman. "That would have been justified, since you tried to lie to them."

Huuq hung his head.

"But they're wiser than you think," said the being. "Wiser than my Wife and I, certainly. I don't think they would have done anything without good cause. They might have been trying to wake you up."

"Wake me?" asked Huuq. Then, after a moment, he understood. "I understand what you mean."

"Yes, you get it," said the Fisherman, nodding. "You were asleep to your true nature, thanks in part to the Enemy."

"The Enemy," muttered Huuq. "Akiraq. Aki. I was his real tool, not Blanket. She's dying because of me. The Egg-Child is dying because of me. My family and folk . . . what will the Enemy do to them, now that I've freed him?"

"Keep feeding on them, I would expect," the being said, "until they become beasts who tear each other apart. Sorry if that bit was blunt."

The Fisherman sighed. "But there is a sliver of good news," he went on. "It seems as if something still keeps the Enemy in check. Even without the Egg being present."

Huuq waited for more.

The Fisherman held his webbed hands out helplessly. "I don't know what it is, Huuq. But something has to be there. An important object. And Strong. Otherwise, the Enemy would not remain stuck in camp, sending out sad little shadows."

"The Egg was all I found," said Huuq. He tried to recall if he had seen another object; anything special, that might have influenced Aki.

"I don't remember seeing anything like the Egg," he said at last.

"It would not have to be like the Egg," said the Fisherman. "It might not even appear Strong. Think hard. Did you leave something with him at your last meeting? Anything at all?"

Huuq could think of nothing. When he and Aki had last spoken, Aki had simply filled his head with lies: all concerning the need to take Qipik. To leave camp. To never come back.

Lest Huuq risk the entire camp attacking him.

Nothing but lies.

A World of deceit.

Huuq's frame shuddered with rage. He began to swear in the colourful manner of his father. A kind man. One who had grown angrier over time. Darker. Like the rest of the camp.

Huuq missed Father. He missed his mother. Sister.

But he had fallen for Aki's deception. He would never see them again.

And then he remembered.

"Yes!" cried Huuq. "I did leave something! A knife. I left a pana-knife."

The Fisherman stared out across the white expanse, seemingly lost in thought.

"Hmm," said the being after a time. "That might be the thing. Many of the nastier Its do not like blades. You'd be surprised how superstitious they can be. If the blade had family meaning, that might have even left some Strength in it."

"It was Father's," said Huuq a bit sadly. "The last thing I stole from him. The knife was the only thing I wasn't going to give back, too. I just thought . . . Aki deserved it. That he was my friend."

Huuq shrugged, feeling foolish again.

"Let me guess," said the Fisherman. "The Enemy didn't touch it, did he?"

Huuq had trouble remembering. Had Aki actually taken the knife in hand? So much had happened in such a short time. How could he be expected to recall every detail?

When Huuq made no answer, the Fisherman asked, "Where is it now? Did you leave the blade with him?"

"I . . . think it fell on the floor of his snow house," said Huuq, trying to remember. "He kept trying to get me to pick it up. I wouldn't do it."

The Fisherman began to laugh in deep, watery gasps.

"Ah! Ah!" he cried in amusement. "Stuck with your Father's knife! Poor monster! No wonder he was only able to send out shadows. Caught in the very camp he thinks he owns.

Serves him right!"

The small being stood laughing for a long moment, in a deep gurgle that made him sound like he was drowning.

Huuq was not sure why it was so funny, though it seemed good that the being was happy.

The Fisherman turned back to Huuq. "But, wonderful as it is, that blade's power won't last. He'll get around it. Unless we find some new way to bind him."

"Or destroy him," snarled Huuq. Now that he knew Aki's true nature, he was filled with hatred.

"Destruction is never a process that one should rush into," said the Fisherman a bit sadly, "but the Enemy did a lot to invite such a fate. Long ago. That was what the Egg was for, I'm afraid."

Huuq made a circular gesture. "Then our words," he said, "are no more important than the wind blowing around us."

Again, the being dismissed him with the wave of a hand. "Never quit, Huuq. Never," said the Fisherman. "It is only by never quitting that we preserve ourselves from an existence that seeks ever to reabsorb us. Do you have any more artifacts such as the knife? Anything from a loved one? Even something as small as a thimble. Even taken against their will."

Huuq opened his mouth to say "no." But then he remembered Mother's comb.

It seemed almost too pitiful to mention, though. How could a comb have power? It wasn't a weapon. Like a knife. But then again, this was about Strength. Not weaponry.

After a moment, Huuq realized that this had nothing to do with practicality. Something in him wanted the comb to remain his secret. He was tired of taking instructions. Sick of listening to others.

Hadn't listening to others put him here? Out on the Sea ice? Without a proper face? Or arms? Or legs?

And the comb was all he had. Not including Qipik, it was the one thing left to remind him of family.

(But wasn't this about saving his family?)

No, he thought to himself. *No one's business but my own.*

"No," Huuq said after a few heartbeats. "I don't have anything else."

The Fisherman sighed.

"Then," he said, "I shall have to think longer. And harder . . . ."

"Wait!" cried Huuq.

The being stood and stared. Only once, his great, goggle eyes blinked.

"I . . . I lied," Huuq told him at last. "I'm sorry. It's just that . . . well, I only have one thing. And it's not mine. I . . . stole it. Like I was trying to tell you. I'm not a good person."

Though he felt that he was about to end up laughed at, Huuq fiddled around with his hood, retrieving the comb from the small pocket hidden in its folds. He now felt embarrassed, remembering such a tiny, dirty little life. It seemed like recalling life as a mosquito.

"I have this," he mumbled, holding the comb out in his Inhabitant hand.

The Fisherman stepped up to look at it with curiosity, then gasped.

The being stood frozen for a long moment, until Huuq felt quite awkward. The Fisherman reached out slowly, pointed fingertips tracing the comb's outline. As though there were a thin, invisible barrier around the comb's surface, he moved his fingers over the carved features, perhaps admiring the fish-like look of the tool. His fingers paused over the comb's teeth, a few of which were broken. The remaining teeth resembled fish spines.

"This is a treasure," whispered the Fisherman.

Huuq was not sure of what to say.

It was a nice comb. That was all.

The Fisherman's eyes met Huuq's own.

"Have you never used the Strong vision to look at this?" the being asked. "Have you never Seen it?"

Huuq sighed, staring at the comb in his open hand. It was a weathered thing. Used. Beaten, but not entirely broken. Somehow, he felt a bit sorry for it.

"I don't really want to," Huuq muttered. "It feels . . . sad in my hand."

The Fisherman studied Huuq's face for a moment.

"And you're afraid," he said, "to See what lies behind the feeling."

"I don't know," Huuq told the being. "Maybe I was wrong when I said 'sad.' I'm afraid it might make me . . . *want* something. But I don't know what. Something good for me. But also bad."

Huuq shrugged.

"That's the only way I can say it."

The Fisherman grunted. "I will let you see the Deep Mother," he said. "Once you've talked to Her, we'll meet again."

"But . . . ." Huuq shut his mouth. He had thought to ask why the comb was so important. It was Strong. He understood that. But knowing that it held Strength was different from knowing how to implement it.

So, he went quiet, noting that the Fisherman had stepped back. The small figure seemed to be hugging himself. He had closed his great, globular eyes. Dimly, Huuq wondered why the being, as a fish, had eyelids. But then it occurred to him that he had a man-shaped body, as well.

Symbols, he reminded himself. *World of symbols.*

Huuq could feel the Strength. It whorled, all around him, though he could not sense any particular source. This Strength was spread out, never still, nothing at all like the roots that he had imagined running through the Land. Within several heartbeats, it began to make Huuq a bit nauseated.

The odd manifestation of Strength continued, even as the Fisherman opened his eyes once again.

"Huuq," he said in a cold, even voice, "you are about to meet Her. Do not expect kindness from Her. In truth, I don't know what She'll do. She dislikes uninvited guests, and Inhabitants most of all. She likes shades of blue, though. Green, as long as it's not too garish. And if you could . . . actually, never mind. I'm sorry, I wish I could be more helpful."

"I have to bring Blanket with me," said Huuq.

"Impossible. You're lucky enough to be—"

The ice began to tremble.

"No!" yelled Huuq. "I'm bringing Blanket! Your Wife has to heal—"

"Don't talk, Huuq! Listen! Remember to use the comb. She'll respect the comb. Use it on Her hair. It will calm Her. Symbols! Remember, everything is a symbol!"

"I'm not seeing Her without Blanket!" Huuq roared over the groan of ice. As he spoke, he placed the comb back in his hood. Then he picked up Qipik, holding her limp weight tight to his chest. She now felt more leaden, more *dead*, than she ever had before. The feeling frightened him.

"Too late!" hollered the Fisherman.

As the being spoke, he pointed to somewhere behind Huuq.

Huuq turned.

Without his noticing, the ice on which he stood had broken away from the frozen part of the Sea. Huuq had no idea how long he had been floating, but the floe edge now seemed quite far away.

He and Qipik and the Fisherman were adrift. The ice pan was like an enormous, white raft.

On all sides, there was black water.

Strange emotions seemed to rise in Huuq's core. Within heartbeats, he realized that the feelings were not his own. He was sensing a life. A great one, pushing ahead tides of passion.

Great, but not friendly.

And it was rising.

21

The Deep Mother

Huuq leapt away just as a massive black tendril erupted out of the ice beneath him. He turned in time to see it lashing, flecking salt water in all directions, in the open air. The tendril seemed to seek him. He dodged left, then back, to avoid its touch. Whenever it got close, the realization of what it was chilled his blood.

Hair? he wondered.

It was.

Hair.

Another lock of hair erupted from the Sea, towering above him. As with the first, he sensed its arrival only by "sniffing out" the odd emotions that preceded it. One seemed to dominate.

Wrath. The locks radiated purest wrath.

Huuq leapt as far away as possible, but two more locks shot upward, seeking him like giant black worms.

He was running out of room.

"Huuq!" cried the Fisherman, who went ignored by the locks. "Stop panicking! You're making it worse."

"This is your Wife?" Huuq called back. "Tell Her to stop!"

"Just relax! Use the comb!" the Fisherman hollered. "Remember what I told you!"

Huuq barely heard. He was already in mid-leap, avoiding another three of the monstrous locks. They had drenched him in briny water. He still felt no cold. But because the splashing water made the ice pan quite slick, he slipped and skidded for some distance on landing.

All the while, he managed to keep a grip on Qipik.

Huuq stood and roared at the tendrils, all waving high over his head. If he had to, he would dodge them for the rest of eternity.

The rage had risen within him. He was sick of being attacked.

Over a dozen locks burst forth under his feet, shattering the ice on which he stood. He was near the edge of the pan. There was nothing left to stand on.

He fell.

Wet blocks of ice battered his head and limbs.

Frigid waters blinded him. Engulfed him.

Black coils pulled him.

Down.

Always down.

There was no way to count the coils—locks of the Mother's hair—around him. Their combined power was impossible. Irresistible. There seemed to be more coils than water around Huuq. They pulled at his limbs so that he lost hold of Qipik within heartbeats.

And the coils were Strong.

Wherever they touched his flesh, passions of the Deep Mother washed into him. As with all sensations based in Strength, they had a material feel to them. They were substances. It was not as though his brain could perceive—or even understand—the Deep Mother's feelings. His mind instead responded to Her like something porous. As if it had become moss. Or peat. Against his own will, a murky part of him drank up the Deep Mother's passions.

His soul steeped in Her.

Huuq opened his mouth to scream in mad, mindless terror—a Strong terror that caught up all thought, making it seem as though someone were sewing random stitches into his brain.

His mouth filled with Sea water.

The Deep Mother's passions continued to saturate him. They were tangible. Tidal. They displaced some of his own heart, so that emotional control was swept from him. His soul suddenly seemed less real before Hers. Ghostly. As though his selfhood were no more than a Strong dream.

Her Strength then turned, forcing him to feel need. Cold, lurking need. A hunger for power to defeat the fear that She had dreamed into him. Huuq's muscles became cramped. His limbs twisted. If he did not make prey of another creature, force it down so as to raise himself up, he would starve in the frigid need.

His lungs filled with Sea water.

The Deep Mother's power withdrew for the barest moment—then crashed against Huuq. She churned, now pouring wrath into him: that of all life combined into one force. There were jaws in the Sea. Snapping mandibles. He sensed their millions within millions. The Mother's collective bite. Huuq could feel the phantom Strength of countless teeth. Each pierced, set, tore at, some aspect of his selfhood whose existence he had never before sensed.

(And, madly, a deep part of him enjoyed it . . . .)

On their own, Huuq's jaws snapped shut. It was as though his wolverine teeth were biting into each other. He struggled against his own flesh. It wanted to move with the Deep Mother's will.

For the span of a heartbeat, Huuq completely agreed with Her. He wanted to rage. To attack other lives.

Even his own.

He regained some flicker of awareness, tried to focus. But he was panicked. He could sense the few, final grains of his will. Like sand under surf, they were washing away from whatever had once been his centre. Whatever had been Huuq. Faced with the madness of conflicting urges—the desire to harm himself and at once escape harm—his awareness again began to collapse.

And his soul howled.

The Deep Mother was not an It. She was a force. Something old. Old beyond age. Like the World itself. And as heavy.

(Yet someone else was there.)

(With him.)

(In the dark . . . .)

Blanket?

The Strength turned again. Instead of pushing, the Deep Mother's mind sucked at him. Passion. Urge. Wrath. Fear. Hunger. Like skin from meat, She seemed to tear all aspects of feeling and impulse from him.

Huuq's identity, on some field where only Strength existed, was at last swallowed. If someone had then asked him his name, he would not have known the answer. He would not have understood the question.

There was only struggle, She insisted.

Birth was struggle.

Fighting others.

Fight oneself.

Life was a word for success.

Death was failure.

The last of Huuq went wild, like an animal scraping its neck raw in order to break a tether. For a moment, he believed that if he fought anything, anyone, that would prove that he lived—and others did not. It would prove him most powerful. Without fear. Or need. Because all other life feared his wrath.

On the same field of Strength, She swallowed his heart.

Time became insignificant as Huuq soaked in the Deep Mother's Strength. His heart and mind seemed to whorl in tatters about each other, amid throbs of Her feelings. Her aggression. He wanted to thrash with Her. To kill for Her. To win against nothing in particular.

Her alone: She was the only thing that he would never bite.

Through Her, he realized that essential life was all that mattered. The fact of it. Of its urges. He was not really separate from the black locks of the Deep Mother. Or the Strong tendrils. Or the Sea's ancient currents—whatever one wished to call them.

He became aware of lives pulsing all around him. The first that slipped into his awareness were whales, calling to each other throughout the blue and black. He then felt the lives of seals. Walruses. Soon, he knew others.

Their numbers were impossible. Overwhelming. Infinite

fish. Shellfish. Urchins. Jellyfish. Sea worms. Krill. Anemones. Coral. Sponges. Seaweed . . . .

He felt lives for which Inhabitants had no name. They were things like plants and animals combined. Too small to see. Yet, in their multitudes, they were mightier than all the life that would ever flourish on Land.

He heard the murmur of Its.

Like all other lives of the great Sea, a vast host of Its sang, played, feasted, and ravaged within the coils of the Deep Mother. Many of the Its had been creatures of the water. Many would return to such a nature. Others had been born only of Strength. They changed their shapes at will. Some were beautiful, like living waves that whorled through endless night. Others were terrible. Like mouths that never ceased to bite.

Once, Huuq had believed that there was a difference between Its and "natural" creatures.

That difference collapsed.

Huuq became aware of a wordless voice. An echo in the depths. It spoke from all around him, using feelings and notions instead of words.

His life as Huuq had failed, it told him.

He believed that to be true.

Would he like to begin a new life? the wordless voice asked.

Are you the Deep Mother? he thought.

A dim sense of amusement.

In its way, the voice answered:

"I AM LIFE."

Huuq knew, then, what the Deep Mother was. Behind all symbols, the play-masks of everything She was called, She was simply the urge of Life. Raw. Murderous and creative. Hideous. Lovely.

She was offering him a new life. A new existence. Further years as something else. Imagery whirled through his consciousness. Would it not be fun to try out a dolphin's skin?

Better yet, a shark? Killer whale seemed the most impressive, though. But why think so small? How about a blue whale?

Then a part of him wondered:

What does Blanket get to be?

"NOTHING," answered the Deep Mother. "SHE IS DEAD."

If Huuq had been allowed to remain mindless, adrift in the Deep Mother's essence, he would not have comprehended such a message. What was Qipik, compared to all of Life? What was Huuq himself?

Yet, in order to communicate, being to being, the Mother had temporarily partitioned Huuq from her soul. And here, in some wink of Strength, was Huuq's chance to find himself again. To seize upon selfhood.

And rebel.

His mind thrashed. He sloughed off some bit of the Deep Mother's passions—the urges of every being in the Sea—that had enslaved him since sinking.

For a precious moment, he owned his own heart.

Fear. Hunger. Wrath. He now drifted apart from those feelings, no longer under Her Strength. But the hearts of so many beings, living, dying: they were loud. How long could he ignore them?

Clarity.

(Finally, he owned a mind again.)

Of course, the Deep Mother had overpowered him.

How could he resist Life?

(She'd embraced him, at least.)

Yet She had condemned his Blanket. To whatever was outside of Her. To whatever Life was not.

Huuq's outrage arose.

(With Strength.)

And his Strength harvested more selfhood back from the Deep Mother.

I condemn You!

The Deep Mother responded with shock. On the Strong field where powers and their symbols met, negotiated, merged, or wrestled, the Mother seemed to spasm.

She expelled Huuq from Her soul.

Once again, he was aware of coils.

Her hair.

All around.

His limbs were being constricted. Both strength and Strength were draining out of him. He willed his eyes to See through the murk.

Coils, more coils, trailing in all directions: they no longer looked exactly like locks of hair. Many pulsed under Huuq's Strong vision, becoming alternately opaque and translucent.

He knew now that they were living tides.

Though the coils had lost their look of actual hair, Huuq nevertheless remembered what the Fisherman had said about the comb. He felt stupid for having allowed himself to drift. He had steeped like a kind of tea in the Mother's primal power. Now he was not even sure if he could use the object.

With great effort, he turned his head toward his Inhabitant hand, which still held the comb. Huuq bent his wrist, trying to touch the comb's teeth to some part of the Mother's hair.

The coils constricted further, breaking the bones of his arm.

There was no pain—just that odd discomfort. Through the Water, he could hear twin snaps.

Unable to grip any longer, his hand went limp. Open.

He watched as the comb tumbled lazily, then drifted upward to the surface.

Huuq was pulled further down.

He opened his jaws to cry out as he finally lost sight of the comb, but his scream was nearly silent. His chest was filled with the Sea. He could feel the Deep Mother, living Water, tickling his lungs from the inside.

So . . . .

Huuq bit Her.

As one of the coils came up to loop over his muzzle, Huuq

thought of Qipik.

He thought of his Mother.

Father.

Sister.

He forced his own emotions to whisk out those of the Deep Mother. His heart swelled with indignity: on behalf of all those, including himself, who had been cheated because of mad powers at play throughout the World. His breast was filled with feelings much like those he had experienced atop the hill, after having been chased by Paa and the bullies.

This time, however, he did not crave power. Or vengeance.

As his jaws clamped down on the Deep Mother's coil, he thought only:

You're unfair . . . .

Life is unfair . . . .

The coil thrashed in his mouth, its power dislodging some of his heavy wolverine teeth. Still, he held on. All the while, he poured his Strength into the tendril. He was not hoping for escape. He thought only of his loved ones. Of how they had been treated unjustly. Of how they deserved better.

He wanted the Deep Mother, who represented Life itself, to feel how he felt.

A snapping sound shot through Huuq's ears, as part of his lower jaw broke under the lashing coil. He closed his eyes . . . .

And *poured.*

All of his Strength, and eventually the stuff of his life, poured into the Deep Mother.

Coils in their hundreds constricted, shattering all of Huuq's bones.

He went slack as his life winked out. But that was all right.

For the first time ever, he was satisfied.

The Many Players

Huuq dreamed that he was a bird. He was a falcon, air caressing his wings as he ranged over a World where Sea and Land blurred into one, far beneath him.

Whenever he chose, his eyes could focus in on the slightest movement of a rodent. On a flash of icicles. A wave. A fleeting shadow.

Tucking his wings in, Huuq dropped from up high on the winds, veering in a wide arc as he lowered himself closer to the Sea. He turned his head long enough to spot storm clouds out of the corner of one eye, but he could avoid them with ease.

Past mountains of ice, over a vast white plain of frozen Water, Huuq soared. With only one or two flaps to add momentum, he was past the floe edge, watching the angular shapes of ice pans adrift on the blackest Sea.

There were odd workings of Strength nearby.

He veered again, searching with perfect eyes until he spotted the comb. It bobbed on dark water, sometimes engulfed by a wave, only to rise up again.

Huuq gauged the distance, flapped, angled his tail to master the approach.

He swooped in a vast arc, caught the comb in both sets of talons.

Huuq's perspective suddenly changed.

He saw the bird that he had been; watched as it flapped to ascend. It went higher, higher, toward a starry patch in the Sky. There, the clouds had parted, so that he could see night Sky, the Many Players drifting like a rainbow ribbon.

Stars filled his vision.

―――――――――――

"Huuq?" called a woman's voice. "Time for you to wake."

He opened his eyes to find that he was already in a sitting position. But he did not recall sitting up. For that matter, he did not recall having lain down.

He sat on hides. On a low bedding platform in a snow house. The home was small, but rich. As his eyes ranged around the walls and floor, the bed on which he sat, he saw pelts from many kinds of animal. All were healthy and thick, whether in the form of spiky black and orange wolverine fur, or curling trails of muskoxen. Silvery whiteness, from mixtures of bear and ermine and caribou belly, made the home seem to shine.

A person stood nearby, somehow blurry at first. Then Huuq's eyes focused, and he realized that he was seeing an old woman.

Her back was to him. She wore light furs tailored into intricate patterns. Her hair was of purest silver. It was tied back into a long trail that hung almost to her ankles, bound by a total of seven knots.

To some degree, Huuq could see around her. He leaned a bit, realizing that she was tending a broad, soapstone lamp, set on a crude pedestal. She used a short stick to position tufts of wild cotton, allowing them to drink up seal oil from the lamp's shallow basin.

The woman noticed Huuq, turned to smile at him.

Somehow, her face seemed familiar. Her skin was of a dark amber colouration, young eyes and smile aglow within aged features. Her facial tattoos—angular bars often placed on young women with a needle and lamp soot—had faded into blue-grey.

She stepped aside, allowing him to admire the long row of perfectly even flames, orange and smokeless, that she had arranged on her lamp. He could feel their heat from where he sat.

The woman put her little stick aside and wiped her hands on a section of bear hide. She said nothing, but regarded Huuq with bright brown eyes. Smiling.

Disoriented, still bearing vivid memories of having flown

as a bird, Huuq said nothing. He realized, after a moment, that his Inhabitant arm was in a leather sling, splinted with driftwood. He fidgeted, looked down at it and wriggled his fingers. Then he gasped.

It hurt.

He gasped again.

Both of his arms were Inhabitant.

As if he had never seen it before, Huuq held up his left arm—that which had been a bear's—examining it from every angle. He flexed his fingers. Bent the arm. Checked for patches of fur.

He felt that he should have already realized, from the fact that he was able to sit properly, that his inhabitant legs had returned.

Then he thought to feel his face.

His humanity had returned.

Tears welled in Huuq's eyes, began to trail down the side of an Inhabitant nose. He had not realized how much he'd missed his original face.

There was a movement to Huuq's left. He spotted something compact and white out of the corner of his eye.

A falcon.

The crisp little bird, feather patterns more perfect than if they had been drawn, regarded him with stern eyes, as though to ask:

"*What?*"

The bird stood on a pile of white caribou hides, a stack of special belly furs that would have been about where Huuq's head had lain, had he been sleeping.

"Your mother's comb is there, too," said the old woman. With a sigh, she sat nearby, amid the largest collection of wolverine hides that Huuq had ever seen.

Huuq suddenly noticed the comb. It lay on the nearest side of the caribou belly heap, quite close to the falcon's talons.

"You can take it," said the old woman. "He won't hurt you."

Huuq reached out a cautious hand, but withdrew it again. He was not so much scared of the bird, as in awe of its presence. It projected majesty. Dignity. Confidence. His eyes flickered from falcon to comb.

Then to the woman.

"How did you know it was my mother's?" he asked. His voice sounded like that of an Inhabitant, with nothing of the guttural It sounds in it. More relief.

"Because I gave it to her," said the woman. "Your father complained that he had nothing nice to give her. He was poor, you see, and they had just married. I had an extra comb by that time. Less fancy, but it was good enough for me. When you're young, having special things matters a lot."

Her smile returned. "Then you get a bit older," she added, "and it's finer to see others enjoy such things. The comb made them sad, though. After I passed. Whenever they saw it, they thought of me."

Huuq paused. He hesitated to speak, lest he misidentify this woman.

"Grandmother?" he asked in a small voice.

Still beaming, she said *yes* with her face.

Then she called him by his name.

Not Huuq.

His true name.

Water continued to well in Huuq's eyes. They were tears of gratitude, though he was not sure why he felt so thankful. He sniffed wetly, trying to sort himself out. He did not want to embarrass himself in front of Father's mother.

He looked around the snow house, as though seeing it for the first time. He remembered: Father's mother had suffered from something to do with her lungs. Like her husband before her, she had died when Huuq was very little.

"So," said Huuq with resignation. "I didn't make it. I died."

"That's right," said Grandmother. "Mostly. You are one of those dead people who sometimes keeps a toe in the living World."

Huuq looked back at the falcon.

"It's not a bird, is it?" he asked.

"No," said Grandmother.

"Symbols. These are symbols again," said Huuq.

"That's right," she answered. She pointed to his arm in the sling. "Memory of harm to the body," she explained.

Huuq indicated the home overall. "Is any of this real?" he asked. "Or am I just seeing Strength again?"

"Not here," Grandmother told him. "Not in the way you've been told to understand it. Here, in the Sky domain, we know another power. Far older than Land. Or Sea. Older than Strength."

"What is it?" asked Huuq.

Grandmother shrugged. "Nothing," she replied. "Everything."

"You're teasing me now," he said.

She said *no* with her face.

"My little, loveable fledgling," said Grandmother. "Your

World is just a petal. One petal. Think of the *paunnait*, those fireweed blossoms that cover summer hills in purple. I used to love walking among them as a girl. Your World, the one that used to be mine, is a petal on a blossom."

"But," said Huuq, "that doesn't make any sense."

"Why?" asked Grandmother. "The Its may have shown you the Land. But did they hold up rocks and soil for you to look at? They showed you the Sea. Was it just tides? So, when we speak of Sky, you know we don't mean that which holds the clouds. So it is with the petals."

Huuq thought for a moment.

"Are you an It?" he asked.

"I'm your Grandmother," she answered, giving a light laugh.

Huuq had grown used to laughter being associated with mockery. Ego. But hearing Grandmother's laughter was like having a warm breeze blow over his heart. It made him smile in return.

"The Its," said Grandmother, "often think they understand the World. But how can you know a World while only being part of it? That would be like a drop of water containing the Sea. A pebble containing the Land. Those are notions. Like those that give rise to Strength. And notions are temporary. As is Strength. Worlds arise. Fade. They're coloured with action. Perfumed with life. Then they drop like petals."

Huuq thought some more.

"Why didn't the Its tell me any of this?"

"You were busy with other matters, weren't you?" Grandmother answered. She sighed, adding, "Its are like that. Always drawing others into their concerns. Its focus on truths that are true to them. They're like Inhabitants, that way. Only a few know how little they know. Those few are wise. The ones to heed. "

Huuq sat thinking about Grandmother's statements. He had always imagined that death would provide an end to questions. Yet here he was. With Grandmother. And she talked as though the Its, the Strength, even his whole World, were quite tiny things. He tried to organize his thoughts, but he was again bothered by the feeling that he had forgotten something.

He sighed. Let the feeling go. It was wonderful to be able to let go of feelings. This place, Grandmother's words, somehow empowered him in an oddly gentle way. Here, relaxation seemed to be a natural state. He felt content.

Is that bad? he thought.

Why would I think that?

Nice to feel good.

For once.

(Am I forgetting something?)

He glanced at the falcon, which returned his look with a fierce stare. Huuq wriggled his fingers, all ten, liking the feel of them. Somehow, he even enjoyed the pain such movement caused in his arm.

"Each flower," Grandmother went on, "is one in a field."

Her voice, to Huuq, felt like listening to a song.

"But each field is a petal on another blossom. A single wind blows over our countless fields. And that wind never changes. It cannot be chilled. Heated. Halted. It is a single breath. It is at once ourselves. Do these images help you, fledgling?"

"Wind," Huuq repeated, weighing the imagery.

He sat up straight.

Was I falling asleep?

Huuq tried to reach out with Strength. To seize on Grandmother's intent. By now, he was used to thoughts and feelings being graspable. Like different materials. Expressed through Strength, they could be shaped. Held. Passed from one place or mind to another.

The Deep Mother's passions, through Strength, had seemed tangible as water. Huuq had ultimately rejected that mind. In harnessing his own Strength, he had defied Her.

Did he also need to break free of the Sky realm?

No.

This place, he wanted to embrace.

But why, he thought, *do I keep feeling like I forgot something?*

He shook his head. Huuq needed to understand the symbols of this realm. Again, he tried to Strengthen his thoughts. To reach out, in his mind's eye, and touch the power of which Grandmother had spoken.

He failed.

Grandmother was right. There simply was no Strength in this place. Neither of Land. Nor Sea.

"When you were with the Deep Mother, fledgling," Grandmother said, looking a bit concerned, "your struggle was with the force of your own life. It was expressed through Her, but it was still you. Your little self. Now you struggle with something different."

"I'm not struggling," Huuq lied.

The falcon next to him gave one flap of its wings, then folded them again, sitting still. Staring. Huuq rubbed at his cheek, where he had felt a gust from its feathers.

"All right, I lied," he told Grandmother. "Sorry. I . . . it's just, I don't know what I feel. I . . . love this place. Somehow. It makes me feel like—I don't know—I belong here. Like I *came* from here. But I also feel like I forgot to do something. Or think about something. Or get something . . . ."

He shook his head.

"I like it here," he said. "But it makes me feel small."

"Of course," Grandmother told him. "Only part of you has passed, fledgling. The living have minds. Thoughts that trick them into being little selves. But your real Self is not made of mind. You are not made of thought."

Huuq thought about her words.

"But . . . I *do* have a mind," Huuq told her. "I know my name. I'm right here. Thinking."

"If thought is what you are," said Grandmother, patiently, "then are you sick when you forget something? Dying when you sleep? Dead when you fall unconscious? Little fledgling. You were never your mind."

"I . . . how else do we speak?" Huuq argued. "Our thoughts must have left our bodies. To die, I mean. Isn't that what death is? Our minds are here in the Sky. Smiling at each other. Meeting."

"We meet through the wind," said Grandmother. "That which stirs the petals. Which the wise have called Sky Time."

Strangely, it now seemed more important to Huuq that he enjoy Grandmother's voice, rather than grasp her meaning. He still felt that he was too unwise. Too new to this Sky Time. Without Strength of some kind, he could never fully understand the special symbols of this place.

But then, for the first time ever, he thought to himself:

Why must I always know?

"Don't bother to listen to me now, fledgling," Grandmother told him. "It will all seem obvious once you pull your toe out of the living World, and join us here."

"Us?"

"You have ancestors beyond count. They're looking forward to having you among them. Though you do not know most of them yet, their love has always shone down on you."

As Huuq stared into Grandmother's eyes, he sensed the surety of her words.

Rest.

Peace.

An end to the dissatisfaction that, for Huuq, meant life itself.

Maybe it was time to pull out the toe.

Then he remembered.

"What about the Enemy?" he asked. "My parents? My sister?"

Grandmother shook her head. "That time is done," she told him. "We tried to drive the camp's evil out. We asked the Sky to send the Egg-Child. The Sky brought the elements of your World together, and the Egg was placed. The plan didn't work. Sometimes, you have to let a World stir as it will."

Memories flooded back to Huuq, leaving him lucid. With the memories came panic.

"Wait!" he cried, sitting straighter. His arm ached with the movement, and it was not enjoyable.

"What happened to the Child? To Blanket?"

Grandmother's face looked troubled. "Like you," she replied, "they have died in their way."

"I don't understand," said Huuq, almost to himself. "Where are they? Where am I? I mean . . . is this really me?"

He began to look at his body with a new distrust. If he had died and joined his ancestors in the Sky realm . . .

"Why am I even imagining all this?" he demanded, as though chastising a disappointing dream. "Why do I no longer look like I did?"

Grandmother's features became somewhat pitying. She sighed, stared at him for a long moment.

"If you mean your monster body," she told him at last, "it lies broken, on the ice. There is still an eyelash's worth of life left in it. The Strength still clings. Apparently, some part of you does not yet believe in death."

She nodded toward the falcon.

"My bird was the one who spotted your comb, afloat on the Sea," she explained. "He brought it to me, and I focused my attention on you. I realized, then, that you were in danger. I had my bird retrieve your body and lay it on the ice. It lies there, as we speak. Like I said. Basically lifeless. Broken."

"It was the Deep Mother," said Huuq.

"Brave of you to try and beg Her for help," said Grandmother, "but She was always volatile."

"I was trying to save Blanket," Huuq explained. "I didn't know what else to do. The Enemy was killing her. After making her eat the Egg-Child."

My poor Blanket, thought Huuq. After all that, he had still failed to save her. Was there at least some consolation in knowing that she no longer suffered? Maybe. He remembered, now. She had been an It. Where did Its go after they died? Did they simply dissolve? Like melting snow?

Wracked with guilt, Huuq rubbed a hand over his face, as though to hide his shame.

Grandmother waited.

"Is there something I should have done differently, Grandmother?" Huuq eventually asked. "Should I have been smarter? Faster?"

"You are just a little fledgling," said Grandmother. "You did well, but all was not within your control. There is both free will and fate, in the Sky Time. You are guilty, in your way. But also innocent. You're here, among those in the Sky, which means that we approve of you."

"Not good enough," said Huuq, staring at his knees. "Doesn't feel right. Doesn't feel . . . fair. If someone had just helped a bit more. Told me about the Land's Egg . . . ."

"My fledgling, that was no Land's Egg," said Grandmother. "An Egg from the Land would have hatched a Child of the Land. What we asked to be planted near your camp was a Sky Egg. A Sky Child would have been an even more powerful being. Did you not see the Egg-Child's colour when it hatched?"

Of all things that Huuq might forget, the last would be the colour of the Child. He had indeed noted it: a marvellous, silvery white, like stolen moonlight.

"I did see," Huuq muttered. "When Aki wanted to know, I lied. Told him it was brown." He shook his head. "I don't know why."

Grandmother smiled. "Qipik moved you to say that," she explained, "to conceal the Child's true nature. If the Enemy had learned that he was threatened by a Sky Child rather than a Land Child, he would have panicked. He would have killed you, Qipik, and the entire camp. Then he would have fled."

Huuq thought some more. "Are you sure?" he asked. "Father's knife. I left it there with Aki. It was Strong and kept him bound, even after the Egg-Child was taken. I think that's what the Fisherman was telling me."

Does she know about the Fisherman? Huuq wondered. Inwardly, he shrugged. Grandmother already seemed to know about the Deep Mother, so Huuq assumed that she knew about Her husband, as well.

"The knife was not Strong," said Grandmother. "It was used to build a home, a snow house, for you and your family. It was a tool your father depended on to keep you all warm. Sheltered. He realized this, and thought of you whenever he used it. The knife was touched by his feelings for you. Strength is more rigid than stone. Colder than ice. But the heart: that is a power under which it always thaws. Always yields. The Enemy regards this power as we would regard something rotten. Filthy. His selfhood would not want to touch such a thing. He would feel sickened, diminished, by its presence."

Grandmother sighed, then stood. She wiped at her front, even though she was the cleanest person Huuq had ever seen.

"Be sure to take the comb," she told him. "It will help you, in case you can't find the knife. The Enemy is clever. He will have found a way to remove the blade from his home by now, if not from camp."

Huuq was taken aback.

"But . . . I thought I was staying here."

Grandmother said *no* with her face.

As Huuq watched, her eyes became like rainbow flames. He was startled, confused, but not horrified. Since waking in this place, a kind of serenity had seemed to flow into him from some unknown source. It remained with him as Grandmother's image dissolved.

The old woman's rainbow eyes widened, expanded rapidly, until they engulfed the snow house and Huuq's entire field of vision. In mere heartbeats, Huuq seemed to float, bodiless as a living breeze, in a field of endless night. Somehow, he could see in all directions.

There were *stars* here. Stars clustered so thick, on night's gentle blanket, that they looked like streams of spilled milk.

A voice, Grandmother's, once again uttered Huuq's true name.

Ribbons of light approached: shades of violet jostling against greens and reds, playing across infinity. As with Grandmother's eyes, the colours expanded to fill Huuq's vision for a moment. Then they pulled back.

And he was able to discern figures.

The figures were impossible to count. They at once stepped and floated forward, a flowing host, each body throbbing with its own arrangement of rainbow lights. The lights were what distinguished them, rather than crude details such as clothing or facial features. Like long, windblown hair, over each head there danced a whorl of bands, burning with every colour that light could produce.

Huuq watched them with awe and love, sensing that they were his ancestors. He had watched them at play in the Sky, since the time when Father had first taken him out under the stars, pointing upward with laughter.

Of course he knew them.

They were the Many Players.

The Sky Child

In delight, Huuq's eyes ranged over the figures before him. Their hazy forms burned with rainbow fires that seemed to continually whorl and blend and flare—even as the beings themselves stood still. Over them arced the greatness of night; the cosmic Sky, mottled with starry clusters.

"I've watched you," whispered Huuq, almost to himself. "The Many Players. I've always felt you. And watched you."

And dreamed of you . . . .

One of the glowing figures drifted especially close. Huuq knew that it was Grandmother, though he could see no distinct face. Only an outline. Coloured flames.

He sensed that the infinite host was watching.

"As you watch us," said Grandmother, "we are those who watch back. I have spoken with you, and it is clear that you are not content with what you have done in the World. Go back to live awhile longer, my fledgling, then return here to Live."

"But," Huuq said helplessly, "the Egg. I couldn't save Blanket. Didn't the Egg-Child die with her?"

"It has been explained to you," said Grandmother, "that they died in their way. The Child may experience the semblance of death, but nothing can destroy an embodiment of Sky."

As Grandmother spoke, a bright, hazy being padded forward to stand at Huuq's left. The more he tried to see the creature—even to See it—the more the creature shed uncanny, silver light, until Huuq felt as if he were squinting under a bright moon. All he knew was that creature seemed to have four legs. It was regarding him. Not necessarily in a friendly way.

"What about Blanket?" pressed Huuq. "She's not dead?"

"She is dead to the Enemy," answered Grandmother. "But, again, she may become alive to you."

As Grandmother spoke, a different creature—glowing blue, but not as bright as the first—padded up to Huuq's right. Though the creature seemed a bit translucent, as if it were sculpted from azure ice, it was clearly a dog.

A heartbeat, and Huuq realized that it was Qipik.

She did not wag her tail, but stood staring, amber eyes looking quite Inhabitant. Before Huuq could greet her, Grandmother added, "You must make Qipik into your Helper. This is a shaman's way, my fledgling. She served the evil power only as a slave. You, she will serve out of love. But she will never be the same dog you thought you knew. You must accept her in whatever new life she assumes."

"Of course," Huuq answered unhesitatingly. Only then did Qipik give a slight wag of her tail.

Overjoyed that his Blanket had a chance to live, Huuq restrained himself from moving toward her. Grandmother was still talking.

"Now, the *Egg*," she said. "We willed the Egg to assist your camp, my fledgling. We failed. Now, we have requested that the Egg-Child make itself available to you. Unhatched. In full. Unshaped to the World. And unrestrained. As such, it is a free Child of the Sky."

Huuq gestured toward the strange four-legged being on his left. For some reason, he did not want to look directly at it. He felt, somehow, that keeping eyes on this creature might be a bit like staring into the Sun.

"This is the Sky Child," he guessed. "Isn't it?"

"Yes," said Grandmother. "Do you accept its assistance? Be warned: nothing can control a Sky Child."

Huuq was confused. "But," he said, "I don't want to control the Sky Child. I just want it to do . . . whatever it's supposed to do. To beat the Enemy. I want it to help my family. My camp."

"It is not your Helper," Grandmother told him. "That is

what I am trying to tell you, my fledgling. Qipik was a Helper. Many other Its are Helpers. But you must accept the Sky Child as it is. You must agree to whatever course it takes, even if it does not offer the help you had in mind."

Huuq thought for a moment. Again, he tried to See the Sky Child. But the fiery silver creature defied his ability to make out details of its appearance. The feel of it was at once noble and fierce. Something in him admired the being.

And feared it.

"If I don't want the Child," he asked, "can I still beat Aki?"

"We do not have that knowledge, my fledgling."

"All right," said Huuq. "I agree to accept the Child's help."

"In whatever way it is offered?"

"Yes."

"THEN FINISH."

The host of Huuq's ancestors, the Many Players, chimed the words in his brain. He became aware of hisses, crackles, as on nights when the Many Players came out most brightly.

"Grandmother . . . "

"Yes, little, loveable fledgling?"

Huuq suddenly felt embarrassed to ask anything further. He really did feel as though Grandmother had teased him, however lightly. He had sampled life—or whatever existence was called—in this Sky realm. Could he return and simply accept the World? His tiny, tiny World. His petal.

But it's time to finish.

He could feel himself changing. Leaving this place. The part of him that had visited with Grandmother—whether mind or something else—was returning to life. Sky Time no longer soothed him. He was no longer content.

"Your mind lives again," said Grandmother. "And living is wondering. The mind is always caught between happiness and sadness. We sense your questions. So ask, loveable one. Hurry!"

"I'm not sure I want to leave!" said Huuq. "I don't want a . . . flower petal life. I want what's real. I want life to mean something. Haven't I always dreamed about you? Dreamed that I was one of you?"

"You are," said Grandmother. "Any difference is in your mind."

"But you said even my mind isn't real."

"Nothing is real," said Grandmother. "Everything is real."

Then, the strange heaviness of Huuq's soul, that which he had borne his entire life, finally burst from him. They were more demands than questions, and they gusted out of him, seeming to come faster than his own thoughts.

"Why does it matter, then?" cried Huuq. "Why does anything matter? Why do anything? Why shouldn't the living all just sit and wait to come here? Why should I go back, Grandmother? Why should I try? Why?"

Grandmother's burning form stood silent. In the background, the great Sky began to move. Its stars drifted, winking with various hues, sometimes streaming; at other times they seemed to blend with the Many Players. Colours fanned out into the vastness.

Grandmother's voice came with the crackle of fire.

"You should try, fledgling," she answered, "because you matter. Like every being, you are a statement. A vow. You exist because you were promised to existence. Never despair at feeling small. Everything is small to something else. Or large. A star makes a Sky. But without every star, it would not be the same Sky. You *are* in order that your Self may hold its place in the World. To be what it decides to become. When you return to us, fledgling, it will seem like less than a heartbeat has passed. So play at life. Find the Self. Enjoy unfolding it. Act. And stir."

"Stir what?" Huuq whispered.

Grandmother's voice chimed with the Many Players:

"WIND."

Huuq shivered. Frigid wind drummed at his ears. He

shifted about, but that made him even colder. He sat up suddenly, loosed a scream of pain.

He ached in every part of his body.

"There you are," said a familiar voice.

The Fisherman.

The peculiar being stepped closer to Huuq and put one fish eye close to his own.

"I believe you're mostly healed," said the Fisherman. "You can thank me for that, later. But you seem to have shifted back to your . . . boy appearance. Would you be insulted if I said that fur suited you better?"

"They're back," said Huuq between chattering teeth. He held up his hands. Both Inhabitant. The sleeve on his left side was still missing, torn away at the shoulder.

He felt his human face and legs, saying, "All back. They returned my parts."

Why was he so cold?

Besides the fact that he was soaked in salt water and lying on ice and in the wind, Huuq supposed that he was cold because he was fully Inhabitant.

"No, no," said the Fisherman. "That's what you've never understood, Huuq. The 'theft' of your parts was an illusion. To wake your shaman self. After your ill-advised attempt to seek help from my Wife—She's angrier than ever, thanks—a very nice bird swooped down and assisted me in retrieving the bodies of you and your friend."

"I'm sorry you've had to do so much for me," Huuq told the being. "Thank you."

"Glad the Stone asked me to help," said the Fisherman. The sides of his wide mouth pulled up into a ghastly smile. "A chance to meet your interesting associates."

While the small being spoke, he gestured toward a furry, wet heap.

Qipik.

Huuq gasped. He suddenly remembered: wasn't she supposed to be alive?

"I . . . didn't dream," said Huuq. "Did I?"

"That's your business," said the Fisherman. "I really thought you were dead. Like your friend. Sorry to be blunt. But I did. It was quite wearying to heal all those broken bones. Unsettling, too, when you began to move around in your sleep. Crunch, crunch."

Huuq sat shivering. Miserable. Disappointed. Questioning reality.

"Must have . . . been a dream," he muttered.

"It was not," said a voice.

The voice was somehow silken while interlaced with harsh tones. As it spoke, warmth flooded into Huuq. Within the span of a heartbeat, he was no longer aware of cold.

He turned, along with the Fisherman, to regard the speaker. The Fisherman gasped, while Huuq cried out in delight.

"Blanket!"

Then his breath froze in his chest. He had cried out, at first, only because he'd spotted the rough form of Qipik climbing to her feet. But then he knew, as the being stood tall:

This was not his dog.

On four legs, where Qipik should have stood, a shimmering creature stared back at Huuq. Its eyes were without whites, irises, or pupils. Instead, they were patches of azure Sky. The creature shook, so that its fur—a million spikes of silver light—shed the last of the Sea water that had soaked Qipik. As though they were beats of a heart, blue streaks seemed to spark across the being's entire frame, from elegant snout to bushy tail. Overall, the creature lit up like a great azure and silver lamp.

Yet its shape was that of a wolf.

And it was not a wolf. Huuq was looking at a wolf made of light. It was three times the size of a normal wolf. It was larger than some bears.

"I am Qipik," said the creature in a resounding voice, "and also the Sky Child."

The Return

he Fisherman's wide mouth was agape. He rubbed at where a chin might have been, muttering,

"By my unfathomable soul . . . ."

Huuq merely sat on the ice, blinking. It was impossible to think that this monster, beautiful as it was, had replaced Qipik.

"I am," resounded the great wolf being, "the assistance you requested."

"Not exactly," muttered Huuq.

Unblinking, the wolf creature kept its eyes, twin patches of clear Sky, on Huuq's own.

"Don't fear me, Huuq," said the being after a long moment. While the voice was not exactly that of Qipik, its sound was Strong, leaving an echo in his heart that at once reminded him of storms and wind and moonlight.

(And Qipik.)

She was there, somehow, in every word the wolf being uttered. He realized, after a moment, that he *had* been frightened of her.

Terrified, in fact.

No longer.

Taking care not to slip on the ice, Huuq rose to his bare feet. As when he had been a monster, his skin did not feel the cold. But he frowned in looking down, realizing that all the hoofed activity had shredded his pants.

"They must have merged," speculated the Fisherman. "Your friend is there. So is the Child. I can feel them both, in perfect balance, as when warm and chill tides touch. This is remarkable. I've heard of Its blending with shamans from time to time. But Its with Its? Only one power could do this . . . ."

With no apparent trace of fear, the Fisherman waddled up to the wolf being. She loomed over him. It seemed as if, with the snap of her jaws, she might have been able to swallow him.

"Are you," the Fisherman asked her, "not a Land Child at all? Are you, in fact, a Child of the Sky?"

"Part of me was," said the wolf being.

"Ah, ah, ah!" cried the Fisherman in delight. He clapped his slimy hands. "Couldn't fool me!"

"But no longer," the wolf being added. "Now I am as much Qipik as Sky Child. At once, I am neither. Never before has the Land seen my like."

"This is fabulous!" babbled the Fisherman. He turned and frowned when he saw Huuq.

Huuq was less enthused, but he approached until he stood close to the wolf being. He reached out a hand to touch the creature.

She leaned toward him, but he changed his mind and clasped his hands together.

"Don't fear, Huuq," said the wolf being. "I still remember you. You remain my cherished boy."

Huuq then placed both hands on the fur of the Blanket Child's shoulder. It was thick. Strong. After a moment, he was no longer simply immune to the cold. An odd power ran through him, like a summer breeze through a field, until even the soles of his feet felt hot.

He reached up to scratch behind the Blanket Child's gigantic ear, pretending that she was once again his dog.

(He might have imagined it, but he thought that he spotted a distinctly un-wolflike wag of her tail.)

After long moments without words, the Blanket Child pulled back from Huuq, saying,

"Your camp is in no less danger than before."

"I know," said Huuq.

In the core of his being, where he could not only See in Strength, but now Feel, he knew that his camp had always been in danger. Even back when he had been a fool, a thief, part of him had known, but remained asleep to the fact. His camp was a place of predator and prey. It was where the strong made food of the weak. He now knew that one being did not necessarily have to devour another to make a meal of them. Some predators preferred the mind. The heart. The soul.

His camp had come to tolerate such predation. Even to encourage it.

Everything about the place was wrong.

"The Qipik part of me," said the Blanket Child, "has ceased to be a slave. She is dead to the Enemy. It is time to move. To break him. Now. The Enemy has been allowed to do too much, already, to insult this Land."

"And Sea," said the Fisherman.

"And Sky," finished Huuq. "Was the talk with my Grandmother real?" he asked. "All of it?"

"Of course," said the Blanket Child.

"Then I need Mother's comb. Grandmother said I'd need that."

"Look in your hood, former thief."

Huuq frowned, then fished about in the folds of his hood. He soon felt something both smooth and prickly.

Still using his right arm out of habit, he held the comb out for the Blanket Child to see.

"She sent it with me," Huuq muttered.

"You brought it with you," corrected the Blanket Child, "by electing to endure and finish this."

Huuq returned the comb to his hood. He looked about him. He was still on the floating ice pan—a raft much smaller than before, since the Deep Mother had torn away about half of it. He regarded the many wide holes, punched by her great locks of hair, and shuddered.

"Not much to fight here," he told the others, "unless one of you can fly."

The Fisherman crossed his arms, eyeing Huuq. "Normally, that's a shaman's talent," he said.

Huuq almost laughed before realizing that the small being

was serious. He expected Huuq to fly.

When Huuq shrugged, the Fisherman let out a sigh.

"Well, you're new to all of this, Huuq," said the being, "and a lot is already being asked of you."

"I can learn," Huuq offered.

"Bad idea," said the Fisherman with a wave of his hand. "A practice matter, flying. Crashing makes a poor start to any fight. More broken bones. Crunch, crunch. Besides, the Enemy must be free by now. I find it hard to believe that a mere blade could hold him for all this time. If he saw you coming, he would attack you in the air. Again, think of your bones."

After taking a moment to consider something, the Fisherman fixed one globular eye on the Blanket Child.

"Do you," he asked, "know how to—?"

The Fisherman made a series of wet, gurgling sounds: *"Khih-looh-rih-uh'kh-sih-ookh-tookh."*

To Huuq, the series of syllables came together to form a word or statement with which he was unfamiliar.

"I was waiting for someone to ask," said the Blanket Child. She turned to Huuq, saying, "But you will have to hold onto my tail, cherished boy."

"Now?" asked Huuq.

"Please do it," she pressed.

"Trust in her, Huuq," urged the Fisherman. "She's your Helper."

"Only in part," muttered the Blanket Child.

For a moment, Huuq wondered what she meant by that. Then he remembered Grandmother's caution: the Qipik part of this creature would remain loyal to him, but the Sky Child served its own strange urges.

Huuq stepped around the great wolf being. He took hold of her tail, far thicker than his own wrists.

She's not going to swim, is she? he wondered.

He eyed the floe edge, now a distant line of white against the black of the Sea.

"What are we doing?" Huuq asked, trying to keep the alarm out of his voice.

"Folding the Land," answered the Blanket Child.

"But we're on the Sea," Huuq argued. Then he wondered why he was arguing at all, since he had no idea what "folding" exactly meant.

"It's an expression, Huuq," said the Fisherman. He smiled as he spoke, then stepped far back. "Symbols. Remember?"

"Symbols," Huuq echoed. His hands, where he gripped the Blanket Child's tail, began to feel numb.

"You're not coming with us?" Huuq called to the Fisherman.

"I'll catch up when I can," the small being answered. He shot an anxious glance at the Water. "I do adore my Wife, and I can't just leave Her. She always calms down, but it can take some soothing. We husbands keep combs of our own. Just in case."

Then the Fisherman waved to Huuq.

"It's been a tremendous joy meeting you, Huuq!" piped the being. "Just saying that in case you die before I catch up. Try to relax. Think of it all as fun. And remember to hang on tight!"

Die? thought Huuq. He sighed. It was true: failure, as with confronting the Deep Mother, was a possibility. But at least he had met his ancestors. At least he knew that they approved of him. That he was trying. And he now knew what to expect when his body, like an old sled or boat, gave up and stopped working.

(It wasn't so bad, after all.)

He was here for those who still lived.

Suddenly, Huuq could feel Strength—the most focused and certain Strength that he had ever felt—flowing from the Blanket Child. She did not seem to be drawing it from any particular source; rather, she was generating it herself.

The sensation, at once warm and cold, shocked Huuq, so that he went rigid. His eyes widened when he saw his hands.

They had blended with the Blanket Child's tail. Fingers and fur were now a silvery blur.

Despite all warnings, Huuq tried to release the tail, only to find that his grip was fixed.

The Sky seemed to fall on Huuq.

The ice curved upward from below.

Left and right collapsed.

In less than a heartbeat, his very being was *pinched*.

In his ears rang the lingering voice of the Fisherman, saying,

"Hold, Huuq! Hold to everything! Hold!"

———————

Wind howled. Snow stung. Long black hair flew about his head. Huuq was still warm, though he stood at the heart of a storm. Though it seemed impossible, the weather had grown much worse since the time he had left camp.

He still held the Blanket Child's tail. His fingers had separated from the fur. So he let go. They were sore, though he did not recall any particular strain from the shift: ice pan to hillside.

He looked up at the Standing Stones, hazy shapes sticking up out of the snow like a giant's fingertips.

"The Land respected our folding," said the Blanket Child over the wind. "That is a good sign. We arrived in only a few steps."

Huuq did not recall any steps. Not at first. Then a kind of Strong insight wafted into his mind, and he understood. He had been part of the process. There was an awakened part of him, deep inside, that had assisted the Blanket Child in travelling. Huuq would not have been able to explain it to anyone else. He had simply gained, from asking the Land's permission to fold—to yield the stuff of reality, so that he and the Blanket Child could pass with short, sharp acts of will—a knowledge of how it was done. After experiencing this form of travel, he wondered if he could now do it by himself . . . .

The Blanket Child turned to face him. "We stand at the edge of your camp," she said. "Stop thinking and *do*. Use your Strength. Go and See. Now."

Huuq was jarred by her commands, but he quickly took her meaning. He began to walk. He intuited the way, squinting but walking steadily through the storm's tight embrace. It almost seemed as though it were trying to slow him, to smother him in a vast, vicious, lightless blanket.

Yet he no longer needed outward eyes to find the camp.

He soon stood at the top of the slope, almost exactly at the point to which he had first climbed, after being chased by Paa and the bullies. At that time, he had still been able to see the tiny community below.

Now he had to See.

He hissed to himself as his Strong vision pierced the storm, at once revealing truths about the camp. His sight could range almost anywhere, focusing in by will alone. He could See the many soul-bubbles: men, women, children, even dogs. The bubbles were still tethered to those who had fallen in the snow— all preserved, by Aki's song, in an evil form of stone.

Huuq recalled the lie with which Aki had driven him from camp: that the camp folk would awake after he'd left. Now that Huuq had come to understand the Enemy better, it made sense to See the camp like this. Why should Aki bother to wake them?

Seeing deeper, he could visualize the life-lamps, flames of living existence, that characterized each person. They were of various colours. All were weak, fluttery, like moths in panic. Huuq's insight told him that they were somehow injured.

The Enemy had been feeding on them.

Huuq tried not to let a pang of guilt weaken his heart. He knew that Aki had only been able to afflict the camp in this way because the Egg-Child had been disturbed.

Then, where a number of souls were clustered, Huuq spotted the life-lamps of his parents. His little sister. He knew them instantly. There was less snow piled on them than over nearby camp folk, but their lights were more diminished, more fluttery, than any soul-lights around them.

Aki had clearly been feeding most often on Huuq's family: an act of simple spite, perhaps, for Huuq having left the pana-knife, maybe for injuring the Strength of his shadow.

Huuq found his teeth grinding in rage.

"Huuq!" barked the Blanket Child. "Rage will put itself in place of your insight. It will trick you. Act in calm!"

Yet Huuq disregarded the advice. His vision ranged until he found the snow house closest to him.

At the outskirts of camp.

Near the bottom of the slope.

Aki's home.

Huuq assumed a wide stance and let his eyes burn down into the Land. Past ice and rock, there was Strength, and its roots twisted up into his legs. His body. His heart and mind.

"Huuq!" cried the Blanket Child once again.

He ignored her.

When Huuq's gaze next fixed on Aki's home, his eyes bled azure, flaming tears. His body had become like a vessel, overfilled, so that the Strength streamed out of him. In a single heartbeat, Huuq gathered up as much Strength as he could bear, using his will to make it harder than rock.

Then, without bothering to ask permission, he *folded* the Land.

Hot hatred guiding him, the stuff of Huuq's being narrowed into a beam—a spear of will that was both weapon and self. Like lightning pulled straight, it shot from hilltop to snow house.

The bolt of Huuq, which was he himself, slammed into and through the snow house. In an explosion of snow and ice, a diagonal half of the snow house ceased to exist. Huuq himself reformed on its opposite side, curled like a fetus.

He leapt to his feet and whirled, hoping to see Aki (preferably injured) looking at him with astonishment.

There was no one.

Huuq went to check the open shell of the snow house.

Where was Aki? His fury subsided a bit, diluted by confusion. He tried to remember why he had come here. What he and the Blanket Child were supposed to be doing.

If I could at least find Father's knife . . . .

He stumbled over some shattered snow blocks, feeling suddenly dizzy. He went down on one knee.

"That," said a voice beside him, "is why one asks permission first. Folding without permission is a good way to shorten one's lifespan."

It was the Blanket Child. Somehow, more quietly, she had made her way down.

"I don't care about my lifespan," mumbled Huuq. "I just want Aki. I Saw my family, when I Looked. What's he been doing to them?"

"Feasting," answered the Blanket Child. "While their souls float out of their bodies, they remain trapped in the deepest of nightmares, unable to access their inua. The most human part of themselves is kept just out of reach. So, their minds wallow in animal imaginings, in worlds of pure fear, hunger, and wrath. A richness of these feelings is what brought the Enemy to your camp in the first place. Your camp is the best of hunting grounds."

"No," argued Huuq. "Aki did this to them. It wasn't like this until he got here."

(But he was unsure.)

The Blanket Child made no reply, but began to walk toward the middle of camp.

"Follow close," she said. "Thanks to your ill discipline, he knows exactly where we are."

"Is he hiding?" asked Huuq, stepping lightly beside the Blanket Child.

"Stalking."

Huuq's dizziness had ended, but he still felt weak. He had lost the strange warmth that the Blanket Child had passed on to him. He could almost feel the cold now. Also, he realized that his body was aching, as though every muscle he owned had become stiff and threatened with cramps.

His Inhabitant body, he remembered, was far more fragile than the monster form to which he'd become accustomed. It could feel *pain*.

Huuq then remembered the pana-knife. He had failed to spot the blade among the ruined blocks of Aki's snow house. He ran back.

"Huuq!" growled the Blanket Child.

"I'll be right there!"

"Huuq!"

"Right there!"

Frustrated that he had to look so quickly, he stepped among the remains of Aki's home, kicking and turning a few snow blocks. A spot on the floor, where he had last seen the blade, was open to Sky.

The knife was gone, and he simply could not find it. He hissed between his teeth, hating the fact that he had to give up.

The Blanket Child had by now moved almost out of sight. Huuq ran to catch up. As he moved deeper into camp, among the homes, he spotted snowy mounds here or there. Over most, there floated shimmering soul-spheres. Over others, there was nothing.

Aki, he wondered, *has he started to kill people?*

The thought made him slow his pace, walking wide-eyed, sometimes shuddering, as though he moved among graves. Only by force of will did he tear his eyes away from a small boy, lying curled on the snow, like a life-sized carving of bloody red stone. He feared pausing long enough to recognize the poor child. No bubble floated over him.

As Huuq stepped past, the sight somehow made him feel as though he had allowed all of this to happen. His dread was mingled with guilt.

But even if he had known about Aki, known that he was a monster, what could he have—

Wait! he thought.

Why had the boy not been covered with snow?

From behind Huuq, there came a shuffling sound. He whirled, rigid with horror.

Aki stood over him. His yellow teeth were warped. Long. Bared in a grin.

The right iris burned.

Red.

Before Huuq could so much as cry out, Aki seized his hair with one hand. The Enemy's physical strength was nightmarish. Greater than that of a bear. Impossible. Unbreakable.

Huuq was surprised that his neck did not snap as his head was pulled forward. The pain was shocking, as was the sound of his own yelp. The Enemy wrenched him about like a cruel child with a puppy.

In one smooth gesture, Aki rammed the opposite hand into Huuq's mouth. He could feel the limb twisting, wet fingers deforming, swelling, dividing, stretching and running like slick fat past his tongue.

Huuq flew into wild panic as the river of flesh coursed down his throat. Toward his stomach. Some of the boneless digits took a different route, coming back up into his sinuses.

Then they flared with Strength.

A thousand barbs seemed to shred his brain, flooding his vision with orange. Violet.

He had murdered his community, the Strength told him. By being inadequate. By stealing. Being a fool. By sleeping too long, when he should have been a shaman.

And he had murdered Qipik. He had chosen to lie about the Egg. Let it fester inside of her. When he should have been thinking of others, he had thought only of himself.

And he had murdered the Sky Child. When it should have hatched. Should have destroyed the Enemy. A plan had been set for so long. So carefully. And all had failed due to Huuq . . .

. . . who was not a thief . . .

. . . or an Inhabitant . . .

. . . or a shaman . . .

. . . but just a monster . . .

. . . and a murderer.

Then Huuq stood gulping at open air.

No one held his head. His mouth was empty. He looked up to see that he stood beside the Blanket Child.

Somehow, she had retrieved him.

"I know," Huuq gasped, "you said to stay close."

The two of them faced Aki. The Enemy stood less than a stone's throw away, between a couple of homes. He was no longer grinning. One limb trailed down to the snow: a cascade of crimson worms, spangling with purple and saffron Strength. They moved sluggishly for a moment, then were drawn upward, reforming into the shape of an Inhabitant hand.

"What adventures you must have had, Little Tooth," Aki yelled above the storm, "to return with this Strong creature. A

Helper, is it? Did you realize what you are, then? Good. You will understand everything that I do to you. To your camp. But where did you find this It of yours?"

"You know her," answered Huuq. "Blanket. She's Blanket. You didn't manage to kill her!"

Aki looked puzzled.

"Evil is often stupid," said the Blanket Child. "Tell him the whole of it."

"She's also the Child," said Huuq, "from the Egg." He searched for words, and his Strong insight returned, assisting. "She is," he explained, "the stuff of it. The . . . suchness. Of what the Egg was meant to symbolize."

"Say it all," advised the Blanket Child.

"She's a promise," Huuq added, letting the Strength speak for him. "Of a future for this place."

Aki took a step back, paused. Then he took two steps forward. And stood tall.

"So, this being arose from the Egg?" asked the Enemy. "And my Helper? You must think I'm a fool, Little Tooth. Where did you really find this monster? What did it tell you? It's some Helper of your own, isn't it? Some pitiful, lost It, that you found on the Land."

The Blanket Child sighed. "As suspected," she muttered. "Huuq, gift the Enemy with no further words. Teach a fool, push air with a stone—neither have any effect."

Huuq held up a hand to the Blanket Child, asking for patience. His Strong insight was still with him. It drove him, somehow, to want Aki to understand.

Why? Huuq wondered.

He knew, by now, that the Enemy would never show kindness. Or compassion. Or remorse. Huuq hoped that there wasn't some part of himself, held secret till now, that still viewed Aki as a friend.

"Release the camp," Huuq demanded. "We don't have to fight."

Yes, we do, he thought to himself.

"Release the camp and you can go."

"Release yourself, Little Tooth," answered Aki with a laugh. "Give me control of your Helper, there. It might be useful to me. Then get on your knees and ask, politely, for your life. I am now unrivalled by any power in this part of the Land. You saw to that. By getting rid of the Land's Egg."

For the first time in long while, Huuq laughed.

"It was a Sky Egg, Aki," he said. "And it *hatched*. But in a different way. This is a Child of the Sky. She's merged with Blanket."

Huuq allowed a heartbeat for the Enemy to absorb his words, before adding, "And she wants to kill you."

Panic seemed to flash across the Enemy's features. His red iris glowed like an ember, shifting left, then right, then left again. It settled on the left.

"Ridiculous," Aki growled. "Pitiful, stunted shaman. Fighting the liar with lies."

Yet, while the Enemy spoke, Huuq's insight found a sudden memory. It was Strong, and fluttered like a startled moth into his consciousness. He recalled part of Aki's song—the one that had paralyzed the camp.

"They see nothing of the one
snarling amid flame and chill,
whose poison dreams rake the
wakeful mind. So may terror
freeze! May appetite scorch!
Never see our monster rearing
its whip, fed fat and fastened
by a left eye of fear and right of
hunger. Wrath's coiling grip!"

Huuq's hand stretched out, so that his fingers curled into the fur of the Blanket Child. And his insight immediately met with hers, so that she spoke his thoughts aloud.

"Yes," she muttered. "The eye. I see it, now. His fear."

Huuq leaned toward the Blanket Child, whispering, "Do something . . . ."

"Like what?" whispered the Child.

"You know, make him *feel* us . . . ."

The Blanket Child said nothing, but looked back at Aki.

Then she pulled in a great breath, and Huuq sensed that odd power—the one that had been present with Grandmother—arriving like a summer breeze. At once, the power became part of him, calming his nerves and helping him focus on the only task that now mattered: saving folk and family.

Much like a dog, the Blanket Child shook herself.

And the storm ended.

The wind ceased to howl. As though it had been pushed outward in a widening vortex, snow stopped falling on the camp. Overhead, the clouds opened to reveal night Sky.

There were the Many Players.

Even Huuq stood in awe for a moment. The Blanket Child's expression of Strength had been gentle. Casual. But the storm had not survived it.

Huuq had not realized that she was quite so Strong.

He turned to Aki. The Enemy was also fixed on the Sky. He turned in a circle, regarding the camp. Not a single flake of snow now fell. The white that had already fallen lay still. Undisturbed by the slightest breeze.

"A Sky Child," Huuq told Aki. He no longer had to shout over the winds. "And like I said, she's here to finish you."

The Finish

Aki stood silent for a long moment, eyes turned upward. A new expression—despair—seemed to ripple across his features. Huuq wanted him to take in the Blanket Child's power. He fully understood the Enemy, now.

It filled him with disgust.

This Enemy was no predator. If Aki had been something like a falcon, or a bear, or killer whale, he would have been . . . tolerable. Natural. One more creature of the Land. Trying to survive.

Yet, the Enemy did not truly hunt. He did not capture prey. Instead, he degraded victims. Sickened them. Rotted them. And, on whatever filth he managed to cultivate in a living being—Aki fed.

Inua was the key, Huuq realized. It was the force that, if stripped away, made a being vulnerable. The Enemy simply weakened the inua of others. He stole their "aware" power, as the She-Stone had called it. The power of the self to know itself. As a self among selves. And once that part of a victim's soul had withered, Aki sucked up the remaining garbage. Blind hunger. Futile wrath. And, like marrow sucked from bone, fear.

No, the Enemy was not a predator.

Just a *thief*.

Though his insight rebelled against it, Huuq's disgust turned to anger. He bared his teeth, as if they were still those of a wolverine. It no longer seemed important that the Enemy be simply removed. Like a dull obstacle. A task to be completed. Before destroying him, why not make Aki feel what he had inflicted on others?

"Now, *you* beg," Huuq told him. He was not shouting. But his voice sounded loud, to him, without the storm's constant howl.

"You cause nothing but hurt," Huuq added. He noticed his own fingers, on his free hand. Shaking with fury. He curled them into a fist.

"I think you should feel some, yourself," he told Aki.

Slowly, the Enemy's eyes lowered from their view of the calm Sky, until they again fixed on Huuq and the Blanket Child. His red iris still burned on the left. Then it switched right. Left again. The red danced between eye sockets.

"No, Huuq," muttered the Blanket Child. "You followed your insight, before. And I respected it. But this way weakens . . . ."

Huuq ignored her.

"On your knees, Aki," Huuq commanded.

Aki's iris settled on the right.

Huuq's Strong insight blew like a storm inside of him.

I'm wrong. I'm wrong. I'm wrong . . . .

"Huuq," warned the Blanket Child.

Huuq's hand twisted in her fur. He knew that she was right. But the effort of collecting himself, gathering his will against the need to make Aki suffer, made his teeth grind together. Whatever had overwhelmed him with the Deep Mother was here. It was right here. Now. Inside of him. Even though he stood on Land. He tried to reason his way through the feelings. To concentrate. But focused thought suddenly seemed impossible.

Where was the Strength of his mind?

Then, a breeze cooled Huuq's cheek. A flicker of contentment, as when he'd visited the Sky domain, passed through him. He opened his eyes, not having realized that he had closed them. His lungs heaved with breath.

How, he wondered, *did I forget to breathe?*

"Yes," whispered the Blanket Child, as though she could sense all the colours of his heart. "Well done."

Huuq let go of the Blanket Child's fur, and blinked at the look of her. She had somehow grown. She was now larger than any bear. He wanted to ask how this had happened, but his bizarre struggle—between self and Self—had left him exhausted.

"Just . . . release the camp, Aki," Huuq said with a sigh. "Let everyone go."

The Enemy's left eye burned. A trace of despair had returned to his features.

Then Aki smiled. "Is that all you wish, Little Tooth?" he asked.

"No!" cried the Blanket Child.

Huuq stood startled. Confused. While the Blanket Child cried out, Aki began to slash at open air in front of him. His grin stretched almost to his ears. The yellow rectangles of his teeth grew even longer, more warped. His thick nails seemed to rake, over and over, at invisible targets.

Huuq tried to See. But whatever the Enemy was cutting was truly invisible. If he could only See deeper . . . .

Then Huuq realized that the Blanket Child's hackles were up. She turned in a half-circle, watching something. He tried to find the objects of her gaze.

The bubbles.

All of the soul-spheres had detached from their hibernating owners. Huuq watched, hair prickling with horror, as they floated upward, lights winking wearily. Some had already become translucent, more like water than light, as though they were fading into nothingness.

Through Strength, Aki had cut their cords.

"No, please!" cried Huuq, wheeling in the direction of his family.

The Blanket Child loosed a howl that shook the air.

Then the air shuddered again.

And once more.

As Huuq watched, the soul-bubbles halted in mid-air. Some of their colours became a bit more pronounced, as though the howls had lent them vitality.

"I must will them to reattach!" cried the Blanket Child, bounding deeper into camp. "Beware the Enemy! You must fight while I work!"

Even as she spoke, there came a hiss and crack, followed

by blinding pain on the back of Huuq's neck. As though he had been bitten by the greatest of mosquitos, he slapped his hand to the wound, then pulled it away.

Blood.

Huuq sidestepped, so that another whiplash caught him on the outside of his left arm. Unfortunately, the arm was bare, sleeveless. Huuq cried out as the lash opened his flesh.

He turned, gripping his wound, to see Aki coiling his whip.

The Enemy took a moment to grin. His red iris had left its eye socket and migrated up to the middle of his forehead. It burned there, making the flesh around it sizzle and smoke. There were no eyes, but only blackness, in either socket.

"Qipik may have been your companion," said the Monster Man, "but *you* were always my dog. You were mine."

As Huuq watched, pulses of violet and orange crept out of the Enemy's hand, winding along the length of the whip.

Aki uncoiled it, a length of Strength, and reared his arm to strike again.

Huuq ran, but the whip caught him across his back. Its Strength made him sick. Dizzy. Scenes of tremendous violence, withering horror, looped through his mind. He seemed to see whole other landscapes, entire worlds and peoples he did not recognize, ruled by cruelty. Despair. He sensed that the images were intended to shatter his will. Barely in time to save his mind, he managed to pull Strength of his own up from the Land, pushing out the waking nightmares.

He threw up. Staggered. Ran.

Aki laughed from behind him. Huuq veered around the snow houses, heading toward the edge of camp. Yet the Enemy always found some way to stay right behind him.

"You might not realize it, Little Tooth," hissed the Monster Man, "but I still respect you as a friend. That's why I'm killing you more cleanly than any foe I've known." He snorted, giggled, in a manner that did not seem at all human.

"But leaving the knife there with me," added Aki in a more serious tone, "that was not the act of a friend. I asked you to remove it, didn't I? What moved you to leave it there, Little Tooth? Was it some part of the shaman in you? The inner Sight?"

"Blanket," croaked Huuq. He gagged as he staggered, but his stomach had nothing left to eject. "She was never really with you. She fought you."

"You made the crafty little pair, yes?" observed Aki. "I gave her to you as my watcher. To make sure I knew when to stunt your growth. A bird without proper wings. That was to be you. Mmm . . . we all get careless."

Something struck Huuq from behind, and he went flying into the snow, face down. He felt Aki pushing on the back of his head, pressing his face deeper into the snow, so that he was smothering in cold and darkness. For a moment, he thought that the Enemy would end him in this manner.

Then he felt fingers gripping his hair.

(If only he could shake off this daze.)

The Strength of the Enemy still spun and bit in his mind.

(At least he could breathe.)

By the hair of his head, he was jerked upright.

(Something about a comb?)

Had someone told him that a comb was useful?

Impossible.

What good was a comb?

"Come!" said the Enemy. "I'll show you what became of your father's little knife."

As he spoke, he dragged Huuq by his hair.

After a time of dragging, of blazing pain and confusion, the Enemy let go.

Huuq dropped, limp as a newborn pup. He opened his eyes a bit, realizing that he was near a jumble of boulders at the edge of camp.

He raised his head, searching, and after a moment spotted the remains of Aki's snow house. Somehow, he always returned to this general area. He wondered if it was where he was fated to die. At least he would see Grandmother again.

And her falcon . . . he thought.

Dimly, he wondered why he had bothered to return.

Why?

Family, he remembered.

"Look, Little Tooth!" called Aki. The Monster Man stood about a dozen paces distant, gesturing toward a cluster of rocks. "I want to return your father's knife to you. Crawl over to it. Crawl." He pointed. "It's right there. Dig in the snow. Dig!"

Huuq forced himself to his feet. His belly hurt. His entire face stung. He was surprised that his scalp hadn't been ripped from his skull.

"No," he said, teetering a bit.

He did not wait for an answer, but turned his eyes up to the Many Players. He knew now that he was not Strong enough to defeat Aki. Not as he was. Injured. Frail. Too human. But at least, while the Enemy had his fun in slaying Huuq, the Blanket Child would work. She would have time to save the camp.

Aki began to roar at Huuq. He circled, commanding him over and over. His hands clawed at the air while he bellowed like a concentrated storm.

Huuq kept his gaze on the Sky.

And waited.

In time, Aki fell silent. And Huuq became aware of odd voices. Tones that seemed at once frightening and familiar.

Huuq noticed that Aki's gaze was turned toward the top of the slope.

Above, as though surveying the camp, there stood three dark figures. The feeling of Strength seemed to enshroud them, running out through the Land in all directions. Their Strength felt deeper than roots, Huuq realized, heavier than mountains.

Their guttural voices went silent as Huuq regarded them.

He knew them instantly. Every one.

Brine Beard.

Fungus Face.

Seagull Skull.

These were the three Its whom Huuq had originally met among the Standing Stones. They had taken his limbs, even his face, defying his lies and awakening him to Strength.

At that time, for Huuq, they had represented purest fear.

Now, smiling as though to familiar friends, he stared through their masks of terror.

And he Saw them.

Brine Beard appeared as a living wave, a whitecap, cresting forever from invisible waters. The It of the Sea sprayed—exploded—outward into small green waves, before all curled back to the centre, then surged again.

Fungus Face was a whorl of sand and soil, lashing about boulders that ground upon themselves like black teeth. The It of the Land roared, flaring with wild internal heat, before cooling again.

Seagull Skull was a tornado. A graceful fury. Dancing left. Right. Flashing belts of blue and silver raced around its middle. The It of the Sky spiralled upward, like a grand narwhal tusk. Towering into forever.

"Monsters!" Aki hollered at the Three. "Am I not allowed to eat? Like any creature? Mind your own business!"

Huuq watched the Three. And he realized now that they were forces. Not beings. They could never be seen (not even Seen) in any true form. It was simply that his mind had found better symbols by which to recognize them.

His smile broadened. They were no longer monsters. Not even simple Its. They were . . . acquaintances. And he further understood that they had followed him, in one way or another, throughout his entire life.

In a fond whisper, he called them by their collective name: "My World . . . ."

As he spoke, Huuq could feel familiar tugs, merging into one force. This was the pull of the Three, their deepest of Strengths moving and moved by the stuff of existence: that which made up a field that Huuq called "World." But they were joined with his own will now, guided by a power that he could never name. It was what he had experienced with Grandmother. The power that was everywhere. And nowhere.

Whatever moved the fields.

With a spark of his will, Huuq's jaws grew into terrible weapons.

Orange and black fur sprouted over a stout neck.

His eyes became black beads of malice.

Another spark, and his left arm swelled, covered from shoulder to digits in creamy-silver fur. His fingers came together into a paw tipped with curving black claws.

A final spark, and his height increased. Bare feet solidified into hooves stronger than stone. He stood on legs ready to spring. To kick.

Again, Huuq was the monster: now a free monster. No longer tethered to the will of another.

True Monster Man.

Shaman.

Aki wheeled, finally noticing Huuq's transformation. His lone eye burned in his forehead. He issued a cry of outrage.

Huuq roared, and the Enemy took a step back.

Aki's Strength surged. Huuq sensed the Enemy's own transformation on the way. As he watched, Aki seized his own lips. In one brutal motion, he yanked the skin back, back further still, until his entire head had been self-skinned.

The Enemy revealed a great bear skull: bone white and yellow with spots of green, as if it had lain rotting in a shallow pond. The red iris, during the change, had wandered down to settle in one black socket, where it floated like a campfire spark.

Aki loosed his own roar: a great warble of wretched tones. His breath stank of bad meat, so Huuq stared into Aki's mouth. Maggots tumbled out.

Before now, Huuq would have cowered from the sight. But he was guided by insight. Not fear. And his renewed Strength, harmonizing all the World's forces, recognized Aki as a sham. A fraud. The Enemy's display was nothing other than an attempt to intimidate him. And the attempt only filled Huuq with anger. The special, bestial rage—that which drove him in monster form—had returned.

In a single motion, Huuq leapt and bit.

His wolverine jaws snapped together over the muzzle of Aki's bear skull. The Enemy's snout shattered. Aki loosed a thin wail—from where, Huuq was unsure—teetering about while

Huuq spat out pieces of bone.

Huuq raised his bear paw, intending to lay down a mighty swat while his Enemy was dazed.

He hesitated.

For some reason, Huuq suddenly remembered the time when Aki had helped him: when Huuq had been filled with the camp arrows, barely able to move his limbs. Then, Aki had explained how to "eat" the things.

The rage began to subside. Huuq's thoughts became clearer. And it occurred to him that, no matter how much he roared at Aki, no matter how savagely he beat him down, Aki would find a way to rise. The Enemy was not a creature, he realized. He, too, was a symbol. A site where certain forces came together, like stagnant water filling a hole.

While Aki staggered about, still wailing, Huuq leapt over to search for his father's knife.

He found it in two pieces, near a tangle of leather cord. There was a dead seagull, also caught up in the cord.

Huuq stood. Staring. Confused.

How did a bird get here?

He let the Strong vision arise in him. He wanted to know how the knife had come to be broken. Why it was here. Among the rocks. With a dead gull.

He Saw into the past. Images arrived like guests. They settled in his mind, feeling like events he had witnessed. Except that he had not actually experienced them.

Aki had not been able to pick up Father's knife.

Its touch was poisonous to him.

So, he had called out to a seagull.

A simple Sea bird.

Flying overhead.

Using Strength, the Enemy had dominated its mind.

Called it down.

Into his snow house.

Huuq stood, "remembering" how Aki had made the bird stand still. He had tied a leather cord—the one now gnarled among the rocks—around the poor bird's foot. Then, the Enemy had forced the gull to drag the knife out of his home.

Both the Fisherman and Grandmother had predicted this. Aki was vile, but clever. He had found a way to remove the knife.

Huuq tried to force the rest of the vision from his mind: that of Aki hurling stones from afar. At knife and bird. Until both lay broken.

Trying not to let anger overtake him again, Huuq acted quickly. He placed the pieces of the knife in his upturned bear paw. Then he fished about in his hood, retrieving the comb.

He let Strength lead him, following it like a stream. His insight, given focus by the Three, and inspiration by the unnamed power that Grandmother had represented, now drifted in a steady tide of guidance. More than ever before, he was sure of what he must do.

Once he had the comb and knife pieces together in his paw, he willed. He did not focus on any power in particular. He simply thought of his Grandmother. His family.

(Which, of course, included Qipik.)

And he *willed*.

His body shuddered violently, as if it had been seized by invisible surf. All the while, he was calm.

The last of the monster rage left him.

He watched as the comb and knife were drawn into his flesh. Without leaving any wound, they disappeared.

Eaten.

Huuq did not feel much different when he again turned to face the Enemy. Aki had managed to recreate a semblance of his Inhabitant head. It was twisted, lopsided, like a hastily formed snow sculpture. Attempts to restore his hair had only partially succeeded. Patches of black, grey-streaked, made him look mangy.

Aki turned to grin at Huuq. Yellow teeth ran up one side of his face, to the fungal ball of an ear. He had only fleshy pits for eyes.

The red iris now burned in his open mouth.

Huuq took a step forward, and Aki's grin faded.

The Enemy took a step back.

Huuq pressed forward, but Aki recoiled as though Huuq carried some lethal disease.

Now there was no way for the Enemy to remove his parents' tools. They had become part of Huuq. Aki would not touch them—and so he would not touch Huuq.

Aki made a mad dash, an attempt to escape. But Huuq's powerful legs brought him over the Enemy's head.

Huuq landed in an explosion of snow, blocking the way.

Again, Aki tried to flee.

Then again.

Each time, Huuq was able to block him with ease. Aki began to wail, guttural voice rising to a high pitch in his panic. A circle formed, with the Enemy racing in one direction after another, only to be cut off by Huuq.

Huuq's flesh, having absorbed comb and knife, was poison to Aki.

Either exhausted or despairing, Aki paused. He had lost much of his shape, looking to Huuq much like a man formed from softened fat. He was like a tumour with limbs.

"Why . . . work at this?" gasped Aki. "After all they've put you through . . . why care so much?"

Huuq stood puzzled.

"What are you talking about?" he asked.

"Your filthy little camp. You must have . . . felt it. All your life. Dull. Foggy. Fear . . . ."

"That was you," said Huuq. "That ends now."

Yet even before Huuq's words were finished, the Enemy was laughing. His laughter seemed especially horrid, clear and sickly, on the open air.

"Why do you think . . . this place was . . . such a feast for me?" Aki asked. "You have broken me, Little Tooth. I fade now. Let me give you . . . one last gift."

"No," snarled Huuq. "Fade and be done."

"You will never . . . know, then," gurgled Aki, "if I lied."

Huuq did not trust the Enemy. But he also did not trust his own mind. What if he went on, tried to resume normal life, always wondering about Aki's last "gift"?

Would that not be like stealing from himself?

Huuq suddenly turned away, disgusted at his own feelings. The Strong insight welled within him, crying out that he only wanted some last token of Aki's friendship. But the Enemy knew him. He knew how Huuq's mind worked. This had to be a last lie. A manipulation. Some final attempt to tether him.

Like a dog.

Yet his heart did not quite agree.

"If you attack," said Huuq, "I'll know it. That will be it for you. Understand?"

Again, Aki chuckled. "I cannot touch you now, Little Tooth. You broke me. I cannot touch . . . unless you allow it. Tie your Strength to mine." He chuckled again. "Take your gift."

Before Huuq could wonder what Aki meant by "tying" Strength, he felt something of himself—moving outward like many shy, slender limbs—to meet a part of Aki. In an instant, he sensed the pus of the Enemy's mind. The sickness.

How could he ever have mistaken this being for an Inhabitant?

Huuq had not realized, before now, how much "monster" was expressed in the mind. The body? That was a shape. An image in a dream. A reflection, like clouds seen on calm water. Only a mind, like the one he now touched with such disgust, could hold true monstrosity.

Yet, it also held truth.

Perhaps, because Aki was so twisted, truths stood out in stark contrast against the rest of his soul. Like blossoms on a grave. These flickered through Huuq's awareness.

Aki *had* told the truth.

He had settled here because there was food.

Delicious fear.

The tasty wants of others.

Satisfying rage.

A memory flickered, and Huuq saw a woman. He recognized her, but had never spoken to her much. He watched as she ate well in secret, seal and fat caribou that she had hidden. She told her children that there was nothing left. When they cried, she fed them what she called "caribou." It was dog flesh.

Another memory flickered, and Huuq witnessed a much older woman. Her husband had gone hunting and never returned. She had a few relatives in camp, but none of them ever visited. He watched as her lamp flame burned low on the last of her seal oil, illuminating tears. It went out.

Another memory came, faster than the last, and Huuq saw a very young child. Almost a baby. Older children twisted his ears and nose, making him cry. The older children laughed. Adults glanced over sometimes, looking concerned. They said nothing.

Another: a husband and wife were sitting in silence. The wife sewed his boots with special care, even though he had not caught anything in some time. She pricked a finger with her bone needle, but remained quiet, since he disliked noise. After a while, he turned to her. "Why are you so ugly?" he asked.

A man walked past a dog. The dog, once a loyal hunter but now lean and hungry, remembered the joy of them going out on the Land together. The dog wagged its tail. The man kicked it.

A great swell of such memories rushed forward, too many for Huuq to process, like a jostling crowd. All were recollections from Aki. Each one had left its impression on the Land, like something filthy that steamed and stank in the snow. It was what wafted from these memories, a ghostly foulness without name, that Aki called "food."

And every bite had been from Huuq's camp.

Huuq stepped back, his mind swatting at Aki's memories as though they were great mosquitoes. There were so many of them. Most were milder than those that had at first stood out. Among them was the incident in which Father had thrown Qipik out of the home. But a few memories were far more rancid: the best evils that Aki had come to cultivate and dine on.

Huuq stood, wolverine eyes tearless. His mind was stunned.

His heart was broken.

Aki began to cackle, a wild, bonfire roar that chilled Huuq's blood. Huuq did not bother to silence the Enemy. He could say nothing. He, after all, had accepted this last gift.

The gift of knowledge.

Of what his camp truly was.

Aki's black laughter filled the air.

"Why, then?" pressed the Enemy. "Why care so much . . . for a camp . . . that cared nothing . . . for you? Were you ever . . . accepted . . . in this place? Cherished? Were you not . . . bullied? Treated . . . as a thief? Outsider? Monster? Why? Why care?"

Huuq looked down, feeling shattered, empty, as the Enemy howled and wobbled and spun in a jellied, boneless dance.

Before Huuq could react, a great shadow loomed.

There was a crunch.

The laughter ceased.

It seemed that Aki had possessed some bones, after all.

The Blanket Child was now more than twice the size of a bear. She had bitten the Enemy in two. Huuq watched as she wolfed down the first half of Aki.

Then the second.

Huuq stood and stared at the site of Aki's last dance. Wordless, the Blanket Child watched him.

In time, Huuq's mind finished its work on the Enemy's final question.

"Because they're mine," he whispered.

EPILOGUE:

Huuq's Sky Time

Every time Huuq looked at the Blanket Child, he wondered about her hugeness. It was barely an hour after Aki's death, and she was almost three times the size of a white bear. He squinted at her, but could not actually see her growing. She seemed to swell whenever his back was turned. Huuq didn't bother to inquire about it. He was too distracted. Anxious. Even a bit nauseated. With what she needed him to do.

In a way, fighting the Enemy had been the easy part.

"These people have already suffered," Huuq pressed. "Haven't they? There's no need for this. Are they really so bad? Aki could have lied."

Huuq knew that he had not.

"You know that he did not," said the Blanket Child. "Asking me until the end of forever will not make it as you wish."

Huuq was very unhappy with the Blanket Child. He stood at the top of the slope with her, watching mottled hills stretch into infinity. The gold of sunlight traced its way along the peaks. Ravens wheeled, hints of blue flashing across their black feathers.

Huuq brushed windblown hair from his eyes. Whenever he so willed, he did not feel the cold. But he allowed himself to feel it now. He had scavenged some better clothes from camp, so the chill wind did not represent death. But he enjoyed being an Inhabitant again, and shivering for a while.

"This must be," said the Blanket Child.

"No," said Huuq. He did not keep the fury from his voice. "It's cruel."

The Blanket Child had not only reattached the souls of

the camp folk to their bodies, but had willed each soul back into its body.

She had not, however, awakened the camp. Not yet.

"You must sing with me," she told Huuq. She had said it many times already.

"I don't want to," Huuq answered. "I . . . never liked them, you know, the camp people. Never liked them, but . . ."

"I know."

"Even hated them, sometimes. But I never wanted to hurt them. This feels like hurting."

"It is helping," said the Blanket Child. "In its way. Help that is wider than a mere camp."

Huuq sighed. A shudder ran through him. After gulping down the defeated Enemy (which Huuq hoped was symbolic rather than gastric), the Blanket Child had given him little time for rest. With the intensity of a hunter, she'd explained their next task. She had to sing a song. A Strong one. One that was the reverse of the Enemy's, yet, in Huuq's opinion, not much kinder.

And he had to help her.

The Child was not just here to fight the Enemy, but to address the problem of Huuq's camp. Aki had settled in this place, she reminded him, for a very good reason: the availability of food. Land, Sea, and Sky—all had made their decision. It was why the Egg had been placed here.

Containment.

Of a bad Enemy.

And a bad camp.

Grandmother had been right. The Child was no Helper to Huuq.

For this last task, he was hers.

"No," Huuq whispered, even as his insight disagreed. The Strong part of him accepted the World's strangeness. Through harsh days, the World healed its future.

He could never grasp such a thing with his head.

(But his heart understood. A little.)

The Blanket Child disregarded him, and began to sing:

"Open eyes by gentle light
given to the human heart.
These poor lives fly and in
every direction, their terror
licks the soul till it seems
no more than ancient bone.
Fearsome flames are liars
and sear no healthy mind!"

Huuq listened, and at once felt the loneliness of her song. She did not like to do what she was doing. So, for the sake of his friend, the being who had been born from Qipik's essence, he helped her. The Strength in Huuq borrowed his throat, so that he sang:

"What laughter there is to be
taken from the highest joy.
Others take, and in taking
from others, so themselves. So
I choke off the hunger that
chokes the heart. May the
senses judge well! May wit
rise, with hope for the wise."

Together, they dismantled the power of the Enemy's song. And, though Huuq disliked his part in it, he returned the assistance of the Blanket Child with assistance of his own. As Grandmother had hinted, it was Huuq's duty to respect the true purpose of the Child: to restore balance to the Land.

So, as one, they sang:

"They see nothing of the ones
guarding amid dark and light,
whose own dreams protect the
wakeful mind. So may terrors
fade! May appetite diminish!
Make no wrong monster here,

with whip fed fat and fastened
by a left eye of fear and right
hunger. We loosen such grip!"

Even the Strength of the Land seemed to sing with them as their song was finished. Huuq could feel a power, at once tremendous and fascinating, moving in the Land. He was fixed upon it with an awareness beyond his mind. This Self, serene and accepting, seemed to watch him from afar. Some distance behind where his body stood, all of the Standing Stones had awakened. He knew that they were babbling to each other.

They could feel the change.

At the Child's request, the Land had been asked to alter the camp.

Huuq's odd awareness, that of Self instead of self, faded, so that he could think again. He hung his head, knowing that they were all awake now: every soul in camp.

He would see them in a moment.

Huuq soon spotted the first of them.

Caribou.

Then he saw more. Running. Here. There. Confused. Near the site that had been Aki's snow house. Many more appeared. Most ran in circles. They were herd creatures—not very good at making personal decisions.

Have to get used to it, Huuq thought.

Their decisions, when they'd lived as Inhabitants, had led them to this.

"You have what you wanted," Huuq told the Blanket Child.

"What was needed," said the Blanket Child.

Huuq loosed a defeated sigh. "I can't believe this," he muttered. "All turned into caribou."

Just the legs were bad enough, he thought.

"Are you sure they have to stay this way?"

"Understand, Huuq, they must be hunted," said the Child stonily. "A wolf pack will move into this valley. Quite soon. Their pups need nourishment. Would you starve a vibrant family to save a sickly one?"

"It's just . . . why did we fight for them, if this is how they end up?"

The Blanket Child snorted.

"You should know by now," she said, not for the first time. "Form means nothing. As caribou, your camp folk will return to the Land's ebb and flow. Before, they were like water trapped in a puddle. Stagnant. Now, they will live, die, as caribou. Perhaps, many times over. But their souls *will* have their chances to migrate. To progress."

"I feel as evil as Aki," Huuq muttered.

"You have it backward, as usual," the Blanket Child insisted. "Your folk are the ones who tainted the Land with their evils. And they drew an even greater evil into their midst. We are lucky that it did not cost us dearly. We are lucky that the evil was as weak as that being calling itself Aki."

Huuq was taken aback. "You think he was weak?" he asked. "You think there's something Stronger?"

"There is always something Stronger," answered the Blanket Child. "In every way."

Huuq did not bother asking what the Child meant. His gaze simply ranged about, watching the caribou disperse. Whenever his eyes settled on an animal, he wondered which of the camp folk he was looking at. Had he already spotted Paa?

I guess, he thought, *not everything about this change is bad.*

"You must control your thoughts better," said the Blanket Child. "See? There is always something agreeable, in every situation. As I said, we are lucky that there were not higher costs."

Huuq crossed his arms. "Too high for me," he muttered.

"That makes no sense," the wolf being replied. "Your parents and sister were exempted from the change. They were the least of the camp's offenders, anyway. They lie free and unaltered as we speak. Asleep. You had best go down to awaken them now, before the cold causes them damage."

"I was talking about Blanket," said Huuq.

The Child remained silent for a long moment. Then she leaned her bulk toward him for a moment, before standing straight again.

"You know that I cannot go with you," she told him. "I must stay and guard this part of the Land. For a time."

"I know."

"I am not Qipik."

"I know," Huuq replied. "But if you're not Blanket, then you're not really the Child, either. Are you? Can't you be whatever you want?"

"Such is your power only," said the Blanket Child.

Huuq stood with the being for another few heartbeats. Without glancing back, he headed down the slope.

At his back, he caught the thoughts of the Child, wafting to him as though carried on the breeze:

Yes. The price was high . . . .

Most of the caribou had run off by the time Huuq awakened his family. The Blanket Child had left just the right number of dogs unchanged, available to pull a dogsled. It was no surprise to find that, once Huuq's family got over their daze, they remembered nothing of what had transpired. Father did not even seem to recall yelling at Huuq.

They were frightened, however, when they saw the empty camp. There was little Huuq could do about that. Almost wordlessly, Mother and Father packed up and left. They took only their closest possessions, as though every other object in camp had become poisonous.

To Huuq's thinking, they were not far off. He wanted to leave.

Huuq noticed an immediate improvement in the moods of his parent, as they travelled. His family seemed to drink in the Land and its beauty. They began to laugh again. Together. Huuq stepped in to help his father whenever he could. This surprised both Huuq and Father, though both got used to it in time. As for

Mother, she sometimes asked Huuq to take care of his baby sister. He was proud to do so, and his parents occasionally laughed about that.

And there eventually came a day, to be followed by others, when Huuq awoke without thinking of horror. Or evil.

Though he seemed content, he still could not see a horizon—whether of Sea, Land, or Sky—without halting. Staring. His eyes were always wide. Unblinking. For a while, his family asked what he saw.

"Nothing," he always said.

In time, they stopped asking.

———————————

One bright Spring day, with the sun shimmering off the Sea ice, Huuq spotted a small figure hunched over a hole.

The Fisherman.

"I noticed," Huuq said as he approached, "that seals are a lot easier to catch now."

"Well, your father is a decent fellow," answered the Fisherman without looking up. "Respectful. Always pretends to give the seal a drink of water after the hunt. Both the Deep Mother and the seal's soul tend to like that gesture."

Huuq stood for a while, before asking, "Something wrong?"

The Fisherman cocked his head (though Huuq could not see a neck), looking up with one goggle eye.

"I should ask that of you," said the small being. "Here it is, a nice chilly Spring. The ice is in good condition. The powers are all happy—though that changes in a blink, trust me—so what are you waiting for?"

Huuq shrugged, uncomprehending.

The Fisherman sighed and set his stick aside.

"You've hardly used any Strength since that camp business," he told Huuq. "You haven't changed at all."

"Yes, I have," said Huuq. "I'm a bit taller, I think."

The Fisherman snorted. "You know what I mean," he

said. "You haven't changed shape. At all. How are you going to learn anything without practice? What would a teacher of Strength think? Imagine, I tell him or her (or it) stories of how wonderful you are, only to have—"

"There are teachers?" interrupted Huuq, smiling.

The Fisherman's own smile stretched across his head.

"Now we're getting somewhere," he said.

Huuq continued to live as an Inhabitant. He enjoyed it. Camp life, especially in a family that treated each other with kindness and respect, left his heart full and his head buzzing with knowledge. And as the Spring moved into Summer, the heavy ice at last thawed. Flowers blazed in purplish reds across low hills.

Huuq began to meet more family. They travelled in their own wandering bands, staying together at times. Breaking up. Rejoining. They enriched his life as the brief Summer passed, bringing Autumn snows. And, despite all the new people Huuq met, he never again encountered that dull, foggy fear that had afflicted his original folk.

He had come to appreciate the ordinary.

Yet, on certain nights, when the Moon rose like a silver torch, he did leap on caribou legs, over snow and rock. He shone with creamy-white bear fur. He smelled the Land through a wolverine's nose.

He laughed only on those secret nights, enjoying his powers, feeling the Land's Strength from every stone.

Yet there were times when he stopped leaping under the Moon.

Then, he sat in respectful silence, listening while strange beings—Its—cast their odd shadows across the snow. And they spoke of the Hidden World. Though he could understand less than half of what the Its went on about, Huuq learned. That was how he came to know that there existed shy creatures, made of living fire. There were also oily horrors, lurking like devourer worms. The Moon, he heard, was alive (and He enjoyed gossip).

The Sun was female (and She disliked whatever Her brother enjoyed). Huuq found out that he might have passed by a giant, without even realizing it. He noted that he should be especially respectful to Little Folk, if they allowed his eyes to find them, since they were Strong and quick to anger.

Later, he learned about the parts of the soul. Its strengths. Weaknesses. Why one should be concerned for a soul. Why one should never be concerned. He learned why dreams are important. Why they are useless. He learned the difference between thought and reality (sometimes, as it turned out, there was none). He learned of how the Sea, Land, and Sky were interrelated. How those relationships were echoed in all of life. He learned of how the great World was many and, at once, one. And of how such concepts meant very little, after all.

He learned about the Sky Time.

He listened, while the Its babbled under the Many Players.

He was content.

That all changed, however, when a strange bird arrived one evening. A falcon. Shining. Silver. It had been Grandmother's Helper, it explained, and had arrived to become Huuq's own. There was much to do, the falcon claimed.

The Sky Time would not allow a shaman to sit idle.

Once Huuq understood the situation, he raised his arms to the Sky, and loosed a long howl.

And he no longer felt contentment.

There was some dread in his heart.

(But mostly joy.)

Afterword

This book is a bit like the Sky power that Huuq's granny was talking about: it is about Inuit beliefs; also, it is not. It is just a little onion, so to speak: layered somethings that make up something, called something depending on which something one is looking at. On one of its somethings, *Why the Monster* is a work of fantasy fiction, accessing Inuit beliefs because . . . well, they're cool. On another something, or two, or several, the book is a work of comparative mysticism, accessing many cultures. Because that's cool, too.

The story is Huuq's, but it is also intended as that of every aware being. Huuq's mystic challenge is to grasp the fact that everything around him is symbolic. His great, wide World is a set of symbols that reflect parts of his own being. The better he understands such symbols (and they can be pretty confusing), the more empowered he becomes. As in the mystic traditions of many cultures, Inuit expressed the soul's journey in terms of *three*. In their case, Water, Land, and Sky. Or, if you like, animal life, aware life, and transcendent life. These three are the soul, as a whole, and a given part is strongest depending on our stage of growth. We're first born into animal instinct: the fear, hunger, and wrath that being a life form is all about. As we grow, we try to find some basis, to cultivate our awareness into something that allows free choice, (hopefully) controlling the impulses floating up from our beastie-brains. When we're aware enough, we can seize onto inspiration, what seems to speak to us from our "soul," and that's where words fail. If we find something higher, it's deeply personal, often confusing (or even frightening) to others. Yet it's the seeker's journey, and whatever is found belongs to that seeker.

In order to tell a made-up story, we've accessed a lot of truth: at least, the way Inuit genius saw it. Once upon a time, the Inuit World was much bigger than it is today. Full of primal powers. Cosmic forces that echoed those in the human heart. That's not unique, though. All belief is just a way of scooping something out of the human heart, and setting up symbols by which to recognize it. Gods, goblins, even superheroes—they're all parts of the mind. At the very least, they represent somethings that are interpreted into other somethings that we think we understand. They are held up as the stuff we hope for. Shunned as what we fear. Our own symbols are what we want to express, whether of ourselves or others. So, this book is not about magic. No, not at all. It is about the intuitive cosmos. The unconscious. The little self. And the higher Self.

As already stated, the framework for *Why the Monster* is that of Inuit tradition. Yes, because it's cool. But the ideas are global. The notions presented in *Why the Monster* should sound familiar to anyone who has read some of *Vasiststha's Yoga*. Or the works of Rumi. Attar's *Conference of the Birds*. The *Patach Eliyahu*. Teresa of Ávila. Aristotle. Ch'an thought. Or Mohawk tradition. (And there are so many more.) On the outer layer of our little onion, it seems mad to think that the speculations of Inuit Elders could echo ideas found worldwide. On a deeper layer, where the symbols are better understood, we recognize each other's souls, on their respective journeys. And that's where words, even concepts, collapse.

After all, our existence is a flower petal. And the fields are infinite.

About the Authors

Rachel Qitsualik-Tinsley was born at the northernmost edge of Baffin Island, in Canada's Arctic. She grew up learning traditional survival lore from her father. Sean Qitsualik-Tinsley was born at the southernmost edge of Ontario. He grew up learning traditional woodcraft. They were brought together by a love of nature and each other. Together, they write Arctic fantasy.